A revised edition of *The Disciple* originally published in 1901 by Scribner.

Printed in the United States of America

Set in Baskerville Typesetting
Cover Design by SILK Studio

ISBN-13: 978-1-951319-15-1

Fiction / French Literature

Wiseblood Books
Milwaukee, Wisconsin
www.wisebloodbooks.com

The Disciple

by

Paul Bourget

Wiseblood Books

Dedication

I DEDICATE this book to you, my young countryman, with whom I am so well acquainted, although I may not know your place of birth, your name, your parents, your fortune or your ambitions—nothing but that you are over eighteen and under twenty-five years of age, and that you will search in our books for the answers to the questions which are troubling you. And the answers which you will find depend a little upon your moral life, a little upon your own soul, for your moral life is the moral life of France itself—your soul is her soul. In twenty years from now you and your brothers will hold in your hands the destiny of this ancient country, which is our common mother— you will be the nation itself. What will you have learned from our teachings? No man of letters, however insignificant he may be, but should tremble at the responsibility.

You will find in *The Disciple* the study of one of these responsibilities. May you find here a proof that the friend who writes these lines has the merit, if he possesses no other, of believing profoundly in the seriousness of his art. May you also find that he thinks of you with great concern. Yes, he has thought of you ever since the days when you were learning to read, when we who are now approaching our fortieth year were scribbling our first verses to the noise of the cannon which roared over Paris. We, in our study chambers, were not gay at that period. The oldest of us had just gone to the war, and those of us who were obliged to remain at college already felt the duty of our country's rehabilitation press heavily upon us. We often thought of you in that fatal year, 1871. Oh! Young Frenchmen of today—all of us who were intending to devote ourselves to literature, my friends and I, repeated the beautiful verses of Théodore de Banville[1]:

---

1. Théodore Faullain de Banville (1823–1891) was a French poet and writer whose work was influential on the Symbolist movement in French literature in the late 19th century.

1

Ye in whom I hail the light,
    All ye who will love me,
O young men of the coming fight,
    O holy battalions!

We wished this dawn of light to be as bright as ours had been gloomy and misty with a vapor of blood. We wished to be worthy of your love, in leaving to you that which we valued more than we valued ourselves. We said that our work was to make of you and for you, by our public and private acts, by our words, by our fervor, and by our example, a new France, a France redeemed from defeat, a France reconstructed in its external and in its internal life. Young as we were then we knew because we had learned it from our masters, and this was their best teaching—that triumphs and defeats from without interpreted the qualities and insufficiencies within; we knew that the resurrection of Germany at the beginning of the century had been above all a work of soul, and we recognized that the soul of France had been terribly hurt in 1870, and that it must be helped, healed and cured. We were not the only ones to comprehend in the generous ingenuousness of our youth that the moral crisis was then as it always is, the great crisis of this country; for in 1873 the most valiant of our leaders, Alexandre Dumas, said in the preface to *La Femme de Claude*, addressing the Frenchmen of his age as I am addressing you, my younger brother:

> Take care, you are passing through troublous times. You have just paid death and are not through paying for your earlier faults. It is no time to be a wit, a trifler, a libertine, a scoffer, a skeptic, or a wanton; we have had enough of these for a time at least. God, nature, work, marriage, love, children, all these are serious, very serious things, and rise up before you. *All these must live or you will die.*

I cannot say of the generation to which I belong, and which kindled the noble hope of reconstructing France, that it has succeeded, or that it has even been sufficiently devoted to its work. But I do know that it has labored, and labored hard. We have plodded away without much method, alas! But

2

with a continuous application which touches me when I think how little the men in power have done for us, how much we have been left to our own resources, of the indifference felt toward us by those who directed affairs, and who never once thought to encourage, support or direct us. Ah! The brave middle class, the solid and valiant *bourgeoisie* which France still possesses! What laborious officers, what skillful and tenacious diplomatic agents, what excellent professors, what honest artisans has this *bourgeoisie* furnished for the past twenty years! I sometimes hear: "What vitality there is in this country! It has survived where another would have perished." Yes, it lives because this young *bourgeoisie* has made every sacrifice in order to serve the country. It has seen the masters of a day proscribe its most cherished beliefs in the name of liberty, chance politicians play universal suffrage as an instrument by which to rule and install their lying mediocrity in the highest places.

This universal suffrage has undergone the most monstrous and the most iniquitous of tyrannies; for the force of numbers is the most brutal of forces, possessing neither talent nor audacity. The young *bourgeoisie* has resigned itself to everything, has accepted everything in order to have the right to do the necessary work. If our soldiers come and go, if foreign powers hold us in respect, if our higher education is being developed, if our arts and our literature continue to assert the national genius, we owe it to the bourgeoisie. It is true that this generation of young men of the war has no victory for its activity. It could not establish a definite form of government, or solve the formidable problems of foreign politics and of socialism. However, young man of today, do not despise it. Learn to render justice to your elders. It is through them that France has lived!

How will she live through you is the question which at the present time troubles all those who have retained their faith in the restoration of France. You have not to see the Prussian cavalry galloping victoriously among the poplars of your native land to sustain you. And of the horrible civil war, you have only the picturesque ruins of the Cour des Comptes[2], or the trees putting forth luxuriant vegetation among the scorched stones which lend

---

2. The Court of Audit is the national French administrative court charged with conducting financial and legislative audits of most public institutions and some private institutions.

poetic attraction to the old palaces. We have never been able to conclude that the peace of '71 has settled everything for all time. How I should like to know if you think as we do! How I should like to be sure that you are not ready to renounce the secret dream, the consolatory hope which each one of us had, even of those of us who never spoke of it! But I am sure that you feel sad whenever you pass the Arc de Triomphe where others have passed, even on those beautiful summer evenings in company with the one you love. You would leave her cheerfully tomorrow to go to the front if it should be necessary, I am sure of it. But it is not enough to know how to die. Have you resolved to know how to live? When you look at this Arc de Triomphe and recall the epoch of the Grande Armée,[3] do you regret that you did not feel the heroic breath of the conscripts of that time? When you recall 1830, and the glorious struggles of Romanticism, do you experience nostalgia at not having, like those of *Hernani*,[4] a great literary standard to defend? Do you feel, when you meet one of the masters of today—a Dumas, a Taine, a Leconte de Lisle[5]—that you are in the presence of one of the depositories of the genius of your race? When you read such books as must be written when it is necessary to depict the criminal passions and their martyrdom, do you wish to love more wisely than the authors of these books have loved? Have you, my brother, more of the Ideal than we have—have you more faith than we have—more hope than we? If you have, give me your hand and let me thank you.

But suppose you have not? There are two types of young men that I see before me, and before you also, like two forms of temptation, equally formidable and fatal. One is cynical and usually jovial. He is about twenty years of age, he appraises life at a discount, and his religion consists in enjoy-

---

3. The Great Army was the imperial army commanded by Napoleon Bonaparte during the Napoleonic Wars.

4. *Hernani* (*Hernani, ou l'Honneur Castillan*) is a drama by Victor Hugo which exalted the Romantic ideals and condemned those of the Classicals.

5. Charles Marie René Leconte de Lisle (1818–1894) was a French poet of the Parnassian movement bridging the Romantic and Symbolist periods. He was involved in the French Revolution of 1848.

ing himself—which may be translated by success. Let him be occupied with politics or business, with literature or art, engaged in sport or in industry, let him be officer, diplomat or advocate—his only God is himself; he is his only principle, his only object. He has borrowed from the natural philosophy of the times the great law of vital concurrence, and he applies it to the advancement of his fortune with an ardor of positivism which makes him a civilized barbarian; the most dangerous kind. Alphonse Daudet,[6] who understands so well how to describe him, has christened him the "struggle-for-lifer." He respects nothing but success, and in success nothing but money. He is convinced when he reads this—for he reads what I write as he reads everything else, if only to be in the current—that I am laughing at the public in tracing this portrait, but that I myself am like him. For he is so profoundly nihilistic in his manner that the Ideal appears to him like a comedy, for example, when he judges it proper to lie to the people to secure their votes. Is not this young man a monster? For one is a monster who is only twenty-five years old and has for a soul a calculating machine in the service of a machine of pleasure.

I fear him less, however, on your account than I do the other one who possesses all the aristocracies of nerves and mind, and who is an intellectual and refined epicurean as the former is a brutal and scientific one. How dreadful to encounter this dainty nihilist, and yet how he abounds! At twenty-five he has run the gamut of all ideas. His critical mind, precociously awake, has comprehended the final results of the most subtle philosophies of the age. Do not speak to him of impiety or of materialism. He knows that the word "matter" has no precise meaning, and besides, he is too intelligent not to admit that all religions have been legitimate in their time. Only, he has never believed, and he never will believe in them, any more than he will ever believe in anything whatever, except in the amusing play of his mind which he has transformed into a tool of elegant perversity. The good and the bad, beauty and deformity, vices and virtues are to him simply objects of curiosity. The human soul so far as he is concerned is a skillful piece of

---

6. Alphonse Daudet (1840–1897) was a French short-story writer and novelist, remembered mainly as the author of sentimental tales of provincial life in the south of France.

mechanism in the dissection of which he is interested as a matter of experience. To him nothing is true, nothing is false, nothing is moral, nothing is immoral. He is a subtle and refined egotist whose whole ambition, as that remarkable analyst, Maurice Barrès,[7] has said in his beautiful romance of *L'Homme Libre*—that *chef-d'oeuvre* of irony which lacks only conclusion—consists "in adoring himself," and to acquire new sensations. The religious life of humanity is to him only a pretext for these sensations, as are also the intellectual and the sentimental life. His corruption is otherwise as profound as that of the voluptuous barbarian; it is differently complicated, and the fine name of dilettantism with which he adorns it, conceals its cold ferocity, its frightful barrenness.

Ah! We know this young man too well; we have all wished to be in his place, for we have been so charmed by the paradoxes of too eloquent teachers; we all have been like him at some time. And so I have written this book to show you, who are not yet like him, you child of twenty years, whose soul is in process of formation, what villainy this egoism may conceal.

Be neither of these young men, my young friend! Be neither the brutal positivist who abuses the world of sense, nor the disdainful and precocious sophist who abuses the world of thought and feeling. Let neither the pride of life nor that of intellect make of you a cynic and a juggler of ideas! In such times of troubled conscience and conflicting doctrines cling as you would to a safe support to Christ's words: "The tree is known by its fruit." There is one reality which you cannot doubt, for you possess it, you feel it, you see it every moment, it is your own soul. Among the thoughts which assail you, are those which render your soul less capable of loving, less capable of desire. Be sure that these ideas are false to a degree, however subtle they seem, adorned as they are with the finest names and sustained by the magic of the most splendid talents.

---

7. Auguste-Maurice Barrès (1862–1923) was a French writer and politician known for his individualism and fervent nationalism; literarily, he is known for his solitary project of self-analysis, a method described in the trilogy of novels entitled *Le Culte du moi* (The Cult of the Ego). This work comprises *Sous l'oeil des Barbares* (Under the Eyes of the Barbarians, 1888), *Un Homme libre* (A Free Man, 1889), and *Le Jardin de Bérénice* (The Garden of Bérénice, 1891).

Exalt and cultivate these two great virtues, these two energies, without which only blight and final agony ensue—Love and Will. The sincere and modest Science of today recognizes that the realm of the Unknowable extends beyond the limit of its analysis. The venerable Littré,[8] who was a saint, has magnificently spoken of this ocean of mystery which beats against our shore, which we see stretching before us, and for which we have neither bark nor sail. Have the courage to respond to those who will tell you that beyond this ocean is emptiness, an abyss of darkness and death; "You do not know that." And since you know, since you feel that there is a soul within you, labor to keep it alive lest it die before you. I assure you, my boy, France has need that you should think thus, and may this book help you so to think. Do not look here for allusions to recent events, for you will not find them. The plan was marked out and a part of the book written before two tragedies, the one French, the other European, occurred, to attest that the same trouble of ideas and of sentiments agitates both high and humble destinies at the present time. Do me the honor to believe that I have not speculated on the dramas in which too many persons have suffered, and still suffer. The moralist, whose business it is to seek for causes, sometimes encounters analogies of situation which attest that they have seen correctly. They would rather have been deceived. I, myself, for example, would wish that there never had been in real life a person like the unfortunate Disciple who gives name to this romance! But if there had not been, if none existed, I should not have said what I am going to say to you, my young countryman, you to whom I wish to be a benefactor, you by whom I so earnestly wish to be loved—and to be worthy of your love.

Paul Bourget

Paris, June 5, 1889

---

8. Émile Maximilien Paul Littré (1801–1881) was a French language scholar, lexicographer and philosopher, best known for his *Dictionnaire de la langue française*, commonly called *le Littré*.

The Disciple

I.

A MODERN PHILOSOPHER

THERE IS A STORY that has never been denied to the effect that the bourgeois of the city of Konigsberg supposed that some prodigious event was disturbing the civilized world simply because the philosopher Emanuel Kant changed the direction of his daily walk. The celebrated author of the *Critique of Pure Reason* had that day learned of the breaking out of the French Revolution. Although Paris may not be very favorable to such naive wonders, a number of the inhabitants of the Rue Guy de la Brosse experienced an astonishment almost as great one afternoon in January, 1887, when they saw go out, toward one o'clock, a philosopher, who if less illustrious than the venerable Kant, was as regular and as peculiar in his habits, not to mention that he was even more destructive in his analysis. It was M. Adrien Sixte, whom the English call the French Spencer.

This Rue Guy de la Brosse, which leads from the Rue de Jussieu to the Rue Linné, forms part of a veritable little province bounded by the Jardin des Plantes, the Hôpitaux de la Pitié, the wine warehouse, and the first rise of Sainte-Genevieve. That is to say, that it permits those familiar inquisitions of glance impossible in the larger districts where the come-and-go of existence ceaselessly renews the tide of carriages and of people. Only persons of small incomes live here, modest professors, employees of the museum, students who wish to study, all young literary people who dread the temptations of the Latin Quarter. The shops are patronized by this clientele, which is as regular as that of a suburb. The butcher, the baker, the grocer, the washerwoman, the apothecary, are all spoken of in the singular by the domestics who make the purchases.

There is little room for competition in this square, which is ornamented by a fountain capriciously encumbered with figures of animals in honor of the Jardin des Plantes. Visitors to the garden seldom enter by the gate, which is opposite the hospital; so that even on fine spring days when crowds of people gather under the trees of the park, which is a favorite resort of the military and of nursemaids, the Rue Linné is as quiet as usual, and so also are the adjacent streets.

If occasionally there is an unusual flow of people into this corner of Paris, it is when the doors of the hospital are opened to visitors, and then a line of sad and humble figures stretches along the sidewalks. These pilgrims of poverty come furnished with dainties for their friends who are suffering behind the gray old walls of the hospital, and the inhabitants of ground floors, lodges, and shops are not interested in them. They hardly notice these sporadic promenaders, and their entire attention is reserved for the persons who go by every day at the same hour. There are for shopkeepers and concierges, as for sportsmen in the country, unfailing indications of the time and of the weather, that there will be in this quarter, where resound the savage calls of some beast in the neighboring menagerie; of an *ara*[1] that cries, an elephant that trumpets, an eagle that screams, or a tiger that mews. When they see the free professor jogging along with his old green leather case under his arm, nibbling at a penny bun which he has bought on his way, these spies know that it is about to strike eight.

When the restaurant boy passes with his covered dishes they know that it is eleven o'clock, and that the retired captain of battalion is soon to have his breakfast, and thus in succession for every hour of the day. A change in the toilette of the women who here display their finery, is noted and critically interpreted by twenty babbling and not overindulgent tongues. In fine, to use a very picturesque expression common in central France, the most trifling movements of the frequenters of these four or five streets are at the end of the tongues, and those of M. Adrien Sixte even more than those of many others. This will be readily understood by a simple sketch of the person. And besides, the details of the life led by this man will furnish to students of human nature an authentic document upon a rare species—that of philosopher by profession. Some examples have been given to us by the ancients,

---

1. *Ara* (an onomatopoeia of the sound a macaw makes) is a Neotropical genus of macaws. The genus was erected by the French naturalist Bernard Germain de Lacépède in 1799.

and more recently by Colerus,[2] in reference to Spinoza, and by Darwin and John Stuart Mill in reference to themselves. But Spinoza was a Hollander of the eighteenth century, Darwin and Mill grew up among the wealthy and active English middle class, whereas M. Sixte lived in the heart of Paris at the end of the nineteenth century. In my youth, when studies of this kind interested me, I knew several individuals just as entirely given up to abstract speculations. I have, however, never met one who has made me comprehend so well the existence of a Descartes—in his little room in the depth of the Netherlands, or that of the thinker of the *Ethics*,[3] who, as we know, had no other distraction from his reveries than smoking a pipe and fighting spiders.

It was fourteen years after the war when M. Sixte came to live in the Rue Guy de la Brosse, where every denizen knows him today. He was at that time a man thirty-four years of age, in whom all physiognomy of youth had been destroyed by the absorption of his mind in ideas, so that his smoothly shaven face indicated neither age nor profession. Some physicians, some priests, and some actors offer to our regard, for different reasons, faces at once cold, smooth, intent and inexpressive. A forehead high and tapering, a mouth prominent and obstinate, with thin lips, a bilious complexion, eyes affected by too much reading and hidden behind dark spectacles, a slim, big-boned body, always clothed in a shaggy cloth overcoat in winter, and in some thin material in summer. His shoes tied with strings, his hair long and prematurely gray and very fine, under one of those hats called a *gibus*,[4] which fold up mechanically—such was the appearance presented by this savant, whose every action was as scrupulously regulated as those of an ecclesiastic. He occupied an apartment at a rent of seven hundred francs on the fourth floor, which consisted of a bedroom, a study, a dining-room about as large as the

---

2. Johannes Nicolaus Colerus (1647–1707) was a German Lutheran theologian and one of the early biographers of the philosopher Baruch de Spinoza (1632–1677).

3. *Ethics, Demonstrated in Geometrical Order* (commonly referred to as the *Ethics*) is a philosophical treatise written by Baruch de Spinoza, one of the great rationalists of 17th-century philosophy.

4. A *gibus* is (also called a chapeau or claque) is a top hat that is collapsible through a spring system, originally intended for less spacious venues, such as the theatre and opera house.

cabin of a wherry,[5] a kitchen and a servant's room, the whole commanding a very extensive view. The philosopher could see from his windows the Jardin des Plantes with the hills of Père Lachaise in the distance; beyond, to the left, a kind of hollow which marked the course of the Seine. The Orléans station and the dome of La Salpêtrière rose directly in front; and, to the right, the mass of cedars looked black against the green or bare trees of the labyrinth. The smoke of factories wreathed upward on a clear or gray sky from every corner of the wide landscape, from which arose a sound like the roar of a distant ocean, broken by the whistlings of steam engines. In choosing this Thebais,[6] M. Sixte had no doubt yielded to a general though inexplicable law of meditative nature. Are not nearly all cloisters built in places which permit an extended view? Perhaps these unlimited and confused prospects favor concentration of the mind, which might otherwise be distracted by details too near and circumstantial? Perhaps recluses find the pleasure of contrast between their dreamy inaction and the breadth of the field in which the activity of other men is developed? Whatever may be the solution of this little problem so closely related to another which is too little studied, namely, the animal sensibility of intellectual men—it is certain that the melancholy landscape had, for fifteen years, been the companion with whom the quiet worker had most frequently conversed. His house was kept by one of those servants who are the ideals of all old bachelors, who never suspect that the perfection of certain services implies a corresponding regularity of existence on the part of the master. On his arrival, the philosopher had simply asked the concierge to find someone to keep his rooms in order, and to recommend a restaurant from which he could order his meals. By this request he risked obtaining a service decidedly bad and a very uncertain sort of nourishment. It resulted, however, in unexpectedly introducing into the home of Adrien Sixte precisely the person who realized his most chimerical wishes, if an extractor of quintessences, as Rabelais calls this sort of dreamer, still

---

5. A wherry is a type of boat that was traditionally used for carrying cargo or passengers on rivers and canals.

6. Thebais (or Thebaid) is used here in reference to the desert region in ancient Egypt which, in the 5th century, became a place of retreat fot numerous Christian hermits and monks.

preserves the leisure to form wishes.

This concierge—according to the use and custom of all such functionaries in small apartment houses—increased the revenue of his lodgings by working at a trade. He was a shoemaker, "in new and old," as a placard read which was pasted on a window toward the street. Among his customers, old man Carbonnet—this was his name—counted a priest who lived in the Rue Cuvier. This aged priest had a servant. Mlle. Mariette Trapenard, a woman nearly forty years old, who had been accustomed for some years to rule in her master's house while still remaining a true peasant woman, with no ambition to play the lady, faithful in her work, but unwilling to enter at any price a house where she would be subject to feminine authority. The old priest died quite suddenly the week preceding the installation of the philosopher in the Rue Guy de la Brosse. Old Carbonnet, in whose register the newcomer had simply signed himself *rentier*, had no trouble in recognizing the class to which this M. Sixte belonged, first from the number of books which composed his library, and also through the account of a servant belonging to a professor of the College of France, who lived on the first floor.

In these *phalausteries*[7] of the Parisian bourgeois everything becomes an event. The maid told her mistress the name of her future neighbor; the mistress told her husband; she spoke of M. Sixte at table in such a way that the maid comprehended enough to surmise that the new lodger was "in books like monsieur." Carbonnet would not have been worthy of drawing the cord in a Parisian lodging-house, if his wife and he had not immediately felt the necessity of bringing M. Adrien Sixte and Mlle. Trapenard together. They felt this the more because Mme. Carbonnet, who was old and almost disabled, had already too much to do to take care of three households, to undertake this one. The taste for intrigue which flourishes in lodging-houses like fuchsias, geraniums, and basils induced this couple to assure the savant

---

7. *Phalausteries* were conceived by François Marie Charles Fourier (1772–1837)—a French philosopher known as one of the founders of utopian socialism—as a type of building designed for a self-contained utopian communities that would abolish national boundaries. Fourier chose the name by combining the French word *phalange* (phalanx, an emblematic military unit in ancient Greece) with the word *monastère* (monastery).

that the cooking at the eating-houses was wretched, that there was not a single housekeeper whom they could recommend in the whole neighborhood, and that the servant of the late M. Abbé Vayssier was a "pearl" of discretion, order, economy, and culinary skill. Finally, the philosopher consented to see this model housekeeper. The visible honesty of the woman pleased him and also the reflection that this arrangement would simplify his existence, by relieving him from the odious task of giving a certain number of positive orders. Mlle. Trapenard entered the service of this master for fifty francs a month, which was soon increased to sixty. The savant gave her fifty francs in New Year gifts beside. He never examined his accounts, but settled them every Sunday morning without question. It was Mlle. Trapenard who did the business with all the tradesmen without any interference on the part of M. Sixte.

In a word she reigned absolute mistress, a situation, as may be imagined, which excited the universal envy of the little world incessantly going up and down the common staircase so zealously scrubbed every Monday.

"I say, Mam'zelle Mariette, you have drawn the lucky number," said Carbonnet as the housekeeper stopped a minute to chat with her benefactor, who was now much older.

He wore spectacles on his square nose, and it was with some difficulty that he adjusted the blows of his hammer to the heads of the nails which he drove into the boot-heels closely pressed between his legs. For some years he had taken care of a cock named Ferdinand—why, no one knew. This creature wandered about among the bits of leather, exciting the admiration of all visitors by his eagerness to peck at the buttons of the boots. In his moments of fright this pet cock would take refuge with his master, plunge one of his feet into the pocket of the cobbler's vest and hide his head under the arm of the old concierge: "Come, Ferdinand, say good-day to Mam'zelle Mariette," resumed Carbonnet. And the cock gently pecked the woman's hand, while his master continued:

"I always say, never despair at one bad year, two good ones are bound to come immediately after."

"There we agree," responded Mariette, "for monsieur is a good man, though as to religion he is a regular pagan; he has not been to mass these fifteen years."

"There are plenty who do go," replied Carbonnet, "who are sad dogs, and lead anything but a quiet life between four and midnight—without your knowing anything about it."

This fragment of conversation perhaps shows the type of opinion which Mariette held in regard to her master; but this opinion would be unintelligible if we did not recall here the works of the philosopher, and the trend of his thought.

Born in 1839 at Nancy, where his father kept a little watchmaker's shop, and remarkable for the precocity of his intellect, Adrien Sixte left among his comrades the remembrance of a child thin and taciturn, endowed with a strength of moral resistance which always discouraged familiarity. At first he was very brilliant in his studies, then mediocre, until in the class in philosophy which then bore the name of Logic, he distinguished himself by his exceptional aptitude. His professor, struck by his metaphysical talent, wished him to prepare for the normal school examination. Adrien refused and declared beside to his father that, taking one trade with another, he preferred manual labor. "I will be a watchmaker like you," was his sole answer to the objurgations of his father, who, like the innumerable artisans, or French merchants whose children attend college, cherished the dream that his son might be a civil officer.

M. and Mme. Sixte could not reproach this son, who did not smoke, never went to the cafe, was never seen with a girl, in fine, who was their pride, and to whose wishes they resigned themselves with a broken heart. They renounced a career for him, but they would not consent to putting him to an apprenticeship, hence, the young man lived at home with no other occupation than to study as suited his fancy.

He employed ten years in perfecting himself in the study of English and German philosophy, in the natural sciences and especially in the physiology of the brain and in the mathematical sciences; finally, he gave himself, as one of the great thinkers of our epoch has said of himself, that "violent inflammation of the brain," that kind of apoplexy of positive knowledge which was the process of education of Carlyle and of Mill, of Taine[8] and Renan, and of nearly all the masters of modern philosophy. In 1868, the son of the watchmaker of Nancy, then twenty-five years of age, published a large volume of five hundred pages entitled: *Psychology of God*, which he did not send to more than fifteen persons, but which had the unexpected fortune of causing a scandalous echo. This book, written in the solitude of the most honest thought, presented the double character of a critical analysis, keen to severity, and an ardor in negation exalted to fanaticism. Less poetic than M. Taine, incapable of writing the magnificent preface to *On Intelligence*, and the essay upon universal phenomena; less dry than M. Ribot,[9] who already preluded by his *English Psychology*[10] the beautiful series of his studies, *Psychology of God*, combined the eloquence of one with the penetration of the other, and it had the chance, unsought, of directly attacking the most exciting problem of metaphysics. A pamphlet by a well-known bishop, an unworthy allusion of a cardinal in a discourse to the senate, a crushing article by the most brilliant critical spiritualist in a celebrated review, sufficed to point out the work to the curiosity of the youth over whom passed a revolutionary wind, the herald of future overthrow. The thesis of the author consisted in demonstrating the necessary production of "the hypothesis—God," by the action of some psychological laws, which are themselves connected with some cerebral modifications of an entirely physical order, and this thesis was established, supported, and developed with an acrimony of atheism which recalled the fury of Lucretius against the beliefs of his time. It happened then to the hermit of Nancy, that his work, which was conceived and written as if in the solitude of a cell, was at once in the midst of the noise of the battle of contemporaneous ideas. For years there had not been seen such power of general ideas wedded to such amplitude of erudition, nor so rich

---

8. Hippolyte Adolphe Taine (1828–1893) was a French critic and historian. He was the primary theoretical influence of French naturalism, a major proponent of sociological positivism, and one of the first practitioners of historical criticism.

9. Théodule-Armand Ribot (1839–1916) was a French psychologist. He is known as the founder of scientific psychology in France and for Ribot's Law regarding retrograde amnesia.

10. A scholarly survey of contemporary English psychology by Ribot (published in 1874).

an abundance of points of view united to so audacious a nihilism. But while the name of the author was becoming celebrated in Paris, his parents were bowed to the earth by his success. Some articles in the Catholic journals filled Mme. Sixte with despair. The old watchmaker trembled lest he should lose his customers among the aristocracy of Nancy.

All the miseries of the province crushed the philosopher, who was about to leave his home, when the German invasion and the fearful national shipwreck turned the attention of his countrymen away from him. His parents died in the spring of 1871. In the summer of the same year, he lost an aunt, and so in the autumn of 1872 having settled his affairs, he came to establish himself in Paris. His resources, thanks to the inheritance of his parents and of his aunt, consisted in eight thousand francs income invested in a life-interest. He had resolved never to marry, never to go into society, never to be ambitious of honor, of place nor of reputation. The whole formula of his life was contained in the words: *To think!*

In order to better define this man of a quality so rare that this sketch after nature will risk appearing untruthful to the reader who is unfamiliar with the biographies of the great manipulators of ideas, it is necessary to give a rapid glance at some of the days of this powerful thinker.

Summer and winter, M. Sixte sat down to his work at six o'clock in the morning, refreshed by a single cup of black coffee. At ten o'clock he took his breakfast, a summary operation which permitted him to be at the gate of the Jardin des Plantes at half-past ten. He walked in the garden until noon, sometimes extending his stroll toward the quays[11] and by the way of Notre-Dame.

One of his favorite pleasures consisted in long séances in front of the cages of the monkeys and the lodges of the elephants. The children and servants who saw him laugh, long and silently, at the ferocities and cynicisms of the baboons and *ouistitis*,[12] never suspected the misanthropic thoughts

---

11. A quay is a concrete, stone, or metal platform lying alongside or projecting into water for loading and unloading ships.

12. An *ouistiti* (imitative of the animal's cry) is a marmoset, any of several small native South American monkeys, which are easily recognizable by their long silky coat and bushy tail.

which this spectacle brought to the mind of the savant who compared in himself the human to the simian comedy, as he compared our habitual folly with the wisdom of the noble animal that, before us, was king of the earth.

Toward noon M. Sixte returned to his home and worked again until four o'clock. From four to six he received three times a week, visitors who were nearly always students, masters occupied with the same studies as himself, or foreigners attracted by a reputation which today is European. Three other days he went out to make some indispensable visits. At six o'clock he dined and then went out again, this time going the length of the closed garden to the Orléans station. At eight o'clock he returned, regulated his correspondence or read. At ten o'clock the lights were extinguished in his house.

This monastic existence had its weekly rest on Monday, the philosopher having observed that Sunday emptied an obstructing tide of pleasure seekers into the country. On these days, he went out very early in the morning, boarded a suburban train, and did not return until evening.

Not once in fifteen years had he departed from this absolute regularity. Not once had he accepted an invitation to dine nor taken a stall in a theater. He never read a newspaper, relying on his publisher for marked copies pertaining to his own works.

His indifference to politics was so complete that he had never drawn his elector's card. It is proper to add, in order to fix the principal features of this singular being, that he had broken off all connection with his family, and that this rupture was founded, like the smallest act of his life, upon a theory. He had written in the preface to his second book, *Anatomy of the Will*, this significant sentence:

> The social attachments should be reduced to their minimum for the man who wishes to know and speak the truth in the domain of the psychological sciences.

From a similar motive this man, who was so gentle that he had not given three commands to his servant in fifteen years, systematically forbade himself all charity. On this point he agreed with Spinoza who has written in the fourth book of the *Ethics*: "Pity, for a wise man who lives according to reason, is bad and useless." This Saint Lais, as he might have been called as justly as the venerable Emile Littré, hated in Christianity the excessive fondness for humanity. He gave these two reasons for it: first that the hypothesis of a Heavenly Father and of eternal happiness had developed to excess the distaste for the real and had diminished the power to accept the laws of nature; second, in establishing the social order upon love, that is, upon sensibility, this religion had opened the way to all the caprices of the most personal doctrines.

He did not suspect that his faithful servant had sewed consecrated medals into all his vests, and his indifference with regard to the external world was so complete that he went without meat on Fridays and on other days prescribed by the Church, without perceiving this effort on the part of the old maid to assure the salvation of a master of whom she sometimes said, repeating unconsciously a celebrated saying: "The good God would not be the good God, if he had the heart to damn him."

These years of continuous labor in this hermitage of the Rue Guy de la Brosse had produced, beside *Anatomy of the Will*, a *Theory of the Passions*, in three volumes, whose publication would have been still more scandalous than that of *Psychology of God*, if the extreme liberty of the press for ten years had not accustomed readers to audacities of description which the mild, technical ferocity of a savant could not equal.

In these two books is found, precisely stated, the doctrine of M. Sixte which it is necessary to take up again here, in some of its general features, for the intelligent understanding of the drama to which this short biography serves as prologue. With the critical school sprung from Kant, the author of these three treatises admits that the mind is powerless to know causes and substances, and that it ought only to coordinate phenomena.

With the English psychologists, he admits that one group among these phenomena, those which are classed under the name of soul, may be the object of scientific knowledge, on condition of their being studied after a scientific method.

Up to this point, as we all see, there is nothing in these theories which distinguishes them from those which Messrs.[13] Taine, Ribot and their disciples have developed in their principal works.

The two original characteristics of M. Sixte's inquiries are found elsewhere. The first resides in a negative analysis of what Herbert Spencer calls the Unknowable. We know that the great English thinker admits that all reality rests upon a First Cause which it is impossible to penetrate; consequently it is necessary to use the formula of Fichte to comprehend this First Cause (*arrière-fonds*) as incomprehensible; but as the beginning of the *First Principles* strongly attests this Unknowable is real to Mr. Spencer. It exists since we derive our existence from it. From this there is only a step to apprehend that this First Cause of all reality involves a mind and a soul since one finds their source in it. Many excellent minds foresee a probable reconciliation between science and religion on this ground of the Unknowable. For M. Sixte this is a last form of metaphysical illusion which he is rabid to destroy with an energy of argument that has not been seen to this degree since Kant.

His second title of honor as psychologist consists in an exposé, quite novel and very ingenious, of the animal origin of human sensibility.

Thanks to an exhaustive reading and a minute knowledge of the natural sciences, he has been able to attempt for the genesis of human thought the work which Darwin attempted for the genesis of the forms of life. Applying the law of evolution to all the facts which constitute the human heart, he has claimed to show that, our most refined sensations, our most subtle moral delicacies as well as our most shameful failures, are the latest development, the supreme metamorphosis of very simple instincts, which are themselves transformations of the primitive cellule; so that the moral universe exactly reproduces the physical and the former is the consciousness, either painful or pleasurable, of the latter.

This conclusion presented under the title of hypothesis because of its metaphysical character, is the result of a marvelous series of analyses, among which it is proper to cite two hundred pages on love, which are so audacious as to be almost ludicrous from the pen of so chaste a man. But has not

---

13. *Messrs.* is an abbreviation of messieurs (plural of monsieur) used as a title to refer formally to more than one man simultaneously.

Spinoza himself given us a theory of jealousy which has not been equaled in brutality by any modern novelist? And does not Schopenhauer rival Chamfort[14] in the spirit of his tirades against women?

It is almost unnecessary to add that the most complete positivism pervades these books from one end to the other. We owe to M. Sixte some sentences which express with extreme energy this conviction that everything in the mind is there of necessity, even the illusion that we are free:

> Every act is only an addition. To say he is free, is to say that there is in the total more than there is in the sum of all the parts. That is as absurd in psychology as it is in arithmetic.

And again:

> If we could know correctly the relative position of all the phenomena which constitute the actual universe, we could, from the present, calculate with a certainty equal to that of the astronomers the day, the hour, the minute when England, for example, will evacuate India, or Europe will have burned her last piece of coal, or such a criminal, still unborn, will assassinate his father, or such a poem, not yet conceived will be written. The future is contained in the present as all the properties of the triangle are contained in its definition.

Mohammedan fatalism[15] itself is not expressed with more absolute precision.

With speculations of this order, only the most frightful aridity of imagination would seem to comport. Thus that which M. Sixte so often said of

---

14. Sébastien Nicolas de Chamfort (1741–1794) was a French writer known for his epigrams and aphorisms. He was secretary to Louis XVI's sister, and of the Jacobin club.

15. Fatalism is a view which generally holds that all events in the history of the world, and, in particular, the actions and incidents which make up each individual life, are determined by fate. *Mohammedan fatalism* places such an emphasis on God as the sole cause of all events that secondary causes, such as action based in the free will of an individual, are practically excluded.

himself: "I take life on its poetic side," appeared to those who heard it the most absurd of paradoxes. And yet nothing is truer with regard to the special nature of the minds of philosophers. What essentially distinguishes the born philosopher from other men is that ideas instead of being formulas of the mind more or less exact, are to him real and living things. Sensibility, with him, models itself upon the thought instead of establishing a divorce more or less complete, between the heart and the brain, as with the rest of us.

A Christian preacher has admirably shown the nature of this divorce when he uttered this strange and profound sentence: "We *know* well that we shall die, but we do not *believe* it."

The philosopher, when he is one by passion and by constitution, does not conceive this duality, this life divided between contradictory sensations and reflections. This universal necessity, this indefinite and constant meta-morphosis of phenomena, this colossal work of nature ceaselessly making and unmaking itself, with no point of departure, no point of arrival, by the play of the primitive cells alone, this parallel work of the human mind reproducing under the form of thoughts and volitions the movement of phys-iological life, was not for M. Sixte a simple object of speculation.

He plunged into the contemplation of these ideas with a kind of vertigo, he felt them with all his being, so that this simple man seated at his table, waited upon by his old housekeeper, in a study whose shelves were laden with books, this man of poor appearance, with his feet in a carriage boot to keep them warm, and his body wrapped in a shabby great coat, participated in imagination in the labor of the universe.

He lived the life of every creature. He slept with the mineral, vegetated with the plant, moved with the rudimentary beasts, confounded himself with the superior organisms, and at last expanded into the fullness of a mind capable of reflecting the vast universe.

These are the delights of general ideas, analogous to those of opium, which render these dreamers indifferent to the small accidents of the exter-nal world, and also—why shall we not say it?—almost absolute strangers to the ordinary affections of life.

We become attached to that which we feel to be very real; now to these singular minds, it is abstraction which is reality, and the daily reality is only a shadow, only a gross and degraded impression of the invisible laws. Perhaps M. Sixte had loved his mother, but surely this was the limit of his sentimental existence.

If he was gentle and indulgent to all, it was from the same instinct which made him take hold of a chair gently, when he wished to move it out of his way; but he had never felt the need of a warm and loving tenderness, of family, of devotion, of love, nor even of friendship. He sometimes conversed with some savants with whom he was associated, but always professionally on chemistry with one, on the higher mathematics with another, and on the diseases of the nervous system with a third. Whether these men were married, occupied in rearing families, anxious to make a career for themselves or not, was of no interest to him in his relations with them; but however strange such a conclusion must appear after such a sketch, he was happy. Given such a man, such a home and such a life, let us imagine the effect produced in this study in the Rue Guy de la Brosse by two events which occurred one after the other in the same afternoon: first, a summons addressed to M. Adrien Sixte, to appear at the office of M. Valette, Judge of Instruction,[16] for the purpose of being questioned, "upon certain facts and circumstances of which he would be informed;" second, a card bearing the name of Mme. Greslou and asking M. Sixte to receive her the next day toward four o'clock, "to talk with him about the crime of which her son was falsely accused."

I have said that the philosopher never read a newspaper. If by chance he had opened one a fortnight before he would have found allusions to this history of the young Greslou which more recent trials have caused to be forgotten. For want of this information the summons and the note of the mother had no definite meaning for him. However, by the relation between them he concluded that they were probably connected, and he thought they concerned a certain Robert Greslou, whom he had known the preceding year, in quite simple circumstances. But these circumstances contrasted too strongly with the idea of a criminal process, to guide the conjectures of the

16. The Judge of Instruction (*Juge d'instruction*, Judge of Inquiry) in France is a magistrate responsible for conducting the investigative hearing that precedes a criminal trial.

savant, and he remained a long time looking at the summons turn by turn with the card, a prey to that almost painful anxiety which the least event of an unexpected nature does inflict on men of fixed habits.

Robert Greslou? M. Sixte had read this name for the first time two years before, at the bottom of a note accompanying a manuscript. This manuscript bore the title: "Contribution to the Study of the Multiplication of Self," and the note modestly expressed the wish that the celebrated writer would glance at the first essay of a very young man. The author had added to his signature: "Veteran pupil of philosophy at the Clermont-Ferrand Lyceum."

This work of almost sixty pages revealed an intellect so prematurely subtle, an acquaintance so exact with the most recent theories of contemporaneous psychology, and finally such ingenuity of analysis, that M. Sixte had believed it a duty to respond by a long letter.

A note of thanks had come back immediately, in which the young man announced that, being obliged to go to Paris for the oral examination of the normal school, he would have the honor to present himself to the master.

The latter had then seen enter his study one afternoon, a young man of about twenty years with fine black eyes, lively and changeable, which lighted up a countenance which was almost too pale. This was the only detail of physiognomy which remained in the memory of the philosopher. Like all other speculative persons, he received only a floating impression of the visible world and he retained but a remembrance as vague as this impression. His memory of ideas was, however, surprising, and he recalled to the smallest detail his conversation with Robert Greslou.

Among the young men whom his renown attracted to him, none had astonished him more by the truly extraordinary precocity of his erudition and his reasoning. No doubt there floated in the mind of this youth much of the effervescence of mind which assimilates too quickly vast quantities of diverse knowledge; but what marvelous facility of deduction! What natural eloquence, and what visible sincerity of enthusiasm.

The savant could see him gesticulating a little and saying: "No, monsieur, you do not know what you are to us, nor what we feel in reading your books. You are the one who accepts the whole truth, the one in whom we can believe. Why, the analysis of love in your *Theory of the Passions* is our breviary. The book is forbidden at the Lyceum. I had it at home and two of my comrades copied certain chapters during the holidays."

As there is the author's vanity hidden in the soul of every man who has had his prose printed, be he even so absolutely sincere as M. Adrien Sixte certainly was, this worship of a group of scholars, so ingenuously expressed by one of them, had particularly flattered the philosopher.

Robert Greslou had solicited the honor of a second visit, and then while confessing a failure at the normal school, he disclosed a little of his projects.

M. Sixte, contrary to all his habits, had questioned him upon the most minute details. He had thus learned that the young man was the only son of an engineer who had died without leaving a fortune, and that his mother had made many sacrifices in order to educate him. "But I will accept no more," said Robert, "it is my intention to take my degree next year, then I shall ask for a chair of philosophy in some college, and I will write an extended work on the variation of personality, of which the essay that I submitted to you is the embryo." And the eyes of the young psychologist grew more brilliant as he formulated this programme of life.

These two visits dated from August, 1885, the second was in February, 1887, and since then, M. Sixte had received five or six letters from his young disciple. The last announced the entrance of Robert Greslou as preceptor, into a noble family that was passing the summer months in a chateau near one of the pretty lakes of the Auvergne Mountains—Lake Aydat.

A simple detail will give the measure of the preoccupation into which M. Sixte was thrown by the coincidence between the letter from the office of the judge and the note of Mme. Greslou. Although there were upon his table, the proofs of a long article for the *Philosophical Review* to correct, he began searching for the correspondence with the young man. He found it readily in the box in which he carefully arranged his smallest papers. It was classed with others of the same kind, under the head: "Doctrines contemporaneous on the formation of mind."

It made nearly thirty pages, which the savant read again with special care, without finding anything but reflections of an entirely intellectual order, various questions upon some readings, and the statements of certain projects for memories.

What thread could connect such preoccupations with the criminal process of which the mother spoke? Was this process the cause of the summons otherwise inexplicable? This boy whom he had seen only twice must have made a strong impression on the philosopher, for the thought that the mystery hidden behind this call from the Palais de Justice was the same as that which caused the sudden visit of this despairing mother kept him awake a part of the night.

For the first time in all these years he was sharp with Mlle. Trapenard because of some slight negligence, and when he passed in front of the lodge at one o'clock in the afternoon his face, usually so calm, expressed anxiety so plainly that Father Carbonnet, already prepared by the letter of citation which had arrived unsealed, according to a barbarous custom, and which he had read, and as was right confided to his wife—it was now the talk of the whole quarter—said:

"I am not inquisitive about other people's business, but I would give years of my life as landlord to know what justice can want of poor M. Sixte that he should come down at this time of day."

"Why, M. Sixte has changed his hour for walking," said the baker's daughter to her mother, as she sat behind the counter in the shop, "it seems that he is going to have a lawsuit over an inheritance."

"Strike me if that isn't old Sixte going by, the old zebra! It appears that justice is after him," said one of the two pupils in pharmacy to his comrade; "these old fellows look very innocent, but at bottom they are all rogues."

"He is more of a bear than usual, he will not even speak to us." This was said by the wife of the professor of the College of France who lived in the same house with the philosopher and who had just met him. "So much the better, and they say he is going to be prosecuted for writing such books. I am not sorry for that."

Thus we see how the most modest men, and those who believe themselves to be the least noticed, can not stir a step without incurring the comments of innumerable tongues, even though they live in what Parisians are pleased to call a quiet quarter. Let us add that M. Sixte would have cared as little for this curiosity, even if he had suspected it, as he cared for a volume of official philosophy. This was for him an expression of extreme contempt.

II.

THE GRESLOU AFFAIR

THE CELEBRATED philosopher was in everything methodically punctual. Among the maxims which he had adopted at the beginning, in imitation of Descartes, was this: "Order enfranchises the mind."

He arrived, therefore, at the Palais de Justice five minutes before the time appointed. He had to wait a half-hour in the corridor before the judge called him. In this long passage, with its long, bare, white walls, and furnished with a few chairs and tables for the use of the messengers, all voices were lowered, as is usual in all official antechambers.

There were six or seven other persons. The savant's companions were an honest bourgeois and his wife, some shopkeepers of the neighborhood who were very much out of their element. The sight of this person, with his smoothly-shaven face, his eyes hidden behind the dark, round glasses of his spectacles, with his long redingote[1] and his inexplicable physiognomy made these people so uneasy that they left the place where they were whispering together:

"He is a detective," whispered the husband to his wife.

"Do you think so?" asked the woman regarding the enigmatic and immovable figure in terror. "*Dieu!* But he has a false look!"

While this profoundly comic scene was being acted, without the professional observer of the human heart suspecting for a moment the effect he was producing, nor even noticing that there was any one beside him awaiting audience, the Judge of Instruction was talking with a friend in a small room adjoining his office.

Adorned with the autographs and portraits of some famous criminals,

---

1. Redingote is a French alteration of the English "riding coat," referring to a loose "great coat" style, replete with overlapping capes or collars.

this apartment served M. Valette for toilet-room, smoking-room, and also a place of retreat when he wished to chat out of the inevitable presence of his clerk.

The judge was a man less than forty years of age, with a handsome profile, clothes cut in the latest fashion and with rings on his fingers, in fact, a magistrate of the new school. He held in his hand the paper on which the savant had written his name in a clear, running hand and passed it to his friend, a simple man of leisure, with one of those physiognomies at once nervous and expressionless which are only seen in Paris. Would you try to read their tastes, habits, or character? It is impossible, so manifold and contradictory are the sensations which have passed over the countenance. This *viveur*[2] was one of those men who are always present at first representations, who visit painters' studios, who attend sensational trials, and who pride themselves on being *au courant*[3] with the affairs of the day, "in the swim," as they say today.

After reading the name of Adrien Sixte, he exclaimed:

"Well, old fellow, have you the chance of talking with that man! You remember his chapter on love in some old book or other. Ah! He's a lascar who knows all about the women. But what the devil are you going to question him about?"

"About this Greslou case," replied the judge; "the young man has often been to his house, and the defense has summoned him as witness for the prisoner. A commission of examination has been issued, nothing more."

"I wish I could see him," said the other.

"Would it give you pleasure? Nothing easier. I am going to have him called. You will go out as he comes in. Well, it is settled that we will meet at Durand's at eight o'clock, is it? Will Gladys be there?"

"Of course. Do you know Gladys' latest? We were reproaching Chris-

---

2. An English expression (from a pseudo-French formation) meaning one who indulges freely or with habitual excess in the pleasures of life, a debauchee.

3. A French expression (literally, in the current) meaning up-to-date, especially in knowledge of current affairs.

tine in her presence for deceiving Jacques, when she said:

"But she must have two lovers, for she spends in one year twice what each one gives her!"

"Faith," said Valette, "I believe that she surpasses, in the philosophy of love, all the Sixtes in the world and in the demi-world too."

The two friends laughed gayly, then the judge gave the order to call the philosopher. The curious one, while shaking hands with Valette and saying: "Goodbye till evening, precisely at eight o'clock," winked his eye behind his single eyeglass in order the better to unmask the illustrious writer whom he knew from having read the piquant extracts from *Theory of the Passions*, in the newspapers.

The appearance of the good man, at once timid and eccentric, who entered the judge's office with the most visible embarrassment, contradicted so plainly the idea of the biting misanthrope, cruel and disillusioned, who was outlined in their imagination, that the man-about-town and the magistrate exchanged a look of astonishment. A smile came irresistibly to their lips, but only for a moment. The friend was already gone. The other motioned to the witness to take a seat in one of the green velvet arm chairs with which the room was furnished, a luxury completed, in the administrative manner, by a green moquette carpet and a mahogany writing desk. The face of the judge had resumed its gravity.

These changes from one attitude to another, are much more sincere than those imagine who observe these contrasts of bearing between the private man and the functionary. The perfect social comedian, who holds his profession in perfect contempt, is happily a very rare monster. We have not this strength of skepticism in the service of our hypocrisies. The witty M. Valette, so popular in the *demi-monde*,[4] the friend of sporting men, emulated by journalists in witticisms, and who had just now commented gayly upon the remark of a bold woman with whom he should dine in the evening, found no trouble to give place to the severe and coolly skillful magistrate

---

4. *Demi-monde* (French for half-world) refers to the world occupied by elite men and the women of doubtful morality and social standing who entertained them. The term derives from a play called *Le Demi Monde*, by Alexandre Dumas *fils*, published in 1855.

whose business it was to find out the truth in the name of the law. If his eye became suddenly acute it was that he might penetrate to the bottom of the consciousness of the newcomer.

In these first moments of conversation with one whom it is their purpose to make talk, even against his own will, born magistrates experience a kind of awakening of their militant nature, like fencers who try the play of an unknown adversary.

The philosopher found that his presentiments had not deceived him, for he saw, written in large letters on the bundle of papers which M. Valette took up these words: "Greslou Case."

Silence reigned in the room broken only by the rustling of paper and the scratching of the clerk's pen. This person was preparing to take down the interrogatory with that impersonal indifference which distinguishes men accustomed to play the part of machine in the drama of judicial life. One case to them is as much like another as one death is like another to an employee of an undertaker, or one invalid like another to a hospital attendant.

"I will spare you, monsieur," said the judge at last, "the usual questions. There are some names and some men of which we are not permitted to be ignorant."

The philosopher did not even incline his head at this compliment. *Not used to the world,* thought the judge, *this is one of those literary men who think it their duty to despise us,* and then aloud: "I come to the fact which was the motive of the summons addressed to you. You know the crime of which young Greslou is accused?"

"Pardon, monsieur," interrupted the philosopher, changing the position which he had instinctively taken to listen to the judge, his elbow on the chair, his chin in his hand, and his index finger on his cheek, as in his grand, solitary meditations, "I have not the least idea."

"It was reported in all the papers with an exactness to which the gentlemen of the press have not accustomed us," responded the judge, who thought it his duty to reply to the scorn of literature for the robe diagnostic by a little persiflage; and he said to himself: *He is dissimulating–Why? To play sharp? How stupid!*

"Pardon, monsieur," said the philosopher again, "I never read the papers."

The judge looked at him keenly and ejaculated an "Ah!" in which there was more irony than astonishment. *Very good*, thought he, *you want to compel me to state the case, wait a little.* There was a certain irritation in his voice as he said:

"Very well, monsieur, I will sum up the accusation in a few words, regretting that you are not better informed of an affair which may very seriously affect your moral if not your legal responsibility." Here the philosopher raised his head with an anxiety which delighted the judge's heart. *Caught, my good man*, said he to himself; and aloud: "In any case, you know, monsieur, who Robert Greslou is, and the position which he held in the family of the Marquis Jussat Randon. I have here among these papers copies of several letters which you addressed to him at the château, and which testify that you were—how shall I express it?—the intellectual guide of the accused." The philosopher again made a motion of the head. "I shall ask you presently to tell me if this young man ever spoke to you of the domestic life of the family and in what terms. I give you no information probably when I tell you that the family was composed of a father, mother, a son who is a captain of dragoons now in garrison at Lunéville, a second son who was Greslou's pupil, and a young girl of nineteen, Mlle. Charlotte.

"The daughter was betrothed to the Baron de Plane, an officer in the same company as her brother. The marriage had been delayed some months for family reasons which have nothing to do with the affair. It had been definitely fixed for the fifteenth of last December.

"Now, one morning of the week which preceded the arrival of the fiancé and of Count André, the brother of Mlle. de Jussat, the maid entering the room of her young mistress at the usual hour found her dead in her bed."

The magistrate made a pause, and while continuing to turn over the papers in his packet, looked with half-closed eyes at the witness. The stupor which was depicted on the face of the philosopher, showed such sincerity that the judge himself was astonished. *He knew nothing about it*, said he to himself, *that is very strange.*

He studied anew, without changing his preoccupied and indifferent air, the countenance of the celebrated man; but he lacked the gifts which would have rendered this abstracted person intelligible, this union of a brain all-powerful in the realm of ideas with an ingenuousness, a timidity almost comical in the domain of facts. He could understand nothing of it, and he resumed his recital.

"Though the physician who was hastily summoned was only a modest, country practitioner, he did not hesitate a minute in recognizing that the appearance of the body contradicted all idea of a natural death. The face was livid, the teeth set, the pupils extraordinarily dilated, and the body, bent in an arch, rested on the nape of the neck and on the heels. In brief, these were the signs of poisoning by strychnine.

"A glass upon the night-table contained the last drops of a potion which Mlle. de Jussat must have taken during the night, as was her custom, for insomnia. She had been suffering for nearly a year from a nervous malady. The doctor analyzed these drops and found traces of *nux vomica*. This, as you know, is one of the forms in which the terrible poison is sold as medicine. A small bottle without any label, containing some drops of a dark color, was picked up by a gardener under the window of the room. This had been thrown from the window that it might be broken, but it had fallen on the soft earth of a freshly dug flowerbed. These brownish drops were also drops of *nux vomica*.[5]

"There was no doubt that Mlle. de Jussat had been poisoned. This was demonstrated at the autopsy. Was it a suicide or a murder? If a suicide, what motive had this young girl, who was soon to be married to a charming man whom she loved, for killing herself? And in such a way, without a word of explanation, without a letter of farewell to her parents! Beside, how had she procured the poison?

"The investigation of this matter put justice on the track of the prisoner. Being questioned, the apothecary of the village deposed that six weeks before the tutor at the chateau had bought some *nux vomica* to take for a disorder of the stomach.

---

5. *Nux vomica* is a tincture that is created from the seeds of the *strychnos nux vomica* tree, also known as poison nut or vomiting nut. In the nineteenth century it was used as a central nervous stimulant.

"Now the tutor went to Clermont under pretext of visiting his sick mother, on the very day of the discovery of the dead body, having been summoned, as he said, by a telegraphic dispatch. It was shown that this telegram had never been received, that on the night of the crime a servant had seen him coming out of Mlle. de Jussat's room; finally, that the bottle of poison which had been bought at the druggist's, and was found again in the room of the young man, had been partly emptied and then refilled with water.

"Other witnesses reported that Robert Greslou had been very assiduous in his attentions to the young girl, without the knowledge of her parents. A letter was even discovered which he had written to her and dated eleven months before, but which might be interpreted as a skillful attempt at a beginning of courtship. The servants and even the young lad who was his pupil testified that, for the past eight days, the relations between Mlle. de Jussat and the tutor had been strained. She would scarcely respond to his salutations. From these facts the following hypothesis was deduced:

"Robert Greslou, being in love with this young girl, had courted her in vain and then poisoned her to prevent her marriage with another. This hypothesis was strengthened by the lies of which the young man had been guilty when he was questioned. He denied that he had ever written to Mlle. de Jussat; the letter was shown him, and even half of an envelope, with his handwriting upon it, was found among the remains of burned papers in the fireplace of the victim's room. He denied going out of Mlle. Charlotte's room on the night in question, and he was brought face to face with the footman who had seen him, and who supported his assertion with the greater energy that he confessed that he had gone to keep an appointment with one of the maids with whom he was in love, at the same hour.

"Beside, Greslou could not explain why he had bought the *nux vomica*. It was proved that he had never before complained of any stomach trouble. He could neither explain the invention of the dispatch, his sudden departure, nor his frightful agitation at the news of the discovery of the poisoning. Beside, no other motive than a lover's vengeance was admissible, from the simple fact that the victim's jewelry and money were not taken and her body bore no mark of violence.

"This is the way it was presumably done: Greslou entered Mlle. de Jussat's room, knowing that she usually slept until two o'clock, when she awoke to take her potion. He put into this potion enough *nux vomica* to so overpower the girl that she had only time to replace the glass upon the table, but was unable to call for help. Then, fearing that his emotion would betray him, he went away before the body was discovered.

"The empty bottle which was found on the ground he had thrown from the study window which opened directly above that of Mlle. Charlotte. The other bottle he had refilled with water by one of those unskillful ruses which betray the novice in crime.

"In brief, Greslou is now confined in the jail at Riom and will appear at the assizes of that city, in February, or early in March, accused of poisoning Mlle. de Jussat-Randon.

"The charge against him is made more overwhelming by his attitude since his arrest. He has shut himself up in absolute silence, since his false-hoods were confounded, and refuses to answer any question put to him, simply saying he is innocent and has no need to defend himself. He has refused counsel and is in a state of so profound melancholy that we must believe that he is haunted by a terrible remorse.

"He reads and writes a great deal, but what seems very strange, and shows the strength of the comedy with this young man of twenty, he reads and writes only on subjects of pure philosophy, no doubt to counteract the bad impression made by his gloominess, and also to prove his entire freedom of mind. The nature of the prisoner's occupations leads me, monsieur, after this prolonged statement, to the reason for which your evidence is desired in this case, by the mother of the young man, who naturally rebels against the evidence, and who is dying of grief, but is unable to overcome her son's silence. Your books, with those of some English psychologists, are the only ones which the prisoner has asked for. I will add that your books were found on the shelves of his library, in a condition which show that they have been most assiduously read, and between the printed leaves there are other leaves filled with comments, sometimes more developed than the text itself. You shall judge for yourself."

While speaking M. Valette handed the philosopher a copy of *Psychology of God*, which the latter opened mechanically. He could see at each printed page a corresponding leaf covered with writing similar to his own, but more confused and nervous.

In the tendency of the lines to fall, a graphologist[6] would have discovered a tendency to easy discouragement. This similarity of writing impressed the philosopher for the first time, and gave him a singularly painful sensation. He closed the book and returning it to the judge said:

"I am painfully surprised, monsieur, at the revelations you have just made to me; but I confess I do not understand what sort of relation exists between this crime and my books or my person, nor what can be the nature of the testimony I can be called upon to give."

"That is very simple," replied the judge, "however grave the charges against Robert Greslou may be they rest upon certain hypotheses. There are terrible presumptions against him, but there is no absolute certainty. So you see, monsieur, to use the language of the science in which you excel, that a question of psychology will rule the contest. What were the thoughts, what was the character of this young man? It is evident that, if he were much interested in abstract studies the chances of his guilt diminish."

While making this assertion, in which the savant did not suspect a snare, Valette seemed more and more indifferent. He did not add that one of the arguments of the prosecution, brought forward by the old Marquis de Jussat was that Robert Greslou had been corrupted by his reading. He wished to bring M. Sixte to characterize the principles with which the young man had been impregnated.

"Question me, monsieur," responded the savant.

"Shall we begin at the beginning?" said the judge. "In what circumstances and at what date did you make the acquaintance of Robert Greslou?"

"Two years ago," said the savant, "in relation to a work of a purely speculative kind upon human personality, which he came to submit to me."

"Did you see him often?"

---

6. Graphology is the analysis of the physical characteristics and patterns of handwriting with attempt to identify the writer, indicate the psychological state at the time of writing, or evaluate personality characteristics.

"Twice only."

"What impression did he make on you?"

"That of a young man admirably endowed for psychological work," replied the philosopher, weighing his words, so that the judge felt convinced that he wished to see and speak the truth; "so well endowed even that I was almost frightened at his precocity."

"He did not converse with you about his private life?"

"Very little," said the philosopher; "he only told me that he lived with his mother, and that he intended to make teaching his profession and at the same time work at some books."

"Indeed," replied the judge, "that was one of the articles laid down in a sort of programme of life which was found among the prisoner's papers, among those that are left. For it is one of the charges against him that, between his examination and his written attestation, he destroyed the most of them. Could you," he added, "give any explanation of one sentence of this programme which is very obscure to the profane who are not conversant with modern philosophy? Here is the sentence," taking a sheet from among the others: "'Multiply to the utmost psychological experiences.' What do you think Robert Greslou understands by that?"

"I am very much puzzled to answer you, monsieur," said M. Sixte after a silence; but the judge began to see that it was useless to use artifice with a man so simple, and he understood that his silence simply showed that he was seeking an exact expression for his thoughts. "I only know the meaning which I myself should attach to this formula, and probably this young man was too well instructed in works of psychology not to think the same. It is evident that in the other sciences of observation, such as physics or chemistry, the counter-verification of any law whatever exacts a positive and concrete application of that law. When I have decomposed water, for example, into its elements, I ought to be able, all conditions being equal, to reconstruct water out of these same elements. That is an experience of the most ordinary kind, but which suffices to summarize the method of the modern sciences. To know by an experimental knowledge is to be able to reproduce at will such or such a phenomenon, by reproducing its conditions.

"Is such a procedure admissible with moral phenomena? I, for my part, believe that it is, and definitely this that we call education is nothing more than a psychological experience more or less well established, since it sums up thus: having given such a phenomenon—which sometimes is called a virtue, such as patience, prudence, sincerity; sometimes an intellectual aptitude, such as a dead or a living language, orthography, calculation—to find the conditions in which this phenomenon produces itself the most easily. But this field is very limited, for if I wished, for instance, the exact conditions of the birth of such passion being once known, to produce at will this passion in a subject, I should immediately come up against insoluble difficulties of law and morals. There will come a time perhaps, when such experiments will be possible.

"My opinion is that, for the present, we psychologists must keep to the experiences established by law and by accident. With memoirs, with works of literature or art, with statistics, with law reports, with notes on forensic medicine, we have a world of facts at our service.

"Robert Greslou had, in fact, discussed this *desideratum*[7] of our science with me. I recollect, he regretted that those condemned to death could not be placed in special conditions, which would permit of experimenting upon them certain moral phenomena. This was simply a hypothetical opinion of a very young mind, who did not consider that, to work usefully in this order of ideas, it is necessary to study one case for a very long time. It would be best to experiment on children, but how could we make any one believe that it would be useful to science to produce in them certain defects or certain vices for example?"

"Vices!" exclaimed the judge astounded by the tranquility with which the philosopher pronounced this phrase.

"I speak as a psychologist," responded the savant who smiled in his turn at the exclamation of the judge; "that is just why, monsieur, our science is not

---

7. A seventeenth-century English term (from Latin, 'something desired'), largely related to Francis Bacon's (1561–1626) philosophic use of the term, *desiderata*, referring to an immense catalogue of that which remained to be discovered, at the conclusion of the 1623 Latin edition of Bacon's *Advancement of Learning* entitled "The New World of Sciences, or Desiderata" (*Novus Orbus Scientiarum, sive Desiderata*).

susceptible of certain progress. Your exclamation proves that if I had needed any proof. Society cannot get beyond the theory of the good and the bad which for us has no other meaning than to mark a collection of conventions sometimes useful, sometimes puerile."

"You admit, however, that there are good actions and bad actions," said M. Valette; then the magistrate asserting himself and turning this general discussion to the profit of his inquiry: "This poisoning of Mlle. de Jussat," he insinuated, "for example, you will admit that this is a crime?"

"From the social point of view, without doubt," responded M. Sixte. "But for philosophy there is neither crime nor virtue. Our volitions are facts of a certain order governed by certain laws, that is all. But, monsieur," and here the naive vanity of the writer showed itself, "you will find a demonstration of these theories, which I venture to think conclusive, in my *Anatomy of the Will.*"

"Did you sometimes approach these subjects with Robert Greslou?" asked the judge, "and do you believe that he shared your views?"

"Very probably," said the philosopher.

"Do you know, monsieur," asked the magistrate, unmasking his batteries, "that you come very near justifying the accusations of monsieur the Marquis de Jussat, who claims that the doctrines of contemporary materialists have destroyed all moral sense in this young man, and have made him capable of this murder?"

"I do not know what matter is," said M. Sixte, "so I am not a materialist. As to throwing upon a doctrine the responsibility of the absurd interpretation which a badly balanced brain gives to it, that is almost as bad as to reproach the chemist who discovered dynamite for the crimes in which this substance is employed. That is an argument which has no force."

The tone in which the philosopher pronounced these words revealed the invincible strength of spiritual resistance which profound faith gives, as a timidity almost infantile, in the midst of the stir of material life, was revealed in the accent with which he suddenly asked:

"Do you believe that I shall be obliged to go to Riom to testify?"

"I think not, monsieur," said the judge who could not help noticing with new astonishment the contrast between the firmness of thought in the first part of his discourse and the anxiety with which this last sentence had been uttered, "for I see that your interviews with the prisoner have been more superficial than his mother believed, if indeed they were limited to those two visits and to a correspondence which appears to have been exclusively philosophical. But have you never received any confidences relating to his life with the Jussats?"

"Never; beside he ceased to write to me almost immediately after he entered that family," said M. Sixte.

"In his last letters was there no trace of new aspirations, of inquietude of a curiosity of unknown sensations?"

"I have not noticed any," said the philosopher.

"Well, monsieur," replied M. Valette after a brief silence, during which he studied anew this singular witness, "I will not detain you any longer. Your time is too precious. Permit me to go over the few responses you have made, to my clerk. He is not accustomed to examinations that bear upon matters so elevated. You will sign afterward."

While the magistrate was dictating to his clerk what he thought would be of interest to justice in the deposition of the savant, the latter, who was evidently confused by the horrible revelation of the crime of Robert Greslou and by his conversation with the judge, listened without making any remarks, almost without comprehending what was being said. He signed his name without looking, after M. Valette had read aloud to him the pages on which his answers were recorded, and once more before taking leave he said:

"Then I can be very sure that I shall not have to go down there?"

"I hope not," said the judge, conducting him to the door; and he added: "in any case it would only be for a day or two," feeling a secret pleasure at the childish anguish depicted on the good man's face. Then when M. Sixte had left his office. "There are some fools that it would be well to shut up," said he to his clerk, who assented by a nod. "It is through ideas like those of this fellow upon crime that young people are ruined. He seems to be sincere. He would be less dangerous if he were a scoundrel. Do you know that he might easily cut off his disciple's head with his paradoxes? But that appears to be all right. He is only anxious to know if he will have to go to Riom. What a maniac!" And the judge and his clerk shrugged their shoulders and laughed.

Then the former after a reverie of some minutes, in which he went over the various impressions he had received in regard to this being absolutely enigmatic to him, added:

"Faith, little did I ever suspect the famous Adrien Sixte was anything like that. It is inconceivable."

III.

SIMPLE GRIEF

THE EPITHET by which the Judge of Instruction condemned the impassibility of the savant would have been more energetic still, if he could have followed M. Sixte and read the philosopher's thoughts during the short time which separated this examination from the rendezvous fixed by the unhappy mother of Robert Greslou.

Having arrived in the great court of the Palais de Justice, he whom M. Valette at that very moment was calling a maniac looked first at the clock, as became a worker so minutely regular.

Quarter-past two, he thought, *I shall not be home before three. Madame Greslou ought to be there at four. I shall not be able to do any work. That is very disagreeable.* And he resolved on the spot to take his daily walk, the more readily that he could reach the Jardin des Plantes along the river and through the city, whose old physiognomy and quiet peacefulness he loved.

The sky was blue with the clear blue of frosty days vaguely tinted with violet at the horizon. The Seine flowed under the bridges green and gayly laborious, with its loaded boats on which smoked the chimneys of small wooden houses whose windows were adorned with familiar plants. The horses trotted swiftly over the dry pavement.

If the philosopher saw all these details in the time that he took to reach the sidewalk of the quay, with the precaution of a provincial afraid of the carriages, it was for him a sensation even more unconscious than usual. He continued to think of the surprising revelation which the judge had just made to him; but a philosopher's head is a machine so peculiar that events do not produce the direct and simple impression which seems natural to other persons. This one was composed of three individuals fitted into one; there was the simple-minded, Sixte, an old bachelor, a slave to the scrupulous care of his servant and anxious first of all for his material tranquility. Then there was the philosophical polemic, the author, animated, unknown to himself, by a ferocious self-love common to all writers. And last, the great psychologist, passionately attached to the problems of the inner life; and in order that an idea should accomplish its full action upon this mind, it was necessary for it to pass through these three compartments.

From the Palais de Justice to the first step on the border of the Seine, it was the bourgeois who reasoned: *Yes*, said he to himself, repeating the words which the sight of the clock had called forth, *that is very disagreeable. A whole day lost, and why? I wonder what I have to do with all that story of assassination, and what information my testimony has brought to the examination!*

He did not suspect that, in the hands of a skillful advocate, his theory of crime and responsibility might become the most formidable of weapons against Greslou.

It was not worth the trouble to disturb me, continued he. *But these people have no idea of the life of a man who writes. What a stupid that judge was with his imbecile questions! I hope I shall not have to go to Riom to appear before some others of the same sort!*

He saw the picture of his departure painted afresh in his imagination in characters of odious confusion which a derangement of this kind represents to a man of study whom action unsettles and for whom physical ennui becomes a positive unhappiness. Great abstract intellects suffer from these puerilities. The philosopher saw in a flash of anguish his trunk open, his linen packed, the papers necessary to his work placed near his shirts, his getting into a cab, the tumult of the station, the railway carriage, and the coarse familiarity of proximity, the arrival in an unknown town, the miseries of the hotel chamber without the care of Mlle. Trapenard, who had become necessary to him, although he was as ignorant of it as a child.

This thinker, so heroically independent that he would have marched to martyrdom for his convictions, with the firmness of a Bruno or a Vanini,[1] was seized by a sort of vertigo at the picture of an event so ordinary.

He saw himself in the Court of Assizes,[2] constrained to answer questions, in the presence of an attentive crowd, and that without an idea to support him against his native timidity.

I will never receive a young man again, he concluded, *yes, I will shut my door henceforth. But I will not anticipate. Perhaps I shall not have to go through this unpleasant task and all is ended. Ended?* And already the home-keeping citizen gave place in this inward monologue to the second person hidden within the philosopher, namely, the writer of books which were discussed with passion by the public. "Ended?" Yes, for him who comes and goes, who lives in the Rue Guy de la Brosse and who would be very much annoyed if he had to go to Auvergne in the winter, it may be. *But what about my books and my ideas? What a strange thing is this instinctive hate of the ignorant for the systems which they cannot even comprehend.*

A jealous young man murders a young girl to prevent her marrying another. This young man has been in correspondence with a philosopher whose works he studies. It is the philosopher who is guilty. And I am a materialist forsooth, I who have proved the nonexistence of matter!

He shrugged his shoulders, then a new image crossed his memory, the image of Marius Dumoulin, the young substitute at the College of France, the man whom he most detested in the world. He saw, as if they were there before his eyes, some of the formulae so dear to this defender of spiritualism:

---

1. Bruno Bauer (1809–1882) was a German philosopher and theologian. As a student of G. W. F. Hegel, Bauer was a radical Rationalist in philosophy, politics and Biblical criticism. He wrote a series of works arguing that Jesus was a 2nd-century fusion of Jewish, Greek, and Roman theology.

Lucilio Vanini (1585–1619) was an Italian philosopher and physician who was one of the first significant representatives of intellectual libertinism. He was among the first modern thinkers who viewed the universe as an entity governed by natural laws and an early literate proponent of biological evolution.

2. The Court of Assizes is the principal criminal court in France and the only court that functions with a jury. It has jurisdiction over the graver felonies, defined as crimes, as distinguished from delits, which are tried in the correctional courts.

"Fatal doctrines. Intellectual poison distilled from pens which one would like to believe are unconscious. Scandalous exposure of a psychology of corruption."

Yes, said Adrien Sixte to himself with bitterness, *if someone does not catch up this chance which makes an assassin of one of my pupils, it will not be he! Psychology will have done it all.*

It is proper to state that Dumoulin had, on the appearance of the *Anatomy of the Will*, pointed out a grave error. Adrien Sixte had based one of his most ingenious chapters upon a so-called discovery of a German physician, which was proved to be incorrect. Perhaps Dumoulin dwelt on this inadvertence of the great analyst with a severity of irony far too disrespectful.

M. Sixte, who rarely noticed criticisms, had replied to this one. While confessing the error, he proved without any trouble, that this point of detail did not affect the thesis as a whole. But he cherished an unpardonable rancor against the spiritualist.

It is as if I heard him! thought Sixte. *What he may say of my books is nothing but psychology? Psychology! This is the science on which depends the future of our beloved France.*

As we see, the philosopher, like all other systematics, had reached the point where he made his doctrines the pivot of the universe. He reasoned about like this: Given a historic fact, what is the chief cause of it? The general condition of mind. This condition is derived from the current ideas. The French Revolution, for example, proceeded entirely from a false conception of man which springs from the Cartesian philosophy and from the *Discourse on Method*.

He concluded that to modify the march of events, it was necessary to modify the received notions upon the human mind, and to install in their place some precise notions whence would result a new education and politics. So in his indignation against Dumoulin he sincerely believed that he was indignant at an obstacle to the public good.

He had some unpleasant moments while thus figuring to himself this detested adversary, taking as a text the death of Mlle. de Jussat for a vigorous sortie against the modern science of the mind.

Shall I have to answer him again? asked Sixte, who already was sure of the attack of his rival, such power have the passions to consider real that which they only imagine. *Yes*, he insisted, and then aloud, "I will reply in my best manner!"

He was by this time behind the apsis of Notre-Dame and he stopped to survey the architecture of the cathedral. This ancient edifice symbolized to him the complex character of the German intellect which he contrasted in thought with the simplicity of the Hellenic mind, reproduced for him in a photograph of the Parthenon, which he had often contemplated in the Library of Nancy. The remembrance of Germany changed the current of his thoughts for a moment. He recalled, almost unconsciously, Hegel, then the doctrine of the identity of contrarieties, then the theory of evolution which grew out of it. This last idea, joined itself to those which had already agitated him, and resuming his walk, he began to argue against the anticipated objections of Dumoulin in the case of young Greslou.

For the first time the drama of the Château Jussat Randon appeared real to his mind, for he was thinking of it with the most real part of his nature, his psychological faculty. He forgot Dumoulin as well as the inconveniences of the possible journey to Riom, and his mind was completely absorbed by the moral problem which the crime presented.

The first question would naturally have been: "Did Robert Greslou really assassinate Mlle. de Jussat?" But the philosopher did not think of that, yielding to this defect of generalizing minds, that never more than half verify the ideas upon which they speculate. Facts are, to them, only matter for theoretic using, and they distort them willfully the better to build up their systems. The philosopher again took up the formula by which he summed up this drama: *A young man who becomes jealous and commits a murder, this is one more proof in support of my theory that the instinct of destruction and that of love awake at the same time in the male.* He had used this principle to write a chapter of extraordinary boldness on the aberrations of the generative faculty in his *Theory of the Passions.*

The reappearance of fierce animality among the civilized would alone suffice to explain this act. It would be necessary also to study the personal heredity of the assassin. He forced himself to see Robert Geslon without any other traits than those which confirmed the hypothesis already outlined in

47

his mind.

Those very brilliant black eyes, those too vivacious gestures, that brusque manner of entering into relations with me, that enthusiasm in speaking to me, there was nervous derangement in this fellow. The father died young? If it could be proved that there was alcoholism in the family, then there would be a beautiful case of what Legrand du Saulle calls épilepsie larvée.[3] *In this way his silence may be explained, and his denials may be sincere. This is the essential difference between an epileptic and the deranged. The last remembers his act, the epileptic forgets them. Would this then be a larval epileptic?*

At this point of his reverie the philosopher experienced a moment of real joy. He had just constructed a building of ideas which he called an explanation, following the habit so dear to his race. He considered this hypothesis from different points, recalling several examples cited by his author in his beautiful treatise on forensic medicine, until he arrived at the Jardin des Plantes, which he entered by the large gate of the Quay Saint Bernard.

He turned to the right into an avenue planted with old trees whose distorted trunks were enclosed in iron and coated with whitewash. There floated in the air a musty smell emanating from the tawny beasts which moved around in their barred cages nearby. The philosopher was distracted from his meditations by this odor, and he turned to look at a large, old wild-boar with an enormous head, which, standing on his slender feet, held his mobile and eager snout between the bars.

And, thought the savant, *we know ourselves but little better than this animal knows himself. What we call our person is a consciousness so vague, so disturbed by operations which are going on within us,* and returning to Robert Greslou: *Who knows? This young man who was so preoccupied by the multiplicity of the self? Did he not have an obscure feeling that there were in himself two distinct conditions, a primary and secondary condition as it were—two beings in fact, one, lucid, intelligent,*

---

3. Legrand du Saulle (1830–1886) was a French psychiatrist and proponent of a theory of latent epilepsy termed *larval epilepsy (épilepsie larvée)* which describes a variety of epilepsy not manifested by the ordinary signs of epilepsy, that is to say by fits, dizziness, convulsions proper, but only by certain delusional phenomena. It asserts that these individuals are suffering from larval epilepsy and that we only find in them an incomplete symptomatology of epilepsy, consisting only of intellectual manifestations.

honest, loving works of the intellect, the one whom I knew; and another, gloomy, cruel, impulsive, the one who has committed murder. Evidently this is a case. I am very happy to have come across it. He forgot that on leaving the Palais de Justice he had deplored his relations with the accused. *It will be a fortunate thing to study the mother now. She will furnish me with facts about the ancestors. That is what is lacking to our psychology; good monographs made with one's own eyes upon the mental structure of great men and of criminals. I will try to write out this one.*"

All sincere passion is egoistic, the intellectual as well as the others. Thus the philosopher, who would not have harmed a fly walked with a more rapid step in going toward the gate at the Rue Cuvier whence he would reach the Rue Jussieu, then the Rue Guy de la Brosse—he was about to have an interview with a despairing mother who was coming, without doubt, to entreat him to aid her in saving the head of a son who was perhaps innocent! But the possible innocence of the prisoner, the grief of the mother, the part which he himself would be called to play in this novel scene, all were effaced by the fixed idea of the notes to be taken, of the little insignificant facts to be collected.

Four o'clock struck when this singular dreamer, who no more suspected his own ferocity than does a physician who is charmed by a beautiful autopsy, arrived in front of his house. On the threshold of the porte cochère[4] were two men—Father Carbonnet and the commissionaire usually stationed at the corner of the street. With their back turned to the side from which Adrien Sixte came, they were laughing at the stumblings of a drunken man on the opposite walk, and saying such things as a spectacle of that character suggests to the common people. The cock Ferdinand, brown and lustrous, hopped about their feet and picked between the stones of the pavement.

"That fellow has taken a drop too much for sure," said the commissionaire.

"What if I should tell you," responded Carbonnet, "that he has not drunk enough? For if he had drunk more, he would have fallen down at the wineseller's. Good! See him stumble up against the lady in black."

---

4. *Porte cochère* (literally, coach gateway) refers to a covered porch-like structure at a main or secondary entrance to a building through which a horse and carriage can pass to provide arriving and departing occupants protection from the elements.

The two speakers, who had not seen the philosopher, continued to bar the way. The last, with the customary amenity of his manners, hesitated to disturb them.

Mechanically he turned his eyes in the direction of the drunken man. He was an unfortunate fellow in rags; his head was covered with a high hat weakened by innumerable falls; his feet danced in his worn-out boots. He had just knocked against a person in deep mourning who was standing at the angle of the Rue Guy de la Brosse and the Rue Linné. Without doubt she was looking at someone on the side of this latter street, someone in whom she was interested, for she did not turn at once.

The man in rags, with the persistence of drunken people, was excusing himself to this woman, who then first became aware of his presence. She drew back with a gesture of disgust. The drunken man became angry, and supporting himself against the wall, hurled at her some offensive language; a crowd of children soon collected around him. The commissionaire began to laugh, and so did Carbonnet. Then turning around to look for the cock, muttering: "Where has he gone to crow, the runaway?" he saw Adrien Sixte, behind whom Ferdinand had taken refuge, and who was also regarding the scene between the drunken man and the unknown lady.

"Ah! Monsieur Sixte," said the concierge, "that lady in black has been twice to ask for you in the last quarter of an hour. She said that you were expecting her."

"Bring her here," responded the savant. "It is the mother," thought he. His first impulse was to go in at once, then a kind of timidity came over him, and he remained at the door while the concierge, followed by the cock, went over to the group collected on the corner of the street.

The woman no sooner heard Carbonnet's words than she turned toward the philosopher's house, leaving Ferdinand's master to scold the drunkard.

The philosopher, instinctively continuing his reasoning, instantly noticed a singular resemblance between the mysterious person and the young man about whom he had been questioned. There were the same bright eyes, in a very pale face, and the same cast of features. There was not the least doubt, and immediately the implacable psychologist, curious only about a case to be studied, gave place to the awkward, simple-minded man, unskillful in practical life, embarrassed by his long body and not knowing how to say the first word. Mme. Greslou, for it was she, relieved him by saying: "I am, monsieur, the person who wrote to you yesterday."

"Very much honored, madame," stammered the philosopher, "I regret that I was not at home earlier. But your letter said four o'clock. And then I have just come from the Judge of Instruction, where I was summoned to testify in the case of this unhappy child."

"Ah! Monsieur," said the mother, touching M. Sixte upon the arm to call his attention to the commissionaire who stood in the angle of the door to listen.

"I beg your pardon," said the savant, who comprehended the cruelty of his abstraction. "Permit me to pass before you to show you the way."

He proceeded to mount the stairs which began to be dark at this time of a winter's day. He went up slowly to suit the lassitude of his companion, who held by the rail, as if she had scarcely energy enough to ascend the four flights. Her short breath which could be heard in the provincial silence of this empty house, betrayed the feebleness of the unhappy woman.

As little sensitive as was the philosopher to the outer world, he was filled with pity when, entering his study with its closed shutters which the fire and the lamp already lighted by his servant softly illumined, he saw his visitor face to face. The wrinkle plowed from the corners of the mouth to the ala of the nose, the lips scorched by fever, the eyebrows contracted, the darkness about the eyelids, the nervousness of the hands in their black gloves, in which she held a roll of paper, without doubt some justifying memoir—all these details revealed the torture of a fixed idea; and scarcely had she fallen into a chair when she said in a broken voice:

"My God! My God! I am then too late. I wished to speak to you, monsieur, before your conversation with the judge. But you defended him, did you not? You said that it was not possible; that he had not done what they accuse him of? You do not believe him guilty, monsieur, you whom he called his master, you whom he loved so much?"

"I did not have to defend him, madame," said the philosopher; "I was asked what had been my relations with him, and as I had seen him only twice, and he spoke only of his studies—"

"Ah!" interrupted the mother with an accent of profound anguish; and she repeated: "I have come too late. But no," she continued, clasping her trembling hands. "You will go before the Court of Assizes to testify that he cannot be guilty, that you know he cannot be? One does not become an assassin, a poisoner, in a day. The youth of criminals prepares the way for their crimes. They are bad persons, gamblers, frequenters of the saloons. But he has always been with his books, like his poor father. I used to say to him: 'Come, Robert run out, you must take the air, you must amuse yourself.' If you could have seen what a quiet little life we lead, he and I, before he went into this accursed family. And it was for my sake that he should not cost me anything more that he went into it, and that he might go on with his studies.

"He would have been admitted in three or four years and then perhaps have taken a position in a lyceum at Clermont. I should have had him marry. I have seen a good *parti*[5] for him. I should have remained with him, in some corner, to take care of his children. Ah! Monsieur!" And she sought in the philosopher's eyes, a response in harmony with her passionate desire; "tell me, if it is possible for a son who had such ideas to do what they say he has done? It is infamous; is it not infamous, monsieur?"

"Be calm, madame, be calm." These were the only words which Adrien Sixte could find to say to this mother who wept over the ruin of her most cherished hopes. Beside, being still under the impression of his conversation with the judge, she seemed to him to be so wildly beyond the truth, a prey to illusions so blind that he was stupefied, and also, why not confess it? The renewed prospect of the journey to Riom frightened him as much as the grief of the mother affected him.

These different impressions showed themselves in his manner by an uncertainty, an absence of warmth which did not deceive the mother. Extreme suffering has infallible intuitions of instinct. This woman understood that the philosopher did not believe in the innocence of her son, and with a gesture of extreme depression, recoiling from him with horror, she moaned:

"Monsieur, you too, you are with his enemies. You—you?"

---

5. Someone who is considered to be a good choice for marriage, because of wealth, status, etc.

"No, madame, no," gently responded Adrien Sixte, "I am not an enemy. I ask nothing better than to believe what you believe. But you will permit me to speak frankly? Facts are facts, and they are terribly against him. The poison bought clandestinely, the bottle thrown out of the window, the other bottle half emptied then refilled with water, the going out of the girl's room on the night of her death; the false dispatch, his sudden departure, those burned letters, and then his denial of it all."

"But, monsieur, there is no proof in all that," interrupted the mother, "no proof at all. What of his sudden departure? He had been wishing for more than a month to get away from the place, I have a letter in which he speaks of his plan, and beside his engagement was almost at an end. He fancied that they wished to retain him and he was tired of the life of a tutor, and then, as he is so timid, he gave a false pretext and invented this unfortunate dispatch that is all. And as to the poison he did not buy it secretly. He has suffered for years from a stomach trouble. He has studied too hard immediately after his meals. Who saw him go out of that room? A servant! What if the real murderer paid this servant to accuse my son? Do we know anything about this girl's intrigues and who were interested in killing her?

"Do you not see that all these and the letters and the bottle are parts of the plan for making suspicion fall on him? How? Why? That will be found out some day. But what I do know is that my son is not guilty. I swear it by the memory of his father. Ah! Do you believe I would defend him like this if I felt him to be a criminal? I would ask for pity, I would weep, I would pray, but now I cry for justice, justice! No, these people have no right to accuse him, to throw him into prison, to dishonor our name, for nothing, for nothing. You see, monsieur, I have shown you that they have not a single proof."

"If he is innocent, why this obstinacy in keeping silent?" asked the philosopher, who thought that the poor woman had shown nothing except her desperation in struggling against the evidence.

"Ah! If he were guilty he would talk," cried Mme. Greslou, "he would defend himself, he would lie! No," added she in a hollow voice, "there is some mystery. He knows something, that I am sure of, something which he does not wish to tell. He has some reason for not speaking. Perhaps he does not wish to dishonor this young girl, for they claim that he loved her. Oh!

Monsieur, I have wanted to see you at any risk, for you are the only one who can make him speak, who can make him tell what he has resolved not to tell. You must promise me to write to him, to go to him. You owe this to me," she insisted in a hard tone. "You have made me suffer so much."

"I?" exclaimed the philosopher.

"Yes, you," replied she bitterly, and as she spoke her face betrayed the strength of old grudges; "whose fault is it that he has lost faith? Yours, monsieur, through your books. My God! How I did hate you then! I can still see his face when he told me he would not commune on All-Soul's day, because he had doubts. 'And thy father?' said I to him, 'All-Soul's day!' said he: 'Leave me alone, I do not believe in that any longer, that is done with.' He was sitting at his table and he had a volume before him which he closed while he was talking to me. I remember. I read the name of the author mechanically. It was yours, monsieur.

"I did not argue with him that day; he was a great savant already, and I a poor, ignorant woman. But the next day, while he was at college I took M. the Abbé Martel, who had educated him, into his room to show him the library. I had a presentiment that it was the reading which had corrupted my son. Your book, monsieur, was still on the table. The abbé took it up and said to me: 'This is the worst of them all.'

"Monsieur, pardon me, if I wound you, but do you see, if my son were still a Christian, I would go and pray his confessor to command him to speak. You have taken away his faith, monsieur, I do not reproach you any more; but what I would have asked of the priest, I have come to ask of you. If you had heard him when he came back from Paris! He said to me, speaking of you: 'If you knew him, *maman*,[6] you would venerate him, for he is a saint.' Ah! Promise me to make him speak. Let him speak for me, for his father, for those who love him, for you, monsieur, who cannot have had an assassin for a pupil. For he is your pupil, you are his master; he owes it to you to defend himself, as much as to me his mother."

"Madame," said the savant with deep seriousness, "I promise you to do all that I can."

---

6. French (informal or childish) for mummy, mom, mum.

This was the second time today that this responsibility of master and pupil had been thrust upon him. Once by the judge, repelled by the resistance of the thinker who repels with disdain a senseless reproach. The words of this good woman, quivering with this human grief to which he was so little accustomed, touched other fibres than those of pride. He was still more strangely affected when Mme. Greslou, seizing his hand with a gentleness which contradicted the bitterness of her last words, said:

"He spoke the truth when he said you were good. I came too," she continued drying her tears, "to requite myself of a commission with which the poor child charged me. And see if there is not in it a proof that he is innocent. In his prison during these two months, he has written a long work on philosophy. He considers it by far his best work and I am charged to hand it to you." She gave the savant the roll of paper which she had held on her lap. "It is just as he gave it to me. They let him write as much as he likes, everybody loves him. They do not allow me to speak to him except in the frightful parlor where there is always the guard between us. "Will you look?" she insisted, and in an altered tone: "He has never lied to me, and I believe whatever he has told me. If, however, he had only thought to write to you what he will not confide to any one else?"

"I will see immediately," said Adrien Sixte, who unfolded the roll. He threw his eyes over the first page of the manuscript and he saw the words: *Modern Psychology*, then on the second sheet another title, *Memoir upon Myself*, and underneath were the following lines:

> I write to my dear master, Monsieur Adrien Sixte, and engage his word to keep to himself the pages which follow. If he does not agree to make this engagement with his unhappy pupil, I ask him to destroy this manuscript, confiding in his honor not to deliver it to anyone whomsoever, even to save my life.

And the young man had simply signed his initials.

"Well?" asked the mother as the philosopher continued to turn over the leaves, a prey to profound anxiety.

"Well!" responded he, closing the manuscript and holding the first page before the curious eyes of Mme. Greslou, "this is only a work on philosophy, as he told you. See."

The mother had a question on her lips, and suspicion in her eyes while she was reading the technical formula which was unintelligible to her poor mind. She had observed Adrien Sixte's hesitation. But she did not dare to ask, and she rose saying:

"You will excuse me for having kept you so long, monsieur. I have placed my last hope upon you, and you will not deceive a mother's heart. I carry your promise with me."

"All that it will be possible for me to do that the truth may be known," said the philosopher gravely, "I will do, madame, I promise you again."

When he had conducted the unhappy woman to the door, and was again alone in his study Adrien Sixte remained for a long time plunged in reflection. Taking up the manuscript, he read and reread the sentence written by the young man, and pushing away the tempting manuscript, he paced the floor. Twice he seized the sheets and approached the fire, but he did not throw them into the flames. A combat was going on in his mind between a devouring curiosity, and apprehensions of very different kinds. To contract the engagement which this reading would impose on him, and to learn what could be learned from these pages would throw him, perhaps, into a horrible situation. If he were going to hold in his hands the proof of the young man's innocence without the right to use it, or what he suspected still more, the proof of his guilt, what then? Without being conscious of it he trembled in his inmost nature, lest he find in this memoir if there were crime, the trace of his own influence, and the cruel accusations already twice formulated, that his books were mixed up with this sinister history. On the other hand, the unconscious egoism of studious men who have a horror of all confusion, forbade him to enter any further into a drama with which he had definitely nothing to do.

No, he concluded, *I will not read this memoir; I will write to this boy as I have promised the mother to do, then it will be ended.*

However, his dinner had come in the midst of his reflections. He ate alone, as always, seated in the corner by a porcelain stove, the weather being very chilly, the heat was his only comfort, and before a little round table, covered with a piece of oilcloth. The lamp which served for his work lighted his frugal repast, consisting, as usual, of soup and one dish of vegetables with some raisins for dessert, and for drink water alone.

Ordinarily he took one of the books which had been exiled from the too-crowded study, or he listened while Mlle. Trapenard exposed the details of the housekeeping. On this evening he did not look for a book, and his housekeeper tried in vain to discover if the lady's visit and the summons had any connection. The wind rose, a winter's wind whose plaint from across the empty space died gently against the shutters. Seated in his armchair after his dinner, with Robert Greslou's manuscript before him, the savant listened for a long time to this monotonous but sad music. His hesitation returned. Then psychology drove away all scruples, and when later Marietta came to announce that his bed was ready, he told her to retire. Two o'clock struck and he was still reading the strange piece of self-analysis which Robert Greslou called a memoir upon himself, but whose correct title should have been: *Confession of a Young Man of the Period.*

IV.

CONFESSION OF A YOUNG MAN OF THE PERIOD

⊞

The Jail at Riom, January, 1887

I WRITE TO YOU, monsieur, this memoir of myself which I have refused to the counsel in spite of my mother's entreaties. I write it to you, who in reality know so little of me, and at what a moment of my life! For the same reason that led me to bring my first work to you. There is my illustrious master, between you and myself, your pupil accused of a most infamous crime, a bond which men could not understand, and of which you yourself are ignorant, but which I feel to be as close as it is indissoluble. I have lived with your thought, and by your thought so passionately, so entirely at the most decisive period of my life! Now in the distress of my mental agony, I turn to the only being of whom I can expect hope, implore aid.

Ah! Do not misunderstand me, venerated master, and believe that the terrible trouble with which I am struggling is caused by the vain forms of justice which surround me. I should not be worthy the name of philosopher if I had not, long ago, learned to consider my thought as the only reality, and the external world an indifferent and fatal succession of appearances. From my seventeenth year, I have adopted as a rule to be repeated in the hours of small or great annoyances, the formula of our dear Spinoza: "The force by which man perseveres in existence is limited, and that of external causes infinitely surpass it."

I shall be condemned to death in six weeks, for a crime of which I am innocent, and from which I can not clear myself, you will understand why, after having read these pages—and I shall go to the scaffold without trembling. I shall support this event with the same effort at composure as if a physician, after having auscultated me, should diagnose an advanced disease of the heart. Condemned, I shall have to conquer first the revolt of the animal nature and then to support myself against the despair of my mother.

I have learned from your works the remedy for such feelings, and in opposing to the image of approaching death the sentiment of inevitable necessity, and in diminishing the vision of my mother's grief by the recollection of the psychological laws which govern consolations, I shall arrive at a relatively calm state of mind. Certain sentences of yours will suffice for this, that, for example, in the fifth chapter of the second volume of your *Anatomy of the Will*, which I know by heart:

> The universal interweaving of phenomena causes each to bear the weight of all the others, in the same way that each portion of the universe, and at each moment, may be considered as a resume of all that has been, of all that is, and of all that will be. It is in this sense that it is permissible to say that the world is eternal in its detail as well as in its whole.

What a sentence, and how it envelops, as well as affirms and demonstrates the idea that everything is necessary in and around us since we too are a parcel and a moment of this eternal world! Alas! Why is it that this idea which is so lucid when I reason, as one ought to reason, with my mind, and in which I acquiesce with all the strength of my being, cannot overcome in me a species of suffering so peculiar, which invades my heart when I recall certain actions which I have willed, and others of which I am the author, although indirectly, in the drama through which I have passed?

To tell you all in a few words, my dear master, though once more I say that I did not kill Mlle. de Jussat, I have been connected in the closest manner with the drama of her poisoning, and I feel remorse, although the doctrines in which I believe, the truths which I know, and the convictions which form the essence of my intellect, make me consider remorse the most silly of human illusions.

These convictions are powerless to procure me the peace of certainty, which once was mine. I doubt with my heart that which my mind recognizes as truth. I do not think that for a man whose youth was consumed by intellectual passions, there can be a worse punishment than this. But why try to interpret by literary phrases a mental condition which I wish to expose to you in detail—to you the great connoisseur in maladies of the mind—in order that you may give me the only aid which can do me any good; some word which shall explain me to myself, which shall attest to me that I am not a monster, which shall sustain me in the disorder of my beliefs, which shall prove to me that I have not been deceived all these years, in adhering to the new faith with all the energy of a sincere being.

Indeed, my dear master, I am very miserable, and I must speak out all my misery. To whom shall I address myself, if not to you, since I should have no hope of being intelligible to any one not familiar with the psychology in which I have been educated.

Since coming to this prison, two months ago, the moment I resolved to write to you has been the only one in which I have been what I was before these terrible events occurred. I had tried to become absorbed in some work of an entirely abstract order, but found myself unable to master it.

I have considered only this for four days, and, thanks to you, the power of thought has returned. I have found something of the pleasure which was mine when I wrote my first essays, in resuming, for this work, the cold severity of my method—your method. I wrote out yesterday a plan of this monograph of my actual self, in practicing the division by paragraphs which you have adopted in your works. I have proved the persistent vigor of my reflection in reconstructing my life from its origin, as I would resolve a problem of geometry by synthesis.

I see distinctly at the present time that the crisis from which I suffer has for its factors, first my heredities, then the medium of ideas in which I was educated, finally the medium of facts into which I was transplanted by my introduction among the Jussat-Randons. The crisis itself and the questions which it raises in my mind shall be the last fragments of a study which I shall strip of insignificant recollections, to reduce it to what a master of our time calls generatrices.[1] At least I shall have furnished you an exact document upon the modes of feeling which I formerly believed to be very precious and very rare, and I shall have proved to you in two ways, first by my confidence in your absolute discretion, and second by my appeal for your philosophical support, what you have been to him who writes these lines, and who asks your pardon for this long preamble and begins at once his dissection.

---

1. Generatrices, in mathematics, is the plural form of the term generatrix: a generator; the point, or the mathematical magnitude, which, by its motion, generates another magnitude, as a line, surface, or solid.

§ I. MY HEREDITIES

AS FAR BACK AS I can remember, I find that my dominant faculty, the one that has been present in every crisis of my life, great or small, and which is present today, has been the faculty, I mean the power and the need of duplication. There have always been in me, as it were, two distinct persons; one who went, came, acted, felt, and another who looked at the first go, come, act, and feel with an impassable curiosity.

At this very hour and knowing that I am in prison, accused of a capital crime, blasted in honor, and overwhelmed in sadness, knowing that it is this very I, Robert Greslou, born at Clermont the 5th of September, 1865, and not another, I think of this situation as a spectacle at which I am a stranger. Is it even exact to say I? Evidently not. For my true self is, properly speaking, neither the one who suffers nor the one who looks on. It is made up of both, and I have had a very clear perception of this duality, although I was not then capable of comprehending this psychological disposition exaggerated to an anomaly, from my childhood, the childhood which I wish to recall with the impartiality of a disinterested historian.

My first recollections are of the city of Clermont-Terrand, and of a house which stood on a promenade now very much changed by the recent construction of the artillery school. The house, like all the houses in this city, was built of Volvic stone, a gray stone which darkens with age, and which gives to the tortuous streets the appearance of a city of the middle ages.

My father, who died when I was very young, was of Lorraine extraction. He held at Clermont the position of engineer of roads and bridges. He was a slender man of feeble health, with a face almost beardless, and marked with a melancholy serenity which touched me, when I think of him, after all these years. I see him again in his study, through whose windows may be viewed the immense plain of the Limagne, with the graceful eminence of the Puy de Crouël quite near, and in the distance the dark line of the mountains of Forez.

The railway station was near our house, and the whistling of the trains was constantly heard in this quiet study. I used to sit on the carpet in the corner by the fire, playing without making any noise, and this strident call produced on my mind a strange impression of mystery, of distance, of the flight of time, and of life which endures to the present.

My father traced with his chalk upon a blackboard enigmatic signs, geometric figures or algebraic formulas, with that clearness of the curves, or the letters which revealed the habitual method of his being. At other times he wrote, standing at an architect's table which he preferred to his desk, a table consisting simply of a white wood board placed on trestles. The large books on mathematics arranged with the most minute care in the bookcase, and the cold faces of savants, engraved in copperplate and framed under glass, were the only objects of art with which the walls were decorated.

The clock which represented the globe of the world, two astronomical maps which hung above the desk, and upon this desk the calculating ruler with its figures and its copper slide, the square, the compass, the T-rule. I recall them all, at will, the smallest details of this room whose whole atmosphere was thought, and these images aid me to comprehend how from my infancy the dream of a purely ideal and contemplative existence became elaborated in me, favored by heredity. My later reflections have shown me, in several traits of my character, the result transmitted under form of instinct of the life of abstract study that my father led. I have, for example, always felt a singular horror of action, so much so that, making a simple visit caused my heart to pant and the slightest physical exercise was intolerable to me, such as wrestling with another person; even to discuss my most cherished ideas appeared to me, and still appears, almost impossible.

This dread of action is explained by the excess of brain-work which, pushed too far, isolates man in the midst of the realities which he hardly endures, because he is not habitually in contact with them. I feel that this difficulty of adapting myself to facts comes to me from this poor father; from him also comes this faculty of generalization, which is the power, but at the same time the mania of my mind; and it is also his work that a morbid predominance of the nervous system has rendered my will so wild at certain times.

My father, who was still young when he died, had never been robust. He was obliged at the growing age to undergo the trial of preparation for the Polytechnic School which is ruinous to the soundest health. With narrow shoulders and with limbs weakened by long sittings at sedentary meditations, this savant with transparent hands seemed to have in his veins, instead of red globules of generous blood, a little of the dust of the chalk which he handled so much.

He did not transmit to me muscles capable of counterbalancing the excitability of my nerves, so that with this faculty of abstraction, I owe to him a kind of ungovernable intemperance of desire. Every time that I have ardently wished for anything it has been impossible to repress this covetousness. This is a hypothesis which has often come to me when I have been analyzing myself, that abstract natures are more incapable than others of resisting passion, when passion is aroused, perhaps because the daily relation between action and thought is broken in them.

Fanatics would be the most signal proofs of this. I have seen my father, usually so patient and gentle, so overcome by the violence of anger as almost to faint. In this I am also his son, and through him the descendant of a grandfather as ill-balanced, a sort of primitive genius, who, half-peasant, had risen by force of mechanical inventions to be a civil engineer, and was then ruined by lawsuits.

On this side of my race there has always been a dangerous element, something wild, at times, by the side of constant intellectuality. I formerly considered this double nature a superior condition; the possible ardor of passion joined with this continuous energy of abstract thought. It was my dream to be at the same time frenzied and lucid, the subject and the object, as the Germans say, of my analysis; the subject who studies himself and finds in this study a means of exaltation and of scientific development. Alas! Whither has thy chimera led me? But it is not the time to speak of effects, we are still with the causes.

Among the circumstances which affected me during my childhood, I believe the following to be one of the most important: Every Sunday morning, and as soon as I could read, my mother took me with her to mass. This mass was celebrated at eight o'clock in the Church of the Capuchins recently built on a boulevard shaded by Plantanes which led from Sablon Court to Laureau Square, along the Jardin des Plantes.

At the door of the church, there used to sit, in front of a portable shop, a cake seller called Mother Girard, with whom I was well acquainted, for I had bought of her little bunches of cherries in the spring. This was the first fruit of the season that I might eat. This dainty, acid and fresh, was one of the sensualities of these days of childhood, and any one who had observed me, might have seen this frenzy of desire of which I have spoken. I was almost in a fever when on my way to this shop.

This was not the only reason why I preferred the Church of the Capuchins with its extremely plain architecture, to the subterranean crypts of Notre-Dame du Port and to the vaults of the cathedral upheld by it elegant clustered columns. At the Capuchins the choir was closed. During the offices, invisible mouths behind the grating chanted the canticles, which strangely effected my childish imagination; they seemed to me to come from so far off, an abyss or a tomb. I looked at my mother praying beside me with the fervor which was shown in her smallest actions, and I thought that my father was not there, that he never came to church. My child's brain was so puzzled by this absence, that, one day, I asked:

"Why does not papa come to mass with us?"

My inquiring child's eyes had no trouble to see the embarrassment into which this question threw my mother. She withdrew from it, however, by an answer analogous to hundreds of others which a woman so essentially enamored of fixed principles and of obedience has since given me.

"He goes to another mass, at an hour which suits him better, and then I have already told you that children ought never to ask why their parents do this or that."

All the difference of mind which separated my mother and myself is found in this sentence, uttered one cold morning in winter, while walking home under the trees of Sablon Court. I can see her now in her pelerine,[1] her hands in her muff lined with brown silk from which her book came

---

1. A pelerine is a woman's cape of lace or silk with pointed ends at the center front, popular in the nineteenth century.

halfway out, and the sincerity of her face even in her pious falsehood. I can see her eyes, which so many times since have regarded me with a look which did not comprehend me, and at this period she did not suspect that for my meditative childish nature to think, was already to ask, always and in relation to everything; why? Yes, why had my mother deceived me? For I knew that my father went to no kind of office. And why did he not go?

While the grave and sad voices of the concealed monks were intoning the responses of the mass, I was absorbed in this question. I knew without being able to appreciate the reasons of the superiority that my father was accounted among the first of the city. How many times in walking were we stopped by some friend, who tapping me on the cheek would say:

"Well, will we get to be a great savant like the father some day?"

When my mother took his advice, she listened with the greatest respect. She thought it natural that he did not perform certain duties which, for us, were obligatory. We had not the same duties. This idea was not formulated then in my childish brain with this positive distinctness, but it developed there the germ of that which later became one of the convictions of my youth—to know that the same rules do not govern intellectual minds that control other men.

It was there in that little church, quietly bending over my prayer book, that the great principle of my life had birth, not to consider as a law for thinking men that which is and ought to be a law for others—just as I received from the conversations with my father, during our excursions, the first germs of my scientific view of the world.

The country around Clermont is marvelous, and although I am the reverse of poetical, a man for whom the external world means very little, I have always retained in my memory the pictures of the landscapes which surrounded these walks. While the city on one side looks toward the plain of the Limagne, on the other it strands on the foothills of the Dome Mountains. The slope of the extinct craters, the undulations caused by old eruptions and the streams of hardened lava give to the outlines of these volcanic mountains a resemblance to the landscapes in the moon as discovered by the telescope in that dead planet.

On one side is the savage and sublime memorial of the most terrible convulsions of the globe, and on the other the prettiest rusticity of stony roads among the vineyards, of murmuring brooks under the willows and chestnuts. The great pleasures of my childhood were the interminable wanderings with my father in all the paths which lead from the Puy de Crouël to Gergovie, from Royat to Durtol, from Beaumont to Gravenoire.

Simply in writing these names, my memory rejuvenates my heart. I see myself again the little boy, whom a portrait represents with long hair, with his legs in cloth leggings, who walks along holding his father's hand. Whence came this love for the fields to him, the learned mathematician, the man of study and of reflection? I have often thought of it since, and I believe I have discovered a law of the development of mind—our youthful tastes persist even when we are developed in a sense contrary to them, and we continue to exercise these tastes while justifying them by intellectual reasons which would exclude such things.

I will explain. My father naturally loved the country because he was brought up in a village, and when he was small had passed whole days on the banks of the brooks among the insects and the flowers. Instead of yielding to these tastes in a simple manner, he mingled them with his present occupations. He would not have pardoned himself for going to the mountains without studying there the formation of the land; for looking at a flower without determining its character and discovering its name; for taking up an insect without recalling its family and its habits.

Thanks to the rigor of his method in all work he arrived at a very complete knowledge of the country; and, when we walked together, this knowledge was the sole subject of our conversation. The landscape of the mountains became a pretext for explaining to me the revolutions of the earth; he passed from that with a clearness of speech which made such ideas intelligible to me, to the hypothesis of Laplace upon nebula,[2] and I saw distinctly in my imagination the planetary protuberances flying off from the burning nucleus, from this torrid sun in rotation.

The heavens at night in the beautiful summer months became a kind of map which he deciphered for me, and on which I distinguished the Pole Star, the seven stars of the Chariot, Vega of the Lyre, Sirius, all those inaccessible and formidable worlds of which science knows the volume, the position and almost the very metals of which they are composed.

It was the same with the flowers which he taught me to arrange in an herbarium, with the stones which I broke with a little iron hammer, with the insects which I fed or pinned up, as the case might be. Long before object lessons were practiced in the college my father applied to my education first this great maxim: "Give a scientific account of anything we may encounter."

Thus reconciling the pleasantry of his first impressions with the precision acquired in his mathematical studies. I attribute to this teaching the precocious spirit of analysis which was developed in me during my early youth, and which, without doubt, would have turned toward the positive studies if my father had lived. But he could not complete this education, undertaken after a prepared plan of which I have since found trace among his papers.

In the course of one of our walks, and on one of the warmest days of summer, in my tenth year, we were overtaken by a storm which wet us to the bones. During the time that it required to reach home in our soaked clothes my father took cold. In the evening he complained of a chill. Two days after an inflammation of the lungs declared itself, and the week following he died.

As I wish, in this summary indication of diverse causes which formed my mind, to avoid at any cost that which I hate most of anything in the world, the display of subjective sentimentality, I will not recount to you, my

---

2. Pierre-Simon, marquis de Laplace's (1749–1827) Nebular hypothesis is the most widely accepted model in the field of cosmogony to explain the formation and evolution of the Solar System. It suggests that the Solar System formed from gas and dust orbiting the Sun. The theory was developed by Immanuel Kant and published in his *Allgemeine Naturgeschichte und Theorie des Himmels* ("Universal Natural History and Theory of the Heavens") in 1755 and then modified in 1796 by Pierre Laplace.

dear master, any further details of this death. They were heartrending, but I felt their sadness only in a far-off way, and that later.

I recollect, though I was a large and remarkably developed boy, to have felt more wonder than sorrow. It is now that I truly regret my father—that I comprehend what I lost in losing him. I believe you have seen exactly what I owe to him; the taste and the facility for abstraction, the love of the intellectual life, faith in science and the precocious management of method—these for the mind; for the character, the first divination of the pride of intellect, and also an element slightly morbid, this difficulty of action which has as its consequence the difficulty in resisting the passions when one is tempted.

I wish also to mark distinctly what I owe to my mother. And from the first I perceive this fact that this second influence acts upon me by reaction, while the first had acted directly. To speak truly, this reaction only began when she became a widow and wished to direct my education. Until then she had entirely given me up to my father.

It may seem strange that, alone in the world, she and I, she so energetic, so devoted, and I so young, we did not live, at least during those years, in perfect communion of heart. There exists in fact, a rudimentary psychology for which these words—mother and son—are synonyms of absolute tenderness, of perfect agreement of soul. Perhaps it is so in the families of ancient tradition, although in human nature I believe very little in the existence of entire sympathy between persons of different ages and sexes.

In any case, modern families present under conventional etiquette the most cruel phenomena of secret divorce, of complete misunderstanding, sometimes of hate, which are too well understood when we think of their origin. They come from the mixture for a hundred years of province with province, race with race, which has charged the blood of nearly all of us with hereditary opposites. So people find themselves nominally of the same family who have not a common trait either in their moral or mental structures; consequently the daily intimacy between persons becomes a cause of daily conflicts or of constant dissimulation. My mother and I are an example of it which I would qualify as excellent, if the pleasure of finding very clear proof of a psychological law was not accompanied by keen regret at having been its victims.

My father, I have told you, was an old pupil of the Polytechnic School and the son of a civil engineer. I have also said he was of Lorraine race. There is a proverb which says: "Lorraine traitor to its king and even to God." This epigram expresses in a unique form the idea that there is something complex in the mind of this frontier population.

The people of Lorraine have always lived on the border of two races and of two existences, the German and the French. What is this disposition to treachery if not the depravity of another taste, admirable from the intellectual point of view, that of sentimental complication? For my part, I attribute to this atavism the power of doubling of which I spoke at the beginning of this analysis. I ought to add that, when I was a child, I often felt a strange pleasure in disinterested simulation which proceeded from the same principle. I recounted to my comrades all sorts of inexact details concerning myself, about my place of birth, my father's birthplace, about a walk which I was intending to take, and this not to boast, but simply to be some one else.

I found singular pleasure later in advancing opinions the most opposed to those which I considered the true ones from the same bizarre motive. To play a role different from my true nature appeared to me an enrichment of my person, so strong was the instinct to resolve myself into a character, a belief, a passion.

My mother is a woman of the South, absolutely rebellious against all complexity, to whom ideas of things alone are intelligible. In her imagination the forms of life are reproduced concrete, precise and simple. When she thinks of religion, she sees her church, her confessional, the communion cloth, the few priests whom she has known, the catechism in which she studied. When she thinks of a career, she sees positive activity and benefits. The professorate, for example, which she desired me to enter, was for her M. Limasset, the professor of mathematics, the friend of my father, and she saw me, like him, going across the city twice a day in an alpaca coat and Panama hat in summer, and my feet protected in winter by clogs, and my body in a furred overcoat, with a fixed salary, the perquisites of private tuition and the sweet assurance of a pension.

I have been able by studying her to learn how completely this order of imagination renders those whom it governs incapable of comprehending other souls. It is often said of such people that they are despotic and personal, or that they have bad characters. In reality, they are before those with whom they associate like a child before a watch. He sees the hands move, he knows nothing of the wheels which make them move. So when these hands do not go to suit his fancy there is the stupidity of impatience to force them and to warp the springs.

My poor mother was like this with me, and that from the week which followed our trouble. I felt almost immediately an indefinable discomfort in her presence. The first circumstance which enlightened me in regard to this separation which had begun between us, so far as my childish mind could be enlightened, dates from an afternoon of autumn, nearly four months after my father's death.

The impression received was so strong that I recall it as if it had happened yesterday. We had changed apartments, and had rented the third floor of a house in the Rue Billard, a narrow lane which distorts the shadows of Des Petits-Abres, in front of the palace of the Prefecture. My mother had chosen it because there was a balcony in which I was playing on this beautiful afternoon. My play—you will here recognize the scientific turn given by my father to my imagination—consisted in taking a pebble, which represented a great explorer, from one end of the balcony to the other, and among other stones which I had taken from the flower pots.

Some of these stones represented cities, others curious animals of which I had read descriptions. One of the parlor windows opened on the balcony. It was partly open, and my play having led me thither I heard my mother talking to a visitor. I could not help listening with that beating of the heart which the hearing my personality discussed has always produced. I learned afterward that between our real nature and the impression produced on our relations, and even on our friends, there is no more similarity than there is between the exact color of the face and its reflection in a blue, green, or yellow glass.

"Perhaps," said the visitor, "you are mistaken in regard to poor Robert, at ten years the character is not at all formed."

"God grant that it may be so," replied my mother, "but I am afraid he has no heart. You cannot imagine how hard he has been since his father's death. The next day even he seemed to have forgotten all about it. And he has never said a word since—such a word as makes you feel that one is thinking of another you now. When I speak to him of his father, he hardly answers me. You would think he had never known the man who was so good to him."

I have read somewhere that when Mérimée[3] was quite a child he was one day scolded by his mother and then sent out of the room. He was scarcely gone when his mother burst out laughing. The child heard the laugh which showed him that the irritation had been feigned, and he felt a feeling of distrust rise in his heart which always remained. This anecdote impressed me very strongly.

The impression of the celebrated writer offered a startling analogy with the effect which this fragment of conversation produced upon me. It was very true that I never spoke of my father, but how false that I had forgotten him! On the contrary, I thought of him constantly. I never walked along the street, I could not look at any piece of our furniture without the remembrance of his death taking such possession of me that I was almost ill. But with this was mingled a fearful astonishment that he had gone forever, and it was all confounded in a kind of anxious apprehension, which closed my mouth when any one talked with me about him.

I know now that my mother could have known nothing of the workings of my mind. But, at that time, as I heard her thus condemn my heart, I experienced a profound humiliation. It seemed to me that she was not acting toward me as it should be her duty to act. I felt that she was unjust, and because I was timid, being still a young boy and shy, I became irritated at her injustice, instead of trying to tell her how I felt.

From that moment it became impossible for me to show myself to her as I was. And whenever her eyes sought mine to learn my emotions I felt an irresistible desire to conceal from her my inmost being.

That was the first scene—if anything so insignificant can be dignified by so big a name—followed by a second which I will notice in spite of its appar-

---

3. Prosper Mérimée (1803–1870) was a French Romantic writer and one of the pioneers of the novella. He is best known for his novella *Carmen*, which became the basis of Bizet's opera *Carmen*.

ent unimportance. Children would not be children if the events important to their sensibility were not puerile.

I was, at this period, already passionately fond of reading, and chance had put into my hands a very different kind of books from those which are given as prizes at school. It was this way: although my father as a mathematician knew little of general literature, he loved a few authors whom he understood in his way; and when afterward I found some of his notes on these authors, I learned to appreciate the degree to which the feeling for literature is a personal, irreducible, incommensurable thing—to borrow a word from his favorite science—there is no common measure between the reasons for which two minds like or dislike the same writer.

Among other works my father owned a translation of Shakespeare in two volumes, which they put on my chair to raise my seat at table. They left me without thinking how these volumes illustrated by engravings would very soon incite my curiosity to read the text. There was a Lady Macbeth rubbing her hands in presence of a frightened physician and a servant, and Othello entering Desdemona's chamber with a poniard in his hand, and bending his black face toward the white, sleeping form, a King Lear tearing his clothing under the zigzags of the lightning, a Richard III, asleep in his tent and surrounded by specters.

From the accompanying text I read, before my tenth year, fragments which made me familiar with all these dramas which exalted my imagination, in so far as I could seize the meaning of them, without doubt because they were written for popular audiences, and admit an element of primitive poetry, and an infantile exaggeration.

I loved these kings, who, joyous or despairing, defiled past at the head of their armies, who lost or gained battles in a few minutes, I enjoyed this slaughter accompanied by a flourish of trumpets behind the scenes, the rapid passages from one country to another, and the chimerical geography. In brief, whatever there is in these dramas and especially in the chronicles that is very much abridged, almost rudimentary, so charmed me, that when I was alone I played with the chairs, imagining them to be Lancaster, Warwick, or Gloucester.

My father, who had an extreme repugnance to the troublesome realities of life, relished in Shakespeare that which is simple and touching, the profiles of women so delicately drawn; Imogene and Desdemona, Cordelia and Rosalind pleased him, though the comparison may seem strange, for the same reason that he enjoyed the romances of Dickens, Topffer and even the child's play of Florian and Berquin.

Here we may see the contrasts which prove the incoherence of artistic judgments which are founded upon sentimental impression. I also read all these books, and those of Walter Scott, as well as the rural tales of George Sand, in an illustrated edition. It would certainly have been better for me not to have nourished my imagination on elements so incongruous and sometimes dangerous. But at my age I could not understand more than a quarter of the sentences, and while my father was toiling at his blackboard, combining his formulas, I believe that the lightning might have struck the house without his knowing it, carried away as he was by the all-powerful demon of abstraction.

My mother, to whom this demon is as much a stranger as the beast of the Apocalypse, did not wait long, after the first hours of our trouble had passed, before she rummaged the room in which I studied; and, under an exercise, she discovered a large, open book—Scott's *Ivanhoe*.

"What book is this?" she asked, "who permitted you to take it?"

"But I have read it once already," I replied.

"And these?" she continued, in looking over the little library where by the side of schoolbooks, were, beside the Shakespeare, *Nouvelles Génevoises* and *Nicholas Nickleby*, *Rob Roy* and *La Mare au Diable*. "These are not suitable for a person of your age," she insisted, "and you may help me carry all these books into the parlor, and put them in your father's library."

So I carried them, three at a time, some almost too heavy for my small arms, into the cool room furnished in haircloth. With her white hands in their black mitts, she took the books and arranged them alongside of the big treatises on mathematics. She closed the glass door of the bookcase, locked it, and put the key on the ring with others, which she always carried with her. Then she added severely: "When you wish a book you may ask me for it."

I ask her for one of those books, but which one? I knew so well that she would refuse me all those which I had any desire to read! I have already shown too plainly that we did not think alike on any point. I complain of her having put a stop to my liveliest pleasure, less perhaps because of the prohibition than for the reason she gave. For she believed it to be her duty to repeat the phrases on the danger of romances, no doubt borrowed from some manual of piety, which appeared to me to express exactly the contrary to that which I had experienced.

She made the danger I had run in this indiscriminate reading the pretext for occupying herself more closely with my studies and directing my education. This was her duty, but the contrast was too great between the ideas into which my father had precociously initiated me and the poverty of her mind, which was furnished with impressions positive, mean, and almost vulgar.

I went to walk with her now, and she talked with me. Her conversation was confined to my bearing, my manners, my little comrades, and their parents. My intellect, which had been too early trained in the pleasure of thought, felt stifled and oppressed.

The motionless landscape of extinct volcanoes recalled to me the grand convulsions of the terrestrial drama which my father formerly traced. The flowers which I plucked my mother would hold for a few minutes, and then let fall almost without looking at them. She was ignorant of their names, as she was of those of the insects which she compelled me to throw down as soon as I had picked them up, saying they were unclean and venomous.

The roads among the vines no longer led to the discovery of the vast world to which the genial word of the dead had invited me. They were simply a continuation of the streets of the city and the misery of daily cares. I seek in vain for suitable words to express the vague and singular ennui of a mutilated mind, of a rarefied atmosphere which these walks inflicted on me.

Language was created by men to express the ideas of men. The terms are lacking which correspond to the incomplete perceptions of children, to their penumbra of soul. How can I tell the suffering, which I did not myself comprehend, of a mind in which were fermenting high and broad conceptions, of a brain upon the border of the great intellectual horizon, and which had to submit to the unconscious tyranny of another brain, narrow and weak, a stranger to all general ideas, to every view either ample or profound?

Now that I have passed through this period of repressed and thwarted youth, I interpret the smallest episodes by the laws of the constitution of mind, and I take into account that fate, in confiding the education of such a child as I was to the woman who was my mother, had associated two forms of thought as irreducible the one to the other as two different species.

These details, in which I find the proof of this constitutive antithesis between our two natures, come to me by thousands. I have said enough on this point so that I may content myself by noting with precision the result of this silent collision of our minds, and to borrow formulas in the philosophic style, I believe, that by this wrong education, two germs were prepared in me: the germ of a sentiment and the germ of a faculty; the sentiment was that of the solitude of the individual, the faculty that of internal analysis.

I have said that in the order of sensibility as in that of thought, I had almost immediately felt that I could not show myself to my mother as I was. I thus learned, though I was scarcely born into the intellectual life that there is in us an obscure incommunicable element. This was in my case a timidity at first—then it grew into a pride. But have not all forms of pride a common origin?

Not to dare to show ourselves is to become isolated; and to become isolated is very soon to prefer one's self. I have since found, in some recent philosophers, M. Renan, for example, this sentiment of the solitude of the soul, but it was transformed into a triumphant and transcendental disdain; I have found it changed into disease and barrenness in the Adolphe of Benjamin Constant,[4] aggressive and ironical in Beyle.[5]

In the poor little collegian of a provincial lyceum, who trotted through the slippery streets of his mountain town in winter, with his cartable under

---

4. Henri-Benjamin Constant de Rebecque (1767–1830) was a Swiss-French political activist and writer on political theory and religion. Constant published only one novella during his lifetime, *Adolphe* (1816), the story of a young, indecisive man's disastrous love affair with an older mistress.

5. Marie-Henri Beyle (1783–1842), better known by his pen name Stendhal, was a 19th-century French writer. Best known for the novels *Le Rouge et le Noir* (*The Red and the Black*, 1830) and *La Chartreuse de Parme* (*The Charterhouse of Parma*, 1839).

his arm and his feet in galoshes, it was only an obscure and painful instinct; but this instinct, after being applied to my mother, grew more and more applying itself to my comrades and to my masters. I felt that I was different from them with this difference: I believed that I understood them perfectly and that they did not understand me. Reflection has taught me that I did not understand them any better than they understood me; but I also see now that there was really this difference between us, that they accepted their person and mine simply, purely, bravely, while I had already begun to complicate myself by thinking too much of myself. If I had very early felt that, contrary to the word of Christ, I had no neighbor, it was because I had begun very early to exasperate the consciousness of my own soul, and consequently to make of myself an exemplar, without analogy, of excessive individual sensibility.

My father had endowed me with a premature curiosity of mind. As he was not there to direct me toward the world of positive knowledge, this curiosity fell back upon myself. The mind is a living creature, and as with all other creatures, every power is accompanied by a want. It would be necessary to reverse the old proverb and say: To be able is to wish. A faculty in us always leads to the wish to exercise it.

Mental hereditary and my early education made an intellectual being of me before my time. I continued to be such a being, but all my intellect was applied to my own emotions. I became an absolute egoist with an extraordinary energy of disdain with regard to everyone else. These traits of my character appeared later under the influence of the crises of ideas though which I have passed and of which I owe you the history.

§ II. THE MEDIUM OF IDEAS

THE DIVERSE INFLUENCES which I have just rather abstractly summarized, but in terms which you will understand, my dear master, had first this unexpected result, to make of me a very pious child, between my eleventh and my fifteenth year. If I had been placed in the college as a boarder, I should have grown like my comrades whom I have since studied and for whom there has never been a religious crisis.

At the period of which I am writing, and which marked the definite advent of the democratic party in France, a great wave of free thought rolled from Paris into all the provinces; but I was the son of a very devout woman, and I was subjected to all the observances of religion. I find a proof of what I have told you of my precocious taste for analysis in the fact that unlike all my young companions, I was delighted with the confessional. I can say that, during the four years of the mystic crisis of youth, from 1876 to 1880, the great events of my life were these long seances in the narrow wooden box in the church Des Minimes, which was our parish church, where I went every fortnight to kneel down and speak in a low voice, with a beating heart, of what was passing within me.

The approach of my first communion marked the birth of this feeling for the confessional, mixed with contradictory elements. I believed, consequently, my little sins appeared to me to be veritable crimes, and to confess them made me ashamed. I repented, and I had the certainty that I rose pardoned, with the delight of a conscience washed from every stain. I was an imaginative and nervous child, and there was for me in the scenery of the sacrament, in the cold silence of the church, in the odor of vault and incense which filled it, in the stammering of my own voice saying, "My father," and in the whispering of the priest responding, "my son," from behind the grating, a poetry of mystery which I felt without understanding.

United with this, there was a singular impression of fear, which was derived from the teaching of Abbé Martel, the priest who prepared us for our first communion. He was a small, short man, with an apoplectic face, and a grave, hard blue eye, a man who had been educated in a provincial seminary still penetrated with Jansenism.[1] His eyes, when from the pulpit of Des Minimes he was talking to us of hell, saw visions of terror, and this sensation he communicated to us.

I rejoice that he is dead, for if he were living I might see him enter my prison, and who knows what might happen then? Perhaps I should suffer a recurrence of those emotions of terror which his presence used to inflict. The constant themes of his discourse were the small number of the elect and the divine vengeance.

"Who could hinder God," said the priest, "since he is all-powerful, from forcing the soul of the man who has committed murder to remain near the body from which it is separated? The soul would be there, in the mortuary chamber, hearing the sobs, seeing the tears of the friends, and yet forbidden to console them. It would be imprisoned in the winding-sheet,[2] and there during days and days and nights and nights it would be present at the corruption of the flesh, which was once its own, there among the worms and the rot."

Such images and such ferocity of invention abounded in his bitter mouth; they followed me into my sleep; the fear of hell was excited in me almost to madness. The Abbé Martel employed the same eloquence in presenting the decisive importance to our salvation which the approach to the communion table would have, and so my fear of eternal punishment led to a scrupulous examination of my conscience.

Soon these close meditations, this looking as through a magnifying glass at my slightest deviations, this continuous scrutiny of my inmost self,

---

1. Jansenism was a theological movement within Catholicism (primarily active in France) that originated from the posthumously published work of the Dutch theologian Cornelius Jansen (1585–1638) It emphasized original sin, human depravity, the necessity of divine grace and predestination; the heretical notion of Jansenism, as stated by subsequent Roman Catholic doctrine, lay in denying the role of free will in the acceptance and use of grace. Jansenism asserts that God's role in the infusion of grace cannot be resisted and does not require human assent.

2. A winding sheet, or burial shroud, is a cloth in which a body is wrapped for burial.

interested me to such a degree that no sport had any attraction for me in comparison. I had found, for the first time since the death of my father, an employment for this power of analysis which was already definitive and almost constitutive in me.

The development thus given to my acute sense of the inner life ought to have produced an amelioration of my moral being. On the contrary, it resulted in a subtility which, in itself alone, was a corruption, at least from the point of view of strict Catholic discipline. I became, in the course of these examinations of conscience, into which entered more of pleasure than of repentance, extremely ingenious, and discovering peculiar motives behind my most simple actions. The Abbé Martel was not a psychologist sufficiently acute to discern this shadow and to comprehend that to cut the soul to pieces in this way would lead me to prefer the fleeting complexities of sin to the simplicity of virtue. He recognized only the zeal of a very fervent child. For example, on the morning of my first communion I went in tears to confess to him once more.

In turning over and over again the soil and the subsoil of my memory, I had discovered a singular sin, the fear of man. Six weeks before, I had heard two boys, my comrades, at the door of the Lyceum, mocking an old lady who was entering the church Des Carmes, just opposite. I had laughed at their words instead of reproving them.

The old lady was going to mass; to ridicule her was to ridicule a pious action. I had laughed, why? From false shame. Then I had participated in it. Was it not my duty to find the two mockers and to show them their impiety, and make them promise to repent? I had not done so. Why? From false shame; from respect for man, according to the definition of the catechism. I passed the whole night preceding the great day of the first communion in wondering if I could see the Abbé Martel early enough the next day to confess this sin. I recall the smile with which he tapped my cheek after having given me absolution in order to quiet me. I hear the tone of his voice which had grown very sweet as he said to me: "May you always be what you are now." He did not suspect that this puerile scruple was the sign of an exaggeratedly unhealthy reflection, nor that this reflection would poison the delights of the Eucharist for which I had so ardently wished. I had not been satisfied, in the course of the preceding weeks, to analyze the conscience to its most delicate fibres, I had abandoned myself to the imagination of sentiment which is the forced consequence of this spirit of analysis. I had anticipated with extreme precision the sentiments which I should experience in receiving the host upon my lips. In my imagination I advanced toward the rail of the altar which was draped in a white cloth, with a tension of my whole being which I have never since experienced, and I felt, in communing, a kind of chilling deception, an ecstatic exhaustion of which I cannot describe the discomfort. I have since spoken of this impression to a friend who was still a Christian and he said: "You were not simple enough." His piety had given to him the insight of a professional observer. It was too true. But what could I do?

The great event of my youth, which was the loss of my faith, did not, however, date from this deception. The causes which determined this loss were very numerous, and I have never clearly comprehended them until now. They were slow and progressive at first, and acted upon my mind as the worm upon the fruit, devouring the interior without any other sign of this ravage than a small speck, almost invisible, on the beautiful purple rind. The first was, it seems to me, the application to my confessor of this terrible critical spirit, a faculty destructive of all confidence, which, from my infancy, had so separated me from my mother.

I pushed my examinations of conscience to the most subtle delicacy and still the Abbé Martel did not perceive this work of secret torture which completely anatomized my soul. My scruples appeared to him, as they were, childish; but they were the childishness of a very complex boy, and one who could not be directed unless he might feel that he was understood.

In my conversations with this rude and primitive priest I soon experienced the contrary feeling. This was enough to deprive this director of my youth of all authority over my mind. At the same time, and this is the second of the causes which detached me from the church, I found among men whom I then considered superior the same indifference to religious observances that I had observed in my father. I knew that the young professors, those who had come from Paris with the prestige of having gone through the Normal School, were all atheists and skeptics. I heard the abbé pronounce these words with concentrated indignation, in the visits which he made to my mother. When I accompanied her to the offices of Des Minimes as I had formerly to those of the Capuchins, I reflected on the poverty of intellect of the devotees who crowd to mass on Sunday mornings and mutter their prayers in the silence of the ceremony, broken only by the noise of displaced chairs. The flame of a clear and living thought had never been lighted in the heads that bowed with so submissive a fervor at the elevation of the host.

I did not at that time formulate this contrast with this distinctness, but I recalled the picture of those young masters as they emerged from the Lyceum, talking with each other in conversations which I imagined were like those of my father, where the smallest sentence was charged with science; and a spirit of doubt arose in my mind as to the intellectual value of Catholic beliefs.

This distrust was fed by a kind of naive ambition which made me desire with an incredible ardor to be as intelligent as the most intelligent and not to vegetate among those of second rank. I confess that a good deal of pride was mingled with this desire, but I do not blush at this avowal. It was a purely intellectual pride, completely foreign to any desire for outward success. And, if I hold myself erect at this moment, and in this fearful drama, I owe it first of all to this pride—it is this which permits me to describe my past with this cold lucidity, instead of running away like an ordinary suspect, from the noisy events of this drama. I can see so clearly that the first scenes of this tragedy began with the college youth in whom was acting the young man of today.

The third of the causes which concurred in this slow disintegration of my Christian faith was the discovery of contemporaneous literature, which dates from my fourteenth year. I have told you that my mother, shortly after my father's death, suppressed certain books. This severity had not relaxed with time, and the key of the paternal bookcase continued to click on the steel ring between that of the pantry and of the cellar. The most evident result of this prohibition was, to heighten the charm of the remembrance which these books had left of the half-comprehended pieces from Shakespeare, and the half-forgotten romances of George Sand.

Chance willed that, at the commencement of my thirteenth year, I should come across some examples of modern poetry in the book of French authors which served for the year's recitations. There were fragments of Lamartine, a dozen of Hugo's pieces, the *Stances à la Malibran* of Alfred de Musset, some bits of Sainte-Beuve, and of Leconte de Lisle.

These pages were sufficient to make me appreciate the absolute difference of inspiration between the modern and the ancient masters, as one can appreciate the difference of aroma between a bouquet of roses and a bouquet of lilacs, with his eyes shut. This difference, which I divine by an unreasoning instinct, resides in the fact that, until the Revolution, writers had never taken sensibility as the subject and the only rule of their works. It has been the contrary since eighty-nine. From this there results among the new writers a certain painful, ungovernable something, a search after moral and physical emotion which has become almost morbid, and which attracted me immediately.

The mystical sensuality of the "Stances du Lac" and of the "Crucifix," the changing splendors of several "Orientales," fascinated me; but above all I was charmed at something culpable which breathes in the eloquence of "L'Espoir en Dieu" and in some fragments of the "Consolations." I began to feel for the rest of the works of these masters that strong and almost insane curiosity which marks the middle period of adolescence. One is then on the border of life, and he hears without seeing, as it were, the murmur of a waterfall through a cluster of trees, and how this sound intoxicates him with expectation! A friendship with a comrade who lived on the first floor of our house exasperated this curiosity still more.

This friend, who died young, and who was named Emile, was also an inveterate reader, but more fortunate than I, he suffered from no surveillance. His father and mother, who were already old, lived on a small income and passed the long hours of the day in playing, in front of the window which opened on the Rue de Billard, interminable games of *bezique*,[3] with cards bought in a cafe and still smelling of tobacco. Emile, alone in his room, could abandon himself to all his fancies in reading.

As we were in the same class, and as we went to and from the Lyceum together, my mother willingly permitted me to pass whole hours with this

---

3. *Bezique* is a 19th-century French melding and trick-taking card game for two players.

charming lad, who soon shared my taste for the verses which I so much admired, and my desire to know more of their authors.

On our way to the college, we took the narrow streets of the old town and passed the stall of an old bookseller of whom we had bought some second-hand classics. We discovered here a copy of the poetry of Musset in rather a bad condition, which would cost forty sous. At first we contented ourselves with occasional readings at the stall, but soon we felt that it was impossible to do without it. By putting together our spending money for two weeks, we were able to buy it, and then, in Emile's little room, he on his bed and I on a chair, we read Don Paez, the Marrons du feu, Portia, Mardoche and Rolla. I trembled as if I were committing a great fault, and we imbibed this poetry as if it had been wine, slowly, sweetly, passionately.

I read afterward in this same room, and also in my own, thanks to the ruses of a lover in danger, many clandestine volumes which I very much enjoyed, from the *Peau de chagrin*[4] of Balzac, to *Les Fleurs du mal*[5] of Baudelaire, not to mention the poems of Heinrich Heine and the romances of Stendhal.

I have never felt an emotion comparable to that of my first encounter with the genius of the author of "Rolla." I was neither an artist nor a historian. Was I therefore indifferent to their value more or less real or their meaning more or less actual? Not at all. This was an elder brother who had come to reveal to me the dangerous world of sentimental experience.

The intellectual inferiority of piety to impiety which I had obscurely felt appeared now in a strangely new light. All the virtues that had been preached to me in my childhood seemed poor and mean and humble, and meaner beside the opulence and the frenzy of certain vices. The devotees who were my mother's friends, sadly old and shriveled, represented faith. Impiety was a handsome young man who awakes and looks at the crimson aurora, and in a glance discovers the whole horizon of history and legends, and then again lays his head on the bosom of a girl as beautiful as his most beautiful dream. Chastity and marriage were the *bourgeois* whom I knew who went to

---

4. *La Peau de chagrin* (1831) is known in English as *The Wild Ass's Skin*.

5. *Les Fleurs du mal* (1857) is a volume of poetry known in English as *The Flowers of Evil*.

hear the music in the Jardin des Plantes, every Thursday and Sunday, and who said the same things in the same way. My imagination painted, in the chimerical colors of the most burning poetry, the faces of the libertines of the Contes d'Espagne[6] and of the fragments which follow. There was Dalti murdering the husband of Portia, then wandering with his mistress over the dark waters of the lagoon among the stairways of the antique palaces. There were Don Paez assassinating Juana after folding her to himself in a fond embrace; Frank and his Belcolore, Hassan and his Namouna, Abbé Cassio and his Luzon.

I was not competent to criticize the romantic falsity of all this fine setting, nor to separate the sincere from the literary portion of these poems. The complete profligacy of soul appeared to me through these lines, and it tempted me; it excited in my mind, already eager for new sensations, the faculty of analysis already too much aroused.

The other works which I have cited were the pretext for a temptation which was similar but not so strong.

In the contemplation of the sores of the human heart which they exposed with so much complaisance, I was like those saints of the middle ages who were hypnotized by contemplation of the wounds of the Saviour. The strength of their piety caused the miraculous stigmata to appear on their hands and the ardor of my imagination, at the age of holy ignorances and immaculate purities, opened in my soul the stigmata of moral ulcers which are draining the life blood of all the great modern invalids.

Yes, in the years when I was only the collegian, the friend of little Emile, I assimilated in thought the emotions which the timid teachings of my masters indicated as the most criminal. My mind was tainted with the most dangerous poisons, while, thanks to my power of duplication, I continued to play the part of a very good child, very assiduous at my tasks, very submissive to my mother, and very pious. But no. However strange this must appear to you, I did not play that role. I was pious, with a spontaneous contradiction which, perhaps, has directed my thought to the psychological work to which

---

6. *Contes d'Espagne et d'Italie* (1829), known in English as *Tales of Spain and Italy*, was Alfred de Musset's (1810–1857) first collection of poems.

I consecrated my first efforts.

When I read in your work on the will those suggestive indications on the theory of the multiplicity of self, I seized upon them immediately, after having passed through such epochs as I am describing to you today and in which I have really been several distinct beings.

This crisis of imaginative sensibility had continued the attack upon my religious faith by offering the temptation of subtle sin and also that of painful skepticism. The sensuality crisis which resulted from it failed to revive this faith in my heart. I ceased to be pure when I was seventeen years old, and this happened as usual, in very dull and prosaic circumstances. From that time, beside the two persons who already existed in me, between the youth who was still fervent, regular, pious, and the youth romantically imaginative, a third individual was born and grew, a sensual being, tormented by the basest desires. However, the taste for the intellectual life was so strong, so definite, that although suffering from this singular condition, I felt a sensation of superiority in recognizing and studying it.

What was more strange, I did not yield to this last disposition more than I did to the others, with a clear and lucid consciousness. I remained a youth through all these troubles, that is to say a being still uncertain and incomplete, a being in whom could be discerned the lineaments of the soul to come.

I did not assert my mysticism, for at bottom I was ashamed to believe, as if to believe were something inferior; nor my sentimental imaginations, for I considered them as simple sports of literature; nor my sensuality for I was disgusted with it. And beside, I had neither the theory nor the audacity of my curiosity in regard to my faults.

Emile, who died the following winter, of disease of the lungs, was very ill at this time and did not go out of the house. He listened to my confidences with a frightened interest which flattered my self-love by making me think that I was different from others. This did not prevent my being afraid, as on the evening before my first communion, at the look which Abbé Martel gave me when he met me. He had without doubt spoken to my mother, so far as the secrecy of the confessional permitted, for she watched my goings out but without the power to hinder them entirely, and above all without suspecting any other than the possible causes of temptation, so well did I envelop myself in hypocrisy.

The illness of my best friend, the surveillance of my mother, the apprehension of the priest's eyes enervated me, and perhaps the more that it seemed in this volcanic country as if the summer's heat drew from the sun a more ardent and intoxicating vapor. I knew at that time, days literally maddening, so made up were they of contradictory hours, days in which I arose a more fervent Christian than ever. I read a little in *The Imitation of Christ*,[7] I prayed, I went to my class with the firm determination to be perfectly regular and good. As soon as I returned I prepared my lessons, then I went down to Emile's room. We gave ourselves up to the reading of some exciting book. His father and mother, who knew that he could not live, humored him in everything and allowed him to take from the library any work that he pleased.

We now had in hand the most modern writers, whose books having recently come from Paris, exhaled an odor of new paper and fresh ink. In this way we brought upon ourselves a chill of the brain which accompanied me all the afternoon after I returned to my classroom. There, in the stifling heat of the day, I could see through the open door, the short shadows of the trees in the yard, and bear the far-off voices of some professor dictating the lessons; I could see the figure of Marianne, and then began a temptation which at first was vague and remote, but which grew and continued to grow. I resisted it, while knowing that I should succumb, as if the struggle against my obscure desire made me the more feel its strength and acuteness.

I went home. I hurried through my duties with a kind of diabolical verve, finding some power in the disorder of my too susceptible nerves. After dinner I went downstairs under pretext of seeing Emile and hastened toward Marianne's. On my return I passed some hours at my window, looking at the stars of the vast sky of summer, recalling my dead father, and what he had said to me of these far-off worlds. Then an extraordinary impression of the mystery of nature would seize me, of the mystery of my own soul, living

---

7. *The Imitation of Christ,* a Christian devotional book by Thomas à Kempis, first composed in Latin as *De Imitatione Christi* c. 1418–1427.

in the midst of nature, and I do not know which I admired more, the depths of the taciturn heavens, or the abysses which a day thus employed revealed in my heart.

Such were the habits of my inner life, my dear master, when I entered the class which would decide my development—the class of philosophy. My enchantment began in the first week of the course. What a course, however, and how crammed with the rubbish of the classic psychology! No matter, inexact and incomplete official and conventional as it was, this psychology enamored me. The method employed, the personal reflection and the minute analysis: the object to be studied, the human "I," considered in his faculties and passions; the result sought, a system of general idea capable of summing up in brief formulas a vast pile of phenomena; all in this new science, harmonized too well with the species of mind which my heredity, my education, and my own tendencies had fashioned in me.

I forgot even my favorite reading and plunged into these works of an order until now unknown with the more frenzy that the death of my only friend which occurred at this time imposed on my mind, which was naturally so meditative, this problem of destiny which I already felt myself powerless to solve by my early faith.

My ardor was so lively that soon I was no longer satisfied to follow the course. I sought other books which would complete the teaching of the masters, and in this way, I one day came upon *Psychology of God*. It impressed me so profoundly that I immediately obtained *Theory of Passions* and *Anatomy of the Will*. These were in the realm of pure thought, the same thunderbolt as were the works of Musset[8] in the realm of delirious sensations. The veil fell. The darkness of the external and of the internal world became light. I had found my way. I was your pupil.

In order to explain to you in a very clear manner how your thought penetrated mine, permit me to pass immediately to the result of this reading, and the meditations which followed. You will see how I was able to draw from your works a complete system of ethics, and which properly arranged

---

8. Alfred Louis Charles de Musset-Pathay (1810–1857) was a French dramatist, poet, and novelist.

in a marvelous manner the scattered elements which were floating about within me.

I found in the first of these three works, *Psychology of God*, a definite alleviation of the religious anguish in which I had continued to live, in spite of temptation and of doubts. Certainly, objections to the dogmas had not been lacking, as I had read so many books which manifested the most audacious irreligion, and I had been drawn toward skepticism, as I have told you, because I found in it the double character of intellectual superiority and of sentimental novelty.

I had felt, among other influences, that of the author of *Life of Jesus*.[9] The exquisite magic of his style, the sovereign grace of his dilettantisms, the languorous poetry of his pious impiety had affected me deeply, but it was not for nothing that I was the son of a geometrician, and I had not been satisfied with what there was of uncertainty, of shadow in this incomparable artist.

It was the mathematical rigor of your book which at once took possession of my mind. You demonstrated with irresistible dialectics, that any hypothesis upon the first cause is nonsense, even the idea of this first cause is an absurdity, nevertheless this nonsense and this absurdity are as necessary to our mind as is the illusion to our eyes of a sun turning around the earth, although we know that the sun is immovable and that the earth itself is in motion. The all-powerful ingenuity of this reasoning charmed my intellect, which docilely yielded to your vision of the lucid and rational world. I perceived the universe as it is, pouring out without beginning, and without end, the tide of inexhaustible phenomena. The care which you have taken to found all your arguments upon facts taken from science corresponded too well with the teaching of my father not to have subdued me.

I read your pages over and over again, summarized them, commented upon them, applied them with the ardor of a neophyte, in order to assimilate

---

9. The enormously popular and controversial *Life of Jesus* (*Vie de Jésus*) was written by Renan in 1863. It depicted Jesus as a man but not God, and rejected the miracles of the Gospel. Renan believed that by humanizing Jesus he was restoring to him a greater dignity; he argued Jesus was able to purify himself of "Jewish traits" and that he became an Aryan—promoting racial ideas and infused race into theology and the person of Jesus.

all the substance. The intellectual pride which I had felt from my childhood became exalted in the young man who learned from you the renunciations of the sweetest, of the most comforting topics.

Ah! How shall I tell you of the fervor of an initiation which was like a first love in the delights of its enthusiasm? I felt it a physical joy to overthrow, with your books in my hand, the entire edifice of beliefs in which I had grown up. Yes, this was the masculine felicity which Lucretius has celebrated, that of the liberating negation, and not the cowardly melancholy of a Jouffroy.[10]

This hymn to science, of which each of your pages is a strophe, I listened to with a delight as much more intense as the faculty of analysis, the principal reason of my piety, had found, thanks to you, another way to exercise itself than at the confessional, and that your two great treatises had enlightened me as to my inner being, at the same time that your *Psychology of God* enlightened me in regard to the external universe, with a light which, even today, is my last, my inextinguishable beacon in the midst of the tempest.

How you explained to me all the incoherences of my youth! This moral solitude in which I had suffered so much with my mother, with the Abbé Martel, with my comrades, with everyone, even Emile—I now understood. Have you not demonstrated, in your *Theory of the Passions*, that we are powerless to get away from Self, and that all relation between two beings reposes, like everything else, upon illusion?

Your *Anatomy of the Will* revealed to me the necessary motives, the inevitable logic of the yielding to the temptations of the senses for which I had suffered remorse so severe. The complications with which I reproached myself as a lack of frankness, you showed to be the very law of existence imposed by heredity. I found also, that, in searching the romancers and poets of the century for culpable and morbid conditions of soul, I had, without suspecting it, followed the inborn vocation of psychologist. Have you not written:

---

10. Théodore Simon Jouffroy (1796–1842) was a French philosopher who critically addressed the relationship between skepticism and the French Revolution; especially in his popular work *Comment les dogmes finissent* (*How Dogmas End*) published in 1823.

All souls must be considered by the psychologist as experiences instituted by nature. Among these experiences, some are useful to society and are called virtues; others are injurious and are called vices or crimes. These last are however, the more significant, and there would lack an essential element to the science of the mind, if Nero, for example, or some Italian tyrant of the fifteenth century had not existed?

On those warm summer days, I walked out, with one of these books in my pocket, and, when alone in the country, I read some of these sentences and became absorbed in meditation on their meaning. I applied to the country which surrounded me the philosophical interpretation of what we agree to call evil. Without doubt the eruptions which had raised the chain of the Domes,[11] at whose feet I wandered, had devastated with burning lava the neighboring plain and destroyed living beings, but they had produced this magnificence of scenery which charmed me, when my eyes contemplated the graceful group of the Pariou, the Puy de Dôme and all the line of these noble mountains.

The road was verdant with euphorbias in bloom, whose stems I broke to see the milk-white poison exuding from them. But these poisonous plants nourished the beautiful tithymal caterpillar, green with dark spots, from which a butterfly would be born, a sphinx with colored wings of the finest tint.

Sometimes a viper glided among the stones of these dusty roads, which I watched as it moved away, gray against the puzzuolana[12] red, with his flat head and the suppleness of his spotted body. The dangerous reptile appeared to me a proof of the indifference of nature whose only care is to multiply life, beneficent or murderous, with the same inexhaustible prodigality.

I learned then, with inexpressible force, the same lesson which I learned from your works, to know that we have nothing for our own but ourselves,

---

11. The Chaîne des Puys is a 40 km (25 mi) long, north-south oriented chain of cinder cones, lava domes, and maars in the Massif Central of France.

12. Puzzuolana is a term for what is known in petrology as laterite: a red or brown superficial deposit of clay or earth which gathers on the surface of rocks.

that the "I" alone is real, that nature ignores us, as do men, that from her as from them we have nothing to ask if not some pretexts for feeling or for thinking. My old beliefs, in a God, the father and judge, seemed like the dreams of a sick child, and I expanded to the extreme limits of the vast landscape, to the depths of the immense void heaven, in thinking that as a youth I had already reflected enough to understand of this world what none of the countrymen whom I saw pass could ever comprehend.

They came from the mountains, leading their oxen harnessed to their large carts, and saluted the cross devoutly. With what delight I scorned their gross superstition, theirs and the Abbé Martel's and my mother's, though I had not decided to declare my atheism, foreseeing too plainly what scenes this declaration would provoke! But these scenes are of no more importance, and I come now to the *exposé* of a drama which would have had no meaning if I had not first admitted you into the intimacy of my mind and its formation.

§ III. TRANSPLANTATION

BY TOO CLOSE attention to study during this year, I brought on quite a serious illness, which forced me to interrupt my preparation for the Normal School. When I had recovered I doubled my lessons in philosophy, at the same time following a part of the rhetorical course.

I presented myself at the school about the time in which I had the honor of being received by you. You are acquainted with the events which followed. I failed at the examination. My compositions lacked that literary brilliancy which is acquired only at the Lyceums of Paris.

In November, 1885, I accepted the position of preceptor in the Jussat-Randon family. I wrote to you then that I renounced my independence in order that I might not be any further expense to my mother.

Joined with this reason there was the secret hope that the savings realized in this preceptorate would permit me, my licentiate once passed, to prepare for my fellowship examination in Paris. A residence in that city attracted me, my dear master, by the prospect of living near the Rue Guy de la Brosse.

My visit to your hermitage had made a profound impression. You appeared to me as a kind of modern Spinoza, so completely identical with your books by the nobility of a life entirely consecrated to thought. I created beforehand a romance of felicity at the idea that I should know the hours of your walks, that I should form the habit of meeting you in the old Jardin des Plantes, which undulates under your windows, that you would consent to direct me, that aided and sustained by you, I could also make my place in science; in fine you were for me the living certainty, the master, what Faust is for Wagner in the psychological symphony of Goethe. Besides, the conditions which this preceptorate offered were particularly easy. I was above all to be the companion of a child twelve years of age, the second son of the Marquis de Jussat.

I learned afterward why this family had retired for the whole winter to this chateau, near Lake Aydat, where they usually passed the autumn months only.

M. de Jussat, who is originally from Auvergne, and who has held the office of minister plenipotentiary under the emperor, had just lost a large sum on the Bourse. His property being hypothecated, and his income greatly diminished, he had let his house on the Champs-Elysées furnished at a very high rent.

He had arrived at his Jussat estate a little earlier, expecting to go directly to his villa at Cannes. An advantageous chance to let this villa also offered. The desire to free his property had tempted him, the more as an increasing hypochondria made it easier to face the prospect of an entire year passed in solitude. He had been surprised by the sudden departure of his son Lacien's preceptor, who without doubt did not care to bury himself in the country for so many months, and so he had come to Clermont. He had studied his mathematics there thirty-five years before, under M. Limasset, the old professor who was my father's friend. The idea had come to him to ask his old master to recommend an intelligent young man, capable of taking charge of Lucien's studies for the whole year. M. Limasset naturally thought of me, and I consented, for the reasons which I have given, to be presented to the marquis as a candidate for the place.

In the parlor of one of the hotels on the Place de Jaude, I found a man quite tall, very bald, with clear gray eyes in a very red face, who did not even take the trouble to examine me. He began at once to talk, and he talked all the time, intermingling the details of his health—he was one of the imaginary invalids—with the most lively criticisms on modern education. I can hear him now using pell-mell phrases which revealed in a way the different phases of his character.

"Well, my poor Limasset, when are you coming down to see us? The air is excellent down there. That is what I need. I cannot breathe in Paris. We never breathe enough. I hope, monsieur," and he turned to me, "that you are not an advocate of these new methods of teaching. Science, nothing but science; and my God, gentlemen scholars, what do you make of it?" Then returning to M. Limasset: "In my day, in our day, I may say, everybody had a respect for authority and for duty. Education was not absolutely neglected for instruction. You remember our chaplain, the Abbé Habert, and how he could talk? What health he had! How he could walk in all sorts of weather without an overcoat! But you, Limasset, how old are you? Sixty-five, hey? Sixty-five, and not an ache! Not one? Do you not think I am better since I have lived among the mountains? I am never very ill, but there is always some little thing the matter with me. Indeed, I would rather be really ill. At least I should get well then."

If I repeat these incoherent words, as they come back to my memory, my dear master, it is first, that you may know the value of the intellect of this man who, as my mother has told me, has brought your venerated name into my case; it is also that you understand with what feelings I arrived, four days after, at the chateau when I ran into so terrible dangers.

The marquis had accepted me at the first visit, and insisted upon taking me with him in his landau.[1] During the journey from Clermont to Aydat, he had leisure to tell me about his family. He explained with his invincible garrulity, constantly interrupted by some remarks about his person, that his wife and daughter did not care much for society, and that they were excellent housekeepers; that his oldest son Count André, was home for a fortnight and that I must not be annoyed at his brusqueness, for it covered the best of hearts, that his other son, Lucien, had been ailing and that his restoration to health was the most important thing of all. Then at the word health he started, and, after an hour of confidences regarding his headaches, his digestion, his sleep, his ailments past, present, and future, being fatigued no doubt by the keen air and the flux of words, he fell asleep in a corner of the carriage.

I recall the plans which I formed when, freed from this tormentor, who was already the object of my contempt, I looked at the beautiful country through which we were passing between mountain ravines and woods, now turning yellow in the autumn, with the Puy de la Vache at the horizon, with the hollow of its crater all plowed up, and quite red with volcanic dust.

---

1. A landau is a term for a type of four-wheeled, convertible carriage. The low shell of the landau provides maximal visibility of the occupants and their clothing.

What I had already seen of the marquis, and what he had told me of his family, had convinced me that I was about to be exiled among people whom I called barbarians. I had given this name to those persons whom I judge to be irreparable strangers to the intellectual life.

The prospect of this exile did not alarm me. The doctrine by which I should regulate my existence was so clear to my mind! I was so resolved to live only in myself, to defend myself against all intrusion from without. The chateau to which I was going, and the people who inhabited it would be only subjects for the most profitable study.

My programme was made out: during the twelve or fourteen months that I should live there I would employ my leisure in studying German, and in mastering the contents of the *Physiology of Beaunis*, which was in my small trunk, bound behind the carriage, together with your works, my dear master, my *Ethics*, several volumes of M. Ribot, of M. Taine, of Herbert Spencer, some analytical romances and the books necessary to the preparation for my licentiate. I intended to pass this examination in July.

A new notebook awaited the notes which I proposed to make upon the character of my hosts. I had promised myself to take them to pieces, wheel by wheel, and I had bought for this purpose a book, closed by a lock and key, upon the fly-leaf of which I had written this sentence from *Anatomy of the Will*:

> Spinoza boasts of having studied human sentiments as the mathematician studies his geometric figures; modern psychology must study them as chemical combinations elaborated in a retort, while regretting that this retort may not be as transparent and as manageable as those of the laboratory.

I tell you this childishness to prove the degree of my sincerity, and to show how little I resemble the poor and ambitious young man that so many romances have described.

With my taste for duplication, I remember to have remarked this difference with pleasure. I recalled Julien Sorel of *Le Rouge et le Noir*, arriving at the house of M. de Rênal, the temptations of Rubempré, in Balzac, in front of the house of the Bargetons, some pages also of *Vingtras de Vallés*. I analyzed the sensations which were concealed behind the lusts and the revolts of these different heroes. There is always a surprise in passing from one society to another, but there was not a trace of envy or maliciousness in me. I looked at the marquis as he slept, wrapped, on this cool November afternoon, in a furred coat whose turned-up collar half-concealed his face. A robe of dark soft wool covered his legs. Dark embroidered skin gloves protected his hands. His hat of felt as fine as silk was pulled down over his eyes. I only felt that these details represented a kind of existence very different from ours with the poor and petty economy of our home which only my mother's scrupulous neatness saved from meanness.

I rejoiced that I did not feel any envy, not the least atom, at the sight of these signs of prosperous fortune, neither envy nor embarrassment. I had myself completely under control, and was steeled against all vulgar prejudice by my doctrine, your doctrine, and by the sovereign superiority of my ideas. I will have traced a perfect portrait of my mind at this time if I add that I had resolved to erase love from the programme of my life. I had had, since my adventure with Marianne, another little experience, with the wife of a professor at the Lyceum, so absolutely silly and withal so ridiculously pretentious that I came out of it strengthened in my contempt for the "Dame," speaking after Schopenhauer, and also in my disgust for sensuality.

I attribute to the profound influences of Catholic discipline this repulsion from the flesh which has survived the dogmas of spirituality. I know very well, from an experience too often repeated, that this repulsion was insufficient to hinder profound relapses, but I depended upon the silence of the chateau to free me from all temptation and to practice in its full rigor the great maxim of the ancient sage: "Force all your sex to mount to the brain." Ah! This idolatry of the brain, of my thinking Self, it has been so strong in me that I have thought seriously of studying the monastic rules that I might apply them to the culture of my mind. Yes, I have contemplated making my meditations every day, like the monks, upon the articles of my philosophic credo, of celebrating every day, like the monks, the *fête*[2] of one of my saints,

---

2. *Fête* is a Old French term for elaborate festival, party or celebration.

of Spinoza, of Hobbes, of Stendhal, of Stuart Mill, of you, my dear master, in evoking the image and the doctrines of the initiative thus chosen, and impregnating myself with his example.

I know that all this was very youthful and very naive, but, you see, I was not such a man as this family stigmatizes today, the intriguing plebeian who was dreaming of a fine marriage, and the idea connecting my life with that of Mlle. de Jussat was implanted, inspired, so to speak, by circumstances.

I do not write to you to paint myself in a romantic light, and I do not know why I should conceal from you that, among the circumstances which urged me toward this enterprise so far from my thought on my arrival, the first was the impression produced on me by Count André the brother of the poor dead girl, whose remembrance, now that I am approaching the drama, becomes almost a torture; but let us go back to this arrival.

It is almost five o'clock. The landau moves rapidly along. The marquis is awake. He points out the frozen bosom of the little lake, all rosy under a setting sun, which empurples the dried foliage of the beeches and oaks; and, beyond the chateau, a large building of modern construction, white, with its slender towers and its pepperbox roof,[3] grows nearer at every turn of the gray road.

The steeple of a village, rather of a hamlet, raises its slates above some houses with thatched roofs. It is passed. We are now in the avenue of trees which leads to the chateau, then before the *perron*[4] and immediately in the vestibule.

We entered the salon. How peaceful it was, lighted by lamps with large shades, with the fire burning gayly in the chimney. The Marquise de Jussat with her daughter was working at some knitting for the poor; my future pupil was looking over a book of engravings, as he stood against the open piano; Mlle. Charlotte's governess and a *religieuse*[5] were seated, farther off, sewing. Count André was reading a paper, which he put down at the moment of our

---

3. A pepperbox roof is a pyramidal slate roof.

4. *Perron* is an Old French term for a platform outside the raised entrance to a church or large building, or the steps leading to such a platform.

5. *Religieuse* is a French term for a woman belonging to a religious order.

arrival.

Yes, this was a peaceful place, and who could have told that my entrance would be the end of all peace for these persons who in an instant were impressed on my memory with the distinctness of portraits?

I noticed first the face of the marquise, a tall and strong woman with features slightly gross, so different from what my imagination had conceived of a great lady. She was truly the model housekeeper whom the marquis had described, but a housekeeper with a finished education, and who put me at once at my ease simply by speaking of the beautiful day that we had had for our journey.

I perceived the inexpressive face of Mlle. Eliza Largeyx, the governess, with its ever-approving smile; she was the innocent type of happy servility, of a life all complaisance and of material happiness.

There was sister Anaclet with her peasant's eyes and her thin mouth. She lived permanently at the chateau that she might serve as nurse for the marquis who was always apprehensive of a possible attack.

There was little Lucien with the fat cheeks of the idle child. There, too, was the young girl, who is no more, with her beautiful form in its light dress, her gentle gray eyes, her chestnut hair, and the delicate outline of her oval face. I can still see the gesture with which she offered her hand to her father and a cup of tea to me. I hear her voice saying to the marquis:

"Father, did you see how rosy the little lake was this evening?"

And the voice of M. de Jussat responding between two swallows of his grog:

"I saw that there was some fog in the meadows and some rheumatism in the air."

And the voice of Count André:

"Yes, but what fine shooting tomorrow!" Then turning to me: "Do you shoot, Monsieur Greslou?"

"No, monsieur," I answered.

"Do you ride?" he asked again.

"I do not."

"I pity you," said he, laughing; "after war, these are the two greatest pleasures that I know of."

This is nothing, this bit of dialogue, and, thus transcribed, it will not explain why these simple phrases were the cause of my regarding André de Jussat as a being apart from any I had known until then; why, when I had gone to my room, where a servant commenced to unpack my trunk, I thought more of him than of his fragile and graceful sister; nor why, at dinner and all the evening, I had eyes only for him.

My naive astonishment in the presence of this proud and manly fellow was derived, however, from a very simple fact; I had grown up in a purely intellectual medium in which the only estimable forms of life were the intellectual. I had had for comrades the first of my class, all as delicate and frail as I was myself, without condescending ever to notice those who excelled in the exercises of the body, and who beside only found in these exercises an excuse for brutality.

All my masters whom I liked best, and the few old friends of my father, were also able men. When I had pictured the heroes of romance, they were always mental machines more or less complicated; but I had never imagined their physical condition.

If I had ever thought of the superiority which the beautiful and firm animal energy of man represents, it was in an abstract manner, but I had never felt it. Count André, who was thirty years old, presented an admirable example of this superiority. Figure to yourself a man of medium size, but lusty as an athlete, with broad shoulders and a slender waist, gestures which betrayed strength and suppleness—gestures in which one felt that the movement was distributed with that perfection which gives adroit and precise agility—hands and feet nervous, showing race, with a martial countenance, one of those bistre[6] complexions behind which the blood flows, rich in iron and in globules; a square forehead under bushy black hair, a mustache of the same color over a firm and tightly closed mouth, brown eyes, very near to a nose which was slightly arched, which gives to the profile a vague suggestion of a bird of prey. Last a bold chin, squarely cut, completed the physiognomy

---

6. Bistre is a pigment made from the soot of burnt Beechwood, boiled and diluted with water. Bistre's appearance is generally of a dark grayish brown, with a yellowish cast. Many Old Masters used bistre as the ink for their drawings.

of a character of invincible will. And the will is the whole person; action made man.

It seemed as if there were in this officer, broken to all bodily exercises, ready for all exploits, no rupture of equilibrium between thought and action, and that his whole being passed entire into his smallest gestures.

I have seen him mount a horse so as to realize the ancient fable of the Centaur, put ten balls in succession at thirty paces into a playing card, leap ditches with the lightness of a professional gymnast, and sometimes, to amuse his young brother, leap over a table, only touching it with his hands.

I knew that, during the war and though only sixteen years old, he had enlisted and made the campaign of the Loire, bearing all fatigues and inspiring even the veterans with courage. As I saw him at dinner this first evening, eating steadily, with that fine humor of appetite which reveals the full life; speaking little, but with a commanding voice, I felt in a surprising degree the impression that I was in the presence of a creature different from myself, but finished and complete of his kind.

It seems to me as though this scene dates from yesterday, and that I am there, while the marquis plays bezique with his daughter, talking with the marquise, and stealthily watching Count André play at billiards alone. I saw him through the open door, supple and robust in his evening dress of some light material, a cigar in the corner of his mouth, pushing the balls about with a precision so perfect that it was beautiful; and I, your pupil, I, so proud of the amplitude of my mind, followed with open mouth the slightest gestures of this young man who was absorbed in a sport so vulgar, with the kind of envious admiration which a learned monk of the middle ages, unskillful in all muscular games, must have felt in presence of a knight in armor.

When I use the word envy I beg you to understand me, and not to attribute to me a baseness which was never mine. Neither this evening nor during the days which followed was I ever jealous of the name of Count André, nor of his fortune, nor of any of the social advantages which he possessed, and of which I was so deprived. Neither have I felt that strange hate of the male for the male, very finely noted by you in your pages on love.

My mother had had the weakness to tell me often in my childhood that I was a pretty boy. Without being a coxcomb, I may say that there was nothing displeasing in me, neither in my face nor in my figure. I say this to you, not from vanity, but to prove that there was not an atom of vanity in the sort of sudden rivalry which made me an adversary, almost an enemy, of Count André from this first evening. There was as much admiration as envy in this antipathy. Upon reflection, I find in the sentiment which I have tried to define the probable trace of an unconscious atavism.[7]

I questioned the marquis later, whose aristocratic pride I thus flattered, upon the genealogy of the Jussat-Randons, and I believe that they are of a pure and conquering race, while in the veins of the descendant of the Lorraine farmers who writes these lines to you flows the blood of ancestors who had been slaves of the soil for centuries. Certainly, between my brain and that of Count André there is the same difference as there is between mine and yours, greater, since I can comprehend you and I defy him to follow my reasonings, even that which I am pursuing now, upon our relations.

To speak frankly, I am a civilized being, he is only a barbarian. But I felt immediately the sensation that my refinement was less aristocratic than his barbarism. I felt there, at once, and in the depths of this instinct of life, into which the mind descends with much difficulty, the revelation of this precedence of race which modern science affirms of all nature and which, by consequence, must be true also of man.

Why even use this word envy, which serves as the label of irrational hostilities like those with which the count immediately inspired me? Why should not this hostility be inherited like the rest? Any human acquisition whatever, that for example of character and of active energy, implies that, during centuries and centuries, files of individuals of which one is the supreme addition, have acted and willed. During this long succession of years, an antipathy, sometimes clear and sometimes obscure, has rendered the individuals of the first group odious to individuals of the second; and when two representatives of this sovereign labor of ages meet, each typical in kind as were the count and myself, why not stand up the one in face of the

---

7. Atavism, in biology, refers to a modification of a biological structure whereby an ancestral genetic trait reappears after having been lost through evolutionary change in previous generations; whereas, in social sciences, atavism refers to the tendency of reversion.

other, like two beasts of different species?

The horse that has never been near a lion trembles with fright when his bed is made of the straw upon which one of these creatures has slept. Then fear is inherited, and is not fear one form of hate?

Why is not all hate inherited? And in hundreds of cases envy would be, as it surely was in mine, only the echo of hates formerly felt by those whose sons we are, and who continue to pursue, through us, the combats of heart begun centuries ago.

There is a current proverb that antipathies are mutual, and if it is admitted my hypothesis upon the secular origin of antipathies becomes very simple. It happens, however, that this antipathy does not manifest itself in the two beings at once. This is the case when one of the two does not deign to notice the other, and also when the other dissimulates.

I do not believe that Count André experienced at first the aversion that he would have felt if he had read to the bottom of my soul. In the beginning he paid very little attention to a young man of Clermont who had come to the chateau to be tutor; then I had decided on a constant dissimulation of my real Self, imprisoned among strangers. I felt no more repugnance for this defensive hypocrisy than the gardener would have had in putting straw around the currant bushes to preserve their fruit against snows and frosts. The falseness of attitude corresponded too well with my intellectual pride to prevent me from giving myself up to it with delight.

On the other hand Count André had no motive for concealing his character from me, and on this same evening, at the hour of retiring, he asked me to come into his study to talk a little. He had hardly looked at me, and I understood plainly that his intention was not to put any more familiarity between us, but to give me his opinions on my role as preceptor.

He occupied a suite of three rooms in a wing of the château, a bedroom, a dressing-room and the smoking-room in which we now found ourselves. A large upholstered divan[8], several armchairs and a massive desk, constituted

---

8. Divan is a Turkish term for a piece of couch-like sitting furniture; primarily, in the Middle East (especially the Ottoman Empire), a divan was a long seat formed of a mattress laid against the side of the room, upon the floor or upon a raised structure or frame, with cushions to lean against.

the furniture of this room.

On the walls glittered arms of all kinds, guns of Tangiers, sabres and muskets of the first empire, and a Prussian helmet, which the count pointed out to me almost as soon as we had entered. He had lighted a short brier-wood pipe, prepared two glasses of brandy mixed with seltzer water, and lamp in hand, he showed me the helmet saying:

"I am very sure that I knocked that fellow over. You do not know anything about the sensation of holding an enemy at the point of your gun, of taking aim, of seeing him fall, and thinking: Another one gone? It happened in a village not far from Orleans. I was on guard at daybreak, in a corner of the cemetery. I saw a head above the wall, it looked over, then the shoulders followed. It was this inquisitive fellow who wanted to see what we were doing. He did not go back to tell."

He put down the lamp, and, after laughing a little at this remembrance, he became serious. I had felt obliged, for the sake of politeness, to moisten my lips in the mixture of gaseous water and alcohol, and the count continued:

"I wished to talk with you about Lucien, monsieur, to explain his character and in what way he is to be directed. His old tutor was an excellent man, but very weak, very indolent. I have encouraged your coming because you are a young man, and a young man is more suitable for Lucien. Teaching, monsieur, is worse than nothing, sometimes, when it falsifies ideas. The great thing in this life, I ought almost say the only thing, is character."

He made a pause as if to ask my opinion, I answered with some banal phrase which supported his view.

"Very well," he continued, "we understand one another. At present, for a man of our name, there is in France only one profession, that of a soldier. So long as our country is in the hands of the *canaille*[9] and so long as we have the Germans to fight, our duty is in the only place that remains to us—the army. Thank God my father and my mother share these opinions. Lucien will be a soldier, and a soldier has no need of knowing all that the people

9. *Canaille* is a French derogatory term for the common people, the lowest class of people, the rabble, the vulgar.

prate about today. Having honor, sangfroid,[10] muscles and loving France, everything is right. I had all the trouble in the world to take my degree. This year must be for Lucien, above everything else, a year of outdoor life; and, for studies, these must be conversations only. It is to your talks with him that I wish to call your attention. You must insist on the practical, on the positive, and on principles. He has some faults which must be corrected. You will find him very good, but very soft; he must learn to endure.

"Insist, for example, upon his going out in all sorts of weather, that he walk two or three hours every day. He is very inexact, and I insist that he shall become as punctual as a chronometer. He also is untruthful. I think this the most horrible of vices. I can pardon everything, yes, many, many follies. I never forgive a falsehood. We have had, from my father's old master, such good recommendation of you, of your life with your mother, of your dignity, of your strictness, that we depend very much on your influence. Your age permits you to be as much a companion as a preceptor for Lucien. Example, you see, is the best kind of teaching. Tell a conscript that it is a noble and fine thing to march up to the fire, and he will listen to you without understanding you. March in front of him, swaggering, and he becomes more of a blusterer than you are.

"As for me, I rejoin my regiment in a few days. but absent or present, you can depend on my support; if it should ever be a question what to do, that this child become what he ought to become, a man who can serve his country bravely, and, if God permit, his king."

This discourse, which I believe I have faithfully reproduced, did not at all astonish me. It was quite natural in a house in which the father was an old monomaniac, the mother a simple housekeeper, the sister young and timid, that the oldest brother should hold a directing place, and talk with the new preceptor. It was also quite natural that a soldier and a gentleman educated in the ideas of his class and of his profession should speak as a soldier and a gentleman.

You, my dear master, with your universal comprehension of natures,

---

10. Sangfroid is a French term (literally, cold blood) for composure or coolness, sometimes excessive, as shown in danger or under trying circumstances.

with your facility in disentangling the line which unites the temperament and the medium of ideas, you would have seen in Count André a very definite and significant case. And for what had I prepared my locked notebook if not to collect documents of this kind upon human nature? And was there not here everything new in the person of this officer, so single and so simple, who manifested a mode of thought evidently identical with his mode of being, breathing, moving, smoking and eating?

Ah! I see too well that my philosophy was not as blood in my veins, as marrow in my bones, for this discourse and the convictions it expressed, instead of pleasing me by this rare encounter of logic, only enlarged the wound of antipathy which bad been already opened, I knew not where, in my self-love perhaps, for I was weak and frail in the presence of the strong—surely in my inmost sensibility.

None of the count's ideas had the least value in my eyes. They were for me pure foolishness, and instead of despising this foolishness, as I should have despised it in any other case, I began to hate it in his mouth.

A soldier's profession? I considered it so wretched, because of its brutal associations and the time lost, that I was glad that I was the son of a widow that I might escape the barbarity of the barracks and the miseries of its discipline.

The hatred of Germany? I had tried to destroy it in myself, as the worst of prejudices, from disgust of the imbecile comrades whom I saw exalt it into an ignorant patriotism, and also from admiration for the people to whom psychology owes Kant and Schopenhauer, Lotze and Fechner, Helmholz and Wundt.

Political faith? I professed an equal disdain for the gross hypotheses which, under the name of legitimism,[11] republicanism, Caesarism, pretended to govern a country *a priori*. I dreamed with the author of *Dialogues Philosophiques,* of an oligarchy of savants, a despotism of psychologists and economists, of physiologists and historians.

Practical life? This was a diminished life form, who saw in the external

---

11. Legitimism is a political term referring to support for a ruler whose claim to a throne is based on direct descent.

world only a field of experiences in which an enfranchised soul ventures with prudence, just far enough to collect emotions. Finally this contempt for falsehood which the count professed struck me as an affront, at the same time that his absolute confidence in my morality, based upon a false impression of me, embarrassed me, chilled me, hurt me.

Certainly the contradiction was piquant; I considered the portrait which my father's old friend had drawn; it pleased me in a certain way that they should believe it like me, and I felt irritated that he, Count André, did not distrust me. But what does that prove, if not that we never thoroughly know ourselves? You have magnificently said, my dear master:

> Our states of consciousness are like islands upon an ocean of darkness whose foundations are forever being removed. It is the work of the psychologist to divine by soundings the ground which makes of these isles the visible summits of a mountain chain, invisible and immovable under the moving mass of waters.

I have not described this first evening at the château because it had any immediate consequences, for I retired after assuring Count André that I was entirely of his opinion in regard to his young brother, and, having reached my room, I confined myself to consigning these words to my notebook, with comments more or less disdainful; but these first impressions will help you to understand some analogous impressions which followed, and the unexpected crisis which resulted from them.

It is one of those submarine chains of which you speak, and which I find today when I throw the sound to the very bottom of my heart. Under the influence of your books, and of your example, I became more and more intellectualized, and I believed that I had definitely renounced the morbid curiosity of the passions which had made me find exquisite pleasure in my guilty readings. Thus we retain portions of the soul which were very much alive, and which we believe to be dead, but which are only drowsing.

And so little by little, after an acquaintance of only fifteen days with this man, my elder by nine or ten years, and who was, all reality, all energy, this purely speculative existence of which I had so sincerely dreamed, began to see—how shall I express it? Inferior? Oh, no, for I would not have consented, at the price of an empire, to become Count André, even with his name, his fortune, his physical superiority, and his ideas. Discolored? Not even that. The word incomplete appears to me the only one which expresses the singular disfavor which the sudden comparison between the count and myself diffused over my own convictions.

It is in this feeling of incompleteness that the principal temptation of which I was the victim resides. There is nothing very original, I believe, in the state of mind of a man who, having cultivated to excess the faculty of thought, meets another man having cultivated to the same degree the faculty of action and who feels himself tormented with nostalgia in presence of this action, however despised.

Goethe has drawn the whole of his Faust from this nostalgia. I was not a Faust. I had not, like the old doctor, drained the cup of Science; and yet, I must believe that my studies of these last years, by over-exciting me in one direction, had left in me unemployed powers, which trembled with emulation at the approach of this representative of another race of men.

While admiring him, envying and despising him at the same time, during the days which followed, I could not prevent my mind from thinking. And I thought: "That man who would value him for his activity and me for my thought, would truly be the superior man that I have desired to become."

But do not action and thought exclude one another? They were not incompatible at the Renaissance and later, Goethe has incarnated in himself the double destiny of Faust, by turns philosopher and courtier, poet and minister; Stendahl was romancer and lieutenant of dragoons; Constant was the author of *Adolphe* and a fiery orator, as well as duelist, actor and libertine.

This finished culture of the "I," which I had made the final result, the supreme end of my doctrines, was it without this double play of the faculties, this parallelism of the life lived and the life thought?

Probably my first regret at feeling myself thus dispossessed of a whole world, that of fact, was only pride. But with me, and by the essentially philosophic nature of my being, sensations are immediately transformed into ideas.

The smallest accidents appear in my mind to state general problems.

Every event of my destiny leads me to some theory on the destiny of all. Here, where another man would have said: "It is a pity that fate should have permitted a single kind of development," I took it on myself to ask if I were not deceived in the law of all development.

Since I had, thanks to your admirable books, freed my soul and cast to earth my vain religious terrors, I had retained only one of my old, pious practices, the habit of daily examining my conscience, under the form of a journal, and from time to time I made what I called an orison.[12] I transported, with a singular enjoyment, the terms of religion into the realm of my personal sensibility. I called that again the liturgy of the "I."

One evening of the second week of my stay at the château, I employed several hours in writing out a general confession, that is to say, in drawing a picture of my diverse instincts since the first awakening of my consciousness. I arrived at this conclusion, that the essential trait of my nature, the characteristic of my inmost being, had always been the faculty of duplication. That means that I had always felt a tendency to be at once passionate and reflective, to live and to see myself live. But by imprisoning myself, as I wished, in pure reflection, by neglecting to live and to have only one eye open upon life, did I not risk resembling that Amiel[13] whose dolorous journal appeared at that time, and sterilizing myself by the abuse of analysis to emptiness?

In vain did your image return to me to reinforce me in my resolution to live an abstract existence. I recall the phrases on love in *Theory of the Passion*, and I saw you, at my age, abandoning yourself to the culpable experiences which already obscurely tempted me. I do not know if this chemistry of soul, so very complex and very sincere, will seem sufficiently lucid. The work by which an emotion is elaborated in us, and ends by resolving itself into an idea, remains so obscure that the idea is, sometimes, exactly contrary to that which simple reason could have foreseen!

Would it not have been natural, for example, that the kind of admiring

---

12. Orison is an archaic term for a prayer.

13. Henri Frédéric Amiel (1821–1881) was a Swiss moral philosopher, poet, and critic. The one book by which Amiel is still known, the *Journal Intime* ("Private Journal") was published a year after his death.

antipathy roused in me by my encounter with Count André should have ended either in a declared repulsion, or in a definite admiration? In the first case, I should have thrown myself more into science, and in the other, have desired a more active morality, a more practical virility in my actions. But the natural for each one, is his own nature. Mine willed that the admiring antipathy for the count should become a principle of criticism, in regard to myself, that this criticism should produce a new theory of life, that this theory should reveal my native disposition for passional curiosity, that the whole should dissolve itself into a nostalgia of sentimental experiences and that, just at this moment, a young girl should enter into my life whose presence alone would have sufficed to provoke the desire to please in any young man of my age.

But I was too intellectual for this desire to be born in my heart without passing through my head. At least, if I felt the charm of grace and delicacy which emanated from this child of twenty years, I felt it while believing that I reasoned about it. There are times when I ask myself if it was so, times when all my history appears more simple, and I say:

"I was honestly in love with Charlotte, because she was pretty, refined and tender, and I was young; then I gave some pretexts of the brain because I was a man proud of ideas and did not wish to love like other men."

Ah! What a comfort when I persuade myself to speak in this way! I can pity myself instead of being a horror to myself, as happens when I recall the cold resolution, which I cherished in my mind, consigned to my notebook, and verified alas! By the event, the resolution, to injure this girl without loving her, from motives of purely psychological curiosity, from the pleasure of acting, of governing a living soul, of contemplating at will and directly this mechanism of passion which I had until then only studied in books, from the vanity of enriching my mind by a new experience.

But it is well, I could not have wished otherwise, impelled as I was by my heredities and my education, removed into the new medium where I was thrown by chance, and bitten, as I was by this ferocious spirit of rivalry against the insolent young man who was my opposite?

But this pure and tender girl was worthy of meeting a man who was not a cold and murderous calculating machine. Only to think of her melts and rends my heart.

I did not notice at first sight that perfection of the lines of the face, that brilliance of complexion, that royalty of bearing which distinguishes the very beautiful woman. Everything in her physiognomy was a delicate demitint,[14] from the shade of her chestnut hair to the misty gray of her eyes and to her complexion which was neither pale nor rosy. One thought of modesty when studying her expression, and of fragility when remarking her feet, and hands, and the almost too minute grace of her movements.

Although she was rather short, she appeared tall because of the noble way in which her head was set on her slender neck. If Count André reproduced one of their common ancestors by an evident atavism, she resembled her father, but with so charming an ideality of lines that one could not admit the resemblance unless they were side by side. It was easy, however, to recognize in her the nervous disposition which produced hypochondria in her father.

Charlotte had a sensibility which was almost morbid, which was revealed at times by a slight tremulousness of hands and lips, those beautiful sinuous lips where dwelt a goodness almost divine. Her firm chin showed a rare strength of will in so frail an envelope, and I now understand that the depth of her eyes, sometimes motionless as if fixed on some object visible to herself alone, betrayed a fatal tendency to a fixed idea.

The first trait that I specially observed was her extreme kindness, and this was brought to my notice by little Lucien. The child told me that his sister had several times wished him to ask me if there was anything lacking in my room.

This is a very puerile detail, but it touched me because I felt very lonely in this great house where no person, since my arrival, had seemed to pay the least attention to me. The marquis appeared only at dinner, wrapped in a *robe-de-chambre* and groaning over his health or politics. The marquise was occupied in making the château comfortable, and held long conferences with an upholsterer from Clermont. Count André rode in the morning, hunted in

---

14. Demitint is an aesthetic term for the shade itself, neither the darkest nor the lightest tone in a composition.

the afternoon, and, in the evening, smoked his cigars without ever addressing a word to me. The governess and the *religieuse* looked at one another and looked at me with a discretion which froze me.

My pupil was an idle and dull boy, who had the redeeming quality of being very simple, very confiding, and of telling me all that I wished to know of himself and the rest of his family. I learned in this way that their stay in the country this year was the work of Count André, which did not astonish me in the least, for I felt more and more that he was the real head of the family; I learned that the year preceding he had wished to marry his sister to one of his comrades, a M. de Plane, whom Charlotte had refused, and who had gone to Tonquin.

In our two daily classes, one in the morning from eight o'clock to half-past nine, the other in the afternoon from three o'clock until half-past four, I had a great deal of trouble to fix the attention of the little idler. Seated on his chair, opposite me on the other side of the table, and rolling his tongue against his cheek, while he covered the paper with his big awkward writing, he would now and then glance up at me.

He noticed on my face the least sign of abstraction. With the animal and sure instinct of children, he soon saw that I would make him go on with his lessons less quickly when he talked to me of his brother or sister, and so this innocent mouth revealed to me that there was, in this cold, strange house, some one who thought of me and of my comfort.

My mother had failed so much in this regard, although I might not wish to confess it! And it was this act of simple politeness which made me regard Mlle. de Jussat with more attention.

The second trait that I discovered in her was a taste for the romantic, not that she had read many romances, but as I have already told you, her sensibility was extreme, and this had given her an apprehension of the real.

Without herself suspecting it she was very different from her father, her mother and her brothers; and she could neither show herself to them in the truth of her nature, nor see them in the truth of theirs without suffering. So she did show herself, and she forced herself not to see them. She formed, spontaneously and ingenuously, opinions of those she loved which were in harmony with her own heart and so directly contrary to the evidence that they would have seemed false or flattering in the eyes of a malevolent observer. She would say to her mother, who was so ordinary and material: "Mamma, you are so quick to see;" to her father so cruelly egotistical: "You are so kind, papa," and to her brother who was so positive, so self-sufficient: "You understand everything," and she believed it. But the delusion in which this gentle creature imprisoned herself, left her a prey to the most complete moral solitude, and deprived her, to a very dangerous degree, of all judgment of character.

She was as ignorant of herself as of others. She languished, unknown to herself, for the society of some one who should have sentiments in harmony with her own. For example, I observed in the first walks that we took together, that she was the only one who could really feel the beauty of the landscape formed by the lake, the woods that surround it, the distant volcanoes and the autumn sky, often more blue than the sky of summer because of the contrast of its azure with the gold of the leaves, and which was sometimes so veiled, so sadly vaporous and distant.

She would fall into silence without any apparent reason, but really because her whole being became dissolved into the charm of things about her. She possessed in the state of pure instinct and unconscious sensation the faculty which makes the great poets and the great lovers, namely, the faculty of forgetting oneself, of dispelling oneself, of losing oneself entirely in whatever touches the heart, whether it be a veiled horizon, a silent and yellow-tinted forest, a piece of music or a touching story.

I did not, at the beginning of our acquaintance, formulate the contrast between that combative animal her brother and this creature of sweetness and grace who ran up the stone staircases of the chateau with a step so light that it seemed scarcely poised, and whose smile was so welcoming and so timid.

I will dare to tell all, since I repeat it, I am not writing in order to paint myself in beautiful colors, but to show myself as I am. I will not say that the desire to make myself beloved by this adorable child, in whose atmosphere I began to feel so much pleasure, was not caused by this contrast between her and her brother.

Perhaps the soul of this young girl became as a field of battle for the secret, the obscure antipathy which two weeks had transformed into hate? Perhaps there was concealed the cruel pleasure of humiliating the soldier, the gentleman, by outraging him in what he held most precious? I know that this is horrible, but I should not be worthy of being your pupil if I did not disclose the lowest depth of my heart. And, after all, this odious cloud of sensations may be only a necessary phenomenon, like the others, like the romantic grace of Charlotte, like the simple energy of her brother, and like my own complexities—so obscure even to myself.

§ IV. THE FIRST CRISIS

I REMEMBER VERY distinctly the day on which the project of winning the love of the sister of Count André presented itself to me, no longer as a romantically visionary idea, but as a precise possibility, near, almost immediate.

After I had been at the chateau two months I went to Clermont to pass the New Year holidays with my mother, and I had been back a week. The snow had been falling for forty-eight hours. The winters in our mountains are so severe that nothing but the marquise's monomania can explain his obstinacy in remaining in this savage lone waste, which is indefinitely swept by sudden and violent gusts of wind.

It is proper to state that the marquise watched over the comfort of the household with a marvelous adjustment of daily resources, and although Aydat is considered isolated by the inhabitants of Saint-Saturnin and Saint-Amand-Tallende, the communication with Clermont remains open even in the worst rigor of the season. Then the season offers sudden and radiant changes, mornings of storm are suddenly succeeded by evenings of incomparable azure in which the country beams as if transformed by the enchantment of light.

This was the case on the day my fatal resolution became fixed and took form. I can see the lake now, covered with a thin sheet of ice, under which the supple shivering of the water could be discerned. I see the vast slope of the Cheyre, white with snow, its whiteness broken by dark spots of lava; and perfectly white, without a spot, rises the circle of mountains, the Puy de Dôme, the Puy de la Vache, that of Vichatel, that of Rodde, that of Mont Redon, while the forest of Rouillet stands out against the background of snow and azure.

Some minute details rise again before my eyes which were then scarcely noticed and have remained concealed, one knows not in what hiding-place of the memory. I see a cluster of birches whose despoiled branches are tinted with rose. I see the crystals which sparkle at the end of a tuft of broom, which, thin and still green, marks the tracks of a fox on the immaculate carpet, and the flight of a magpie which cries out in the middle of the road, and this sharp cry renders the silence of this immense horizon almost perceptible. I see some yellow and brown sheep which are driven by a shepherd clothed in a blue blouse, wearing a large, low, round hat, and accompanied by a red and shaggy dog with shining yellow eyes, very near together.

Yes, I can see all this landscape, and the four persons who are walking on the road which leads toward Fontfrède: Mlle. Largeyx, Mlle. de Jussat, my pupil and myself. Charlotte wore an Astrakhan[1] jacket; a fur boa was wrapped around her neck, making her head appear still more petite and graceful under its Astrakhan toque. After the long imprisonment in the château the keen air seemed to intoxicate her. Her cheeks were red, her small feet plunged bravely into the snow, where they left their slight trace, and her eyes sparkled with delight at the beauty of nature—a privilege of simple hearts which is never felt when the soul has become desiccated by force of reasoning, abstract theories and certain kinds of reading.

I walked beside her and so rapidly that we were soon far ahead of Mlle. Largeyx, whose clogs slipped on the road. The child, sometimes in front, sometimes behind, stopped or ran on with the vivacity of a young animal. In the company of these two gay creatures I grew gloomy and taciturn. Was this the nervous irritation which makes us at certain times antipathetic to the joy which we see around us without sharing it? Was it the half-unconscious outline of my future plan, and did I wish to force the young girl to notice me by a kind of hostility against her pleasure?

During the whole of this walk, I, who had formed the habit of talking a great deal with her, scarcely responded by monosyllables to the admiring remarks which she addressed to me, as if she wished me to share in the pleasure of her emotions.

By brusque replies, and by silence, my bad humor became so evident that Mlle. de Jussat, in spite of her enthusiasm, could not fail to notice it. She glanced at me two or three times, with a question on her lips which she did

---

1. Astrakhan is a Russian term for newborn karakul lamb pelts, and the hats and coats made from these pelts.

not dare to formulate, then her face became sad. Her gaiety fell little by little at contact with my sulkiness, and I could trace upon her transparent face the passage, by which she ceased to be sensible to the beauty of things and was conscious only of my sadness.

The moment came when she could no longer control the impression which this sadness made upon her, and, in a voice which timidity rendered a little stifled, she asked:

"Are you suffering, Monsieur Greslou?"

"No, mademoiselle," I replied with a brusquerie which must have wounded her, for her voice trembled as she said:

"Then some one has done something to you? You are not as you usually are."

"No one has done anything to me," I answered, shaking my head; "but it is true," I added, "that I have reasons for being sad, very sad, today. It is the anniversary of a great grief, which I cannot tell you."

She looked at me again, and I could follow in her eyes the movements which agitated her, as one follows the movements of a watch through a glass case. I had seen her so uneasy at my attitude that she lost her feeling for the divine landscape. I saw her now, comforted that I had no cause for grief against her, but touched by my melancholy, curious to know the cause, and not daring to ask me. She only said:

"Pardon me for questioning you." Then she was silent.

These few minutes sufficed to show me the place which I already occupied in her thoughts. Ah! Before the proof of this delicate and noble interest, I should have been ashamed of my falsehood, for so it was, this *soi-disant*[2] recollection of a great grief—a gratuitous and instantaneous falsehood whose sudden invention has often astonished myself.

Why had I suddenly thought to clothe myself in the poetry of a great grief, I whose life, since the death of my father, had been so quiet, so free from any sacrifices? Had I yielded to the innate taste for duplicating myself always so strong? This romantic affectation, did it show the hysteria of vanity which urges some children to lie, without reason and with so much unex-

---

2. *Soi-disant* is a French term (from *soi* 'oneself' + *disant* 'saying') meaning self-styled.

pectedness? Did a vague intuition cause me to see in this play of deception and melancholy the surest means of interesting the Count's sister?

I cannot tell the precise motives which governed me at that moment. Assuredly I did not foresee either the effect of my assumed sadness or of my falsehood, but I remember that as soon as the effect was known a resolution was formed in my mind to go on to the end and see what impression I could produce on the soul of this young girl, by continuing, with consciousness and calculation, the comedy half-instinctively begun in this luminous afternoon of January in presence of a magnificent landscape, which should have served as a frame for other dreams.

Now that the irreparable is accomplished, and by a retrospective penetration, horribly painful—for it convicts me of ignorance and of cruelty—I understand that I had already inspired Charlotte with the truest and the tenderest feelings. All the diplomatic psychology which I employed was only the odious and ridiculous work of a scholar in the science of the heart. I understand that I did not know how to inhale the flowers which bloomed naturally for me in this soul. I had only to let myself know and enjoy the emotions which presented themselves, to live a sentimental life as exalted and extended as that of my intellect.

Instead, I paralyzed my heart by ideas. I wished to conquer a soul already conquered, to play a game of chess, where I needed only to be simple, and I have not even the proud consolation of saying to myself that I have, at least, directed the drama of my destiny as I pleased, that I have combined the scenes, provoked the episodes, conducted the intrigue.

It was played entirely in her, and without my comprehending it in the least, this drama in which Death and Love, the two faithful workers of implacable nature, acted without my order while mocking at the complication of my analysis.

Charlotte loved me for reasons quite different from those which my ingenious psychology had arranged. She died in despair, when by the light of a tragic explanation she saw me in my true nature. Then I was so horrible to her that she thus gave me irrefutable proof that my subtle reflections were nothing to her.

I believed I could solve in this amour a problem of mental mechanism. Alas! I had simply met, without feeling its charm, a sincere and profound tenderness. Why did I not then divine what I see today with the clearness of the most cruel evidence?

Misled by the romantic side of her character, it was natural that this child should be deceived in me. My long studies had given me the appearance of not being quite well, which always interests a woman who is truly feminine. Having been brought up by my mother, my manners were gentle, my voice and gestures refined, and I was scrupulously careful of my person.

I had been introduced by the old master who recommended me, as a person of irreproachable nobility of ideas and character. This was enough to cause a very sensitive young girl to become interested in me in a very particular manner. Ah, well! I had no sooner recognized this interest than I thought how to abuse it instead of being touched by it.

Any one who had seen me in my room on the evening which followed this afternoon, seated at my table and writing, with a big book of analysis near me, would never have believed that this was a young man of scarcely twenty-two years, meditating on the sentiments which he inspired or wished to inspire in a young girl of twenty.

The château was asleep. I could hear only the steps of the footman as he extinguished the lamps on the staircase and in the corridors. The wind enveloped the vast building in its groanings, now plaintive, now soothing. The west wind is terrible on these heights, where, sometimes, it carries away in a single breath all the slates of a roof.

This lamentation of the wind has always increased in me the feeling of internal solitude. My fire burned gently, and I scribbled in my notebook, which I burned before my arrest, the occurrences of the day and the programme of the experience which I proposed to attempt upon the mind of Mlle. de Jussat. I had copied the passage on pity which is found in your *Theory of the Passions*; you remember it, my dear master, it begins:

> There is in the phenomenon of pity a physical element, and which, especially in women, is confined to the sexual emotion.

It was through pity then, that I proposed to act first upon Charlotte. I would profit by the first falsehood by which I had already moved her, combining with it a succession of others, and thus make her love me by making her pity me. There was, in this use of the most respected of human sentiments for the profit of my curious fancy, something particularly contrary to the general prejudice, which flattered my pride most exquisitely.

While I wrote out this plan with philosophical text to support it, I imagined what Count André would think, if he could, as in the old legends, from the depths of his garrison town decipher the words which I had traced with my pen.

At the same time, the idea alone of directing at will the subtle movements of a woman's brain, all this sentimental and intellectual clockwork so complicated and so tenuous, made me compare myself to Claude Bernard,[3] to Pasteur and to their pupils. These savants vivisected animals. Was not I going to vivisect at length, a human soul?

In order to draw from this pity which had been surprised rather than provoked, all the result demanded, it must first be prolonged. To this end, I resolved to keep up the comedy of sadness by preparing for the day of an explanatory conversation, more or less distant, a long, touching romance of false confidences.

I devoted myself, during the week following our walk, to feigning a melancholy more or less absorbing, and to feigning it, not only in the presence of Charlotte, but also during the hours in which I was alone with my pupil, sure that the child would report to his sister the impressions of our tête-à-tête.

You see here, my dear master, the proof of the useless machinery I was preparing to employ. Was there any need of involving this boy, who had been confided to me, in this sad intrigue, and why should I join this ruse with the others, when Mlle. de Jussat did not for a moment doubt my sincerity?

We had our lessons, Lucien and I, in a large room dignified by the name of library, because of the shelves which furnished one side of the wall. There,

---

3. Claude Bernard (1813–1878) was a French physiologist known for his effort in establishing the use of the scientific method in medicine.

behind the gratings lined with green linen, were innumerable volumes bound in sheepskin, notably all the volumes of the Encyclopedia. This was a legacy from the founder of the château, a great philosopher, who had built this habitation among the mountains for the purpose of bringing up his children in the midst of nature and after the precepts of Emile.[4]

The portrait of this gentleman freethinker, a mediocre painting in the taste of the period, with its powder, and a smile both skeptical and sensible, adorned one side of the door; on the other side was that of his wife, quite coquettish under a high coiffure and with patches on her cheeks. In looking at these two paintings, while Lucien translated a bit from Ovid or from Titus Livius, I asked myself what my ancestors were doing for me during the century in which these two persons lived who were represented in these portraits. I imagined, these rustics from whom I am descended pushing the plow, pruning the vine, harrowing the ground in the foggy plains of Lorraine, like the peasants who passed on the road in front of the château, in all weathers, and who with boots to their knees, dragged a metal-tipped stick fastened to the wrist by a strap.

This mental picture gave the charm of a kind of lawful vengeance to the care I took to compose my physiognomy. It is a singular thing, that although I might detest in theory the doctrines of the Revolution and the mediocre spiritualism which they conceal, I became again a plebeian in my profound joy in thinking that I, the great-grandson of these farmers, should perhaps by the force of my mind alone bring to disgrace the great-granddaughter of this great lord and this great lady.

I leaned my chin upon my hand, I forced my brow and my eyes to look sad, knowing that Lucien was watching the expression of my face, in the hope of interrupting his task by a talk. When he had several times observed that he did not see the welcoming smile, nor the indulgent look, he himself became very anxious. As is natural, the poor boy took my sadness for sever-

---

4. *Emile, or On Education* (*Émile, ou De l'éducation*) is a treatise on the nature of education and man written by Jean-Jacques Rousseau in 1762. *Emile* was banned in Paris and Geneva and was publicly burned in the year of its first publication. During the French Revolution, *Emile* served as the inspiration for what became a new national system of education.

ity, my silence for displeasure. One morning he ventured to ask:

"Are you angry with me, monsieur?"

"No, my child," I replied, patting his fresh cheek with my hand; and I continued to preserve my troubled look, while contemplating the snow which beat against the panes. It fell now from morning till evening in large whirling stars, covering and putting to sleep the whole country, and in the warm rooms of the chateau there was the silent charm of intimacy, a distant death of all the noises of the mountains; while through the window panes, covered with frost on the outside and a vapor within, the light sifted languorously.

This gave a background of mystery to the figure of melancholy which I made, and which I imposed on the observation of Charlotte whenever we met. When the breakfast bell reunited us in the dining room, I was surprised by the eyes with which she received me, the same timid and compassionate curiosity which I had noticed during our walk, whence dated what I called in my journal my entrance into my laboratory.

She regarded me with the same look when we were all again together, in the salon at tea, under the light of the early lamps, then at the dinner table and again in the long solitude of the evening, unless, under pretext of having work to finish, I retired to my room.

The monotony of life and of conversation was so complete that there was nothing to help her to shake off the impression of mournful mystery which I had inflicted upon her.

The marquis, a prey to the contrasts of his character, cursed his fatal resolution to remain in this isolation. He announced for the next clear day a departure which he knew would be impossible. It would cost too much now, and beside, where could he go? He calculated the chances of seeing his Clermont friends who had several times breakfasted with him, but it was before the four hours between Aydat and the city had been doubled by the bad weather.

Then he installed himself at the card table, while the marquise, the governess and the *religieuse* applied themselves to their unending work.

It was my duty to look after Lucien who turned the leaves of a book of engravings or played at patience. I placed myself so that when she raised her eyes from the cards which she held in her hands while playing with her father, the young girl was obliged to see me. I had been interested in hypnotism, and I had in particular studied in all its details, in your *Anatomy of the Will*, the chapter devoted to the singular phenomena of certain moral denominations, which you have entitled: "Some demi-suggestions." I depended on taking possession of this unoccupied mind, until the propitious moment in which, to complete this work of daily intercourse, I should decide to relate to her mystery which, justifying my sadness, should end by engrossing her imagination.

This story I had manufactured upon two principles which you lay down, my dear master, in your beautiful chapter on Love. This chapter, the theories of the *Ethics* on the passions, and M. Ribot's book *Maladies of the Will*, had become my breviaries. Permit me to recall these two principles, at least in their essence.

The first is that the majority of beings have sentiment only by imitation; abandoned to simple nature, love, for example, would be for them as for the animals, only a sensual instinct, dissipated as soon as satiated.

The second is that jealousy may exist before love; consequently, it may sometimes create it, and may often survive it. Much struck by the justness of this double remark, I argued that the romance which I should relate to Mlle. de Jussat ought to excite her imagination and irritate her vanity. I had succeeded in touching the cord of pity, I wished to touch that of sentimental emulation and that of self-love.

I had then, founded my story on this idea, that every woman interested in a man, is wounded in her vanity if this man shows that he is thinking of another woman. But twenty pages would be necessary to show you how I studied over the problem of the invention of this fable.

The occasion to relate it to her was furnished by the victim herself, fifteen days after I had begun to put at work what I proudly called my experience. The marquis had been told that one volume of the Encyclopedia was devoted to cards. He wished to find there how to play some old games such as Impériale, Ombre, and Manilla. This brilliant idea had come to him after breakfast, on seeing in a journal a report of a new game called Poker, apropos of which the journalist gave a list of old-fashioned games.

When this maniac had conceived a fancy he could not wait, and his daughter was obliged to go at once to the library, where I was occupied in taking notes. I laid aside Helvétius' *On Mind*,[5] which I had discovered among some other books of the eighteenth century. I placed myself at the disposition of Mlle. de Jussat to take down the volume which she desired, and, when she took it from my hands, she said with her habitual grace:

"I hope that we shall find here some game in which you can take a hand with us. We are so afraid that you do not feel at home here, you are always so sad."

She said these words as if asking pardon for an indelicacy, which had impressed me before, and escaping the familiarity of her remark by a "we" which I too well knew to be untruthful. Her voice was so gentle, we were so alone that the time seemed to have come to explain my feigned sadness.

"Ah! Mademoiselle," I answered, "if you only knew my history."

If Charlotte had not been the credulous creature, the romantic child that she was, in spite of her two or three seasons in Paris, she would have seen that I was beginning a tale prepared beforehand, by this introduction, by the turn of the sentences with which I continued. I was too clumsy, too awkwardly affected.

I told her then that I had been betrothed at Clermont to a young girl, but secretly. I thought to make this adventure more poetical in her eyes by insinuating that this girl was a foreigner, a Russian visiting one of her relations. I added that this girl had allowed me to tell her that I loved her, and she had also told me that she loved me. We had exchanged vows, then she had gone away. A rich marriage offered, and she had betrayed me for money.

I was careful to insist on my poverty, and let her understand that my mother lived almost entirely on what I earned. This was a detail invented on the spot, for hypocrisy doubles itself in expression. In truth this was a scene of a childish and rascally comedy, which I played with very little skill. But the

---

5. Claude Adrien Helvétius published his work titled *De l'esprit* (*On Mind*) in 1758. It claimed that all human faculties are attributes of mere physical sensation, and that the only real motive is self-interest, therefore there is no good and evil, only competitive pleasures. Its doctrines raised a public outcry, and the Sorbonne publicly burned it in 1759, forcing Helvétius to issue several retractions.

reasons which determined me to lie in this fashion were so special that they exacted an extraordinary penetration to be comprehended, a total attention of my mind, almost your genius, my dear master. The visible embarrassment of my position could so easily be attributed to the trouble inseparable from such remembrances. As I was perfectly cool while I was telling this fable, I could observe Charlotte. She listened without any sign of emotion, her eyes lowered on the big book which supported her hand. She took the book when I had finished, and replied in a blank voice, as they say, one of those voices which betrays no sentiment of the speaker:

"I do not understand how you could have had any confidence in this young girl, since she listened to you without the knowledge of her parents."

And she went away with a simple inclination of her graceful head, carrying the book with her. How pretty she was in her dress of fine, light cloth, with her slender form, her small waist, her face quite long and lighted up by her thoughtful gray eyes! She was like a Madonna engraved after Memling, whose profile I had formerly so much admired, fervent, lovely and mournful, on the first page of a large copy of *The Imitation of Christ,* belonging to the Abbé Martel.

Explain to me this other enigma of the heart, you, the great psychologist; never have I felt more the charm of this pure and gentle being than at the moment when I had just lied to her, and lied so uselessly as I imagined from her response.

Yes, I took this response literally, which, on the contrary, should have encouraged me to hope. I did not guess that to have only listened to a confidence so intimate was for a being so proud and so reserved, so far above me, a proof of a very powerful sympathy. I did not consider that this almost severe remark was dictated in part by the secret jealousy which I had desired to arouse in her, in part by a need to strengthen herself in her own principles so as to justify to herself her excessive familiarity.

As she had not been able to read the falsehood in my story, so I had not seen the truth behind her reply.

I felt all the hopes which I had been building up for the past fortnight crumble before me. No. She was not interested in me with a genuine interest which I could transform into passion. I drew up the balance sheet of our relations. What proof had I of this interest? The delicacy of the material cares with which she had surrounded me? This was a simple effect of her goodness. Her attempt to find out the cause of my melancholy? Ah, well! She had been curious, that was all. The timid accent of her voice when she questioned me? I had been a fool not to recognize the habitual modesty of a delicate girl. Conclusion: my comedy of these two weeks, my grimaces *à la* Chatterton,[6] the falsehood of my so-called drama, so many ridiculous maneuvers, had not advanced me a line in the heart I wished to conquer.

I turned again to my book, but I was no longer capable of fixing my attention on the abstract text of Helvétius. I recall this childishness, my dear master, that you may the better perceive what a strange mixture of innocence and depravity was elaborated in my mind.

What did this unexpected deception prove, if not that I had imagined I could direct the thought of Charlotte, by applying to her the laws of psychology borrowed from the philosophers, as absolutely as her brother directed the billiard balls? The white touches the red a little to the left, goes on the cushions, and returns to the other white. That is outlined by the hand on the paper, that is explained by a formula, that is foreseen and is done ten times, twenty times, a hundred times, ten thousand times.

In spite of my enormous reading, perhaps because of it, I saw the play of the passions in this state of ideal simplicity. I did not comprehend till later how much I was deceived. In order to define the phenomena of the heart we must go to the vegetable, and not to the mechanical world for analogies, and to direct these phenomena we must employ the methods of the botanist, patient grafting, long waiting, careful training.

A sentiment is born, grows, expands, withers like a plant, by an evolution sometimes retarded, sometimes rapid, but always unconscious. The germ of pity, of jealousy, and of dangerous example planted by my ruse in the soul of Charlotte must develop its action, but only after days and days, and this action would be the more irresistible as she believed me to be in love with another and that in consequence she would not think to defend herself against me.

---

6. Thomas Chatterton (1752–1770) was an influential, English Romantic poet.

But to account in advance for this work and to discount the hope of it, one would have to be a Ribot, a Horwicz, an Adrien Sixte, that is, a connoisseur of souls, instead of one like me, ignorant that the plain over which he is walking will be covered with grain and not suspecting the approaching harvest.

The conviction that I had definitely failed in my first effort increased during the days which followed this false confidence. For Charlotte scarcely spoke to me.

I know now, from her own confession, that she concealed under this coldness a growing agitation which disconcerted her by its novelty, its force and its depth. In the meantime she appeared absorbed in the game of backgammon which the marquis had discovered in the Encyclopedia.

Recollecting that this had been the favorite pastime of his grandfather, the *emigré*, he had given up all other games. A merchant of Clermont had been able to send him the necessary articles with which to satisfy this caprice.

The backgammon table was installed in the salon and father and daughter passed their evenings in throwing the dice, which made a dry noise against the wooden ledge. The cabalistic terms of little table, big table, outer table, double ace, double threes, two fives, were intermingled now with the words of the marquise and her two companions.

Sometimes the *curé* of Aydat,[7] the Abbé Barthomeuf, an old priest who said mass in the chapel of the château on Thursdays when the weather was very severe, would relieve Charlotte by playing with the marquis. Although the marquis treated me with irreproachable politeness, he had never asked me if I wished to learn to play. The difference which he established between the abbé and myself humiliated me, by the oddest contradiction, for I much preferred to remain in my low chair reading a book, or observing the character of the different persons from their physiognomies.

Is it not always so when one is in a position which is thought to be inferior? Any inequality of treatment wounds the self-love. I took my revenge in observing the ridiculousness of the abbé, who professed, for the château in general and the marquis in particular, an almost idolatrous admiration. His

---

7. *Curé* is a French term for a priest bearing the responsibility of a parish.

face which was always red became apoplectic when he took his seat opposite the marquis, and the prospect of winning the silver coins designed to make the game more interesting made the dice-cup tremble in his hand at the decisive throws.

This observation did not occupy me long, and I turned to follow the young girl, who seated herself at her work near her mother.

The failure of my attempt to win her love had made me more cruel, in proportion to the admiration I had before felt for the innocent grace of this child. To confess all, I began to feel, in her atmosphere, emotions of an order more sensual than psychological. I was a young man, and I had in my flesh, in spite of my philosophical resolutions, the memory of sex of which you have so authoritatively analyzed the persistent fatality and the invincible reviviscence.

How long this period of inertia at once impassioned and discouraged, might have lasted, I do not know. We were, Mlle. de Jussat and I, in a very peculiar situation, impelled one toward the other, she by a budding love of which she was ignorant, I by all the confused reasons which I have analyzed. Although we were together so many hours of the day, neither of us then suspected the sentiments of the other. In such circumstances, one does not consider whether the events which mark a new crisis are effects or causes, whether their importance resides in themselves or whether they simply serve to manifest the latent conditions of the soul. But may we not put this question apropos of each destiny taken in its whole? How many times, above all since I consume my hours in this cell between these four white-washed walls, seeing only the empty sky through four openings at the edge of the roof, in searching and searching again into my short history, have I asked myself if our fate creates our mind, or if it is not our mind which creates our fate, even our external destiny?

It happened one evening that the marquis, seated with his back to the fire in the *robe-de-chambre*, which he sometimes wore all day, spoke at length to his wife of an article in the morning paper. I was holding this paper at the time, and M. de Jussat said to me quite suddenly:

"Would you read this article, Monsieur Greslou?"

I admired, once more, the art with which this grand seigneur rendered the most trifling demands insolent. His tone alone was sufficient to chill me. I obeyed however, and began to read this chronicle, more finely written than such articles usually are, and in which were revived all the picturesqueness and coloring of a fancy ball, with a curious mixture of reporting and poetry.

During the reading the marquis regarded me in astonishment. I must tell you, my dear master, that at the time of my friendship with Emile, I had acquired a real talent for diction. During his illness my little comrade had no greater pleasure than to hear me read.

"You read very well, very well!" cried M. de Jussat when I had finished.

His astonishment made his eulogy a new wound to my self-esteem. It was too plain that he did not expect to find much talent in a silent and timid young man of Clermont, who had come to the château on the recommendation of old Limasset, to be a *valet de lettres.* Then, following as usual, the impulse of his caprice, he continued:

"That is an idea. You shall read for us in the evening. That will amuse us a little better than this *trictrac.*[8] Little *jan*, big *jan*, it is always the same thing, and then the noise of the dice sets my teeth on edge. This beastly country! If the snow ever stops again, we will not stay here eight days. And what book are you going to begin with?"

Thus I found myself promoted to a new service, without even being allowed to consider whether it would interfere with my studies or not, for I often brought into the salon some of my books that I might study a little without leaving Lucien. But I did not for a moment think of evading this task. First the brusqueness of the marquis had brought me a glance almost supplicating from Charlotte, one of those glances by which a woman knows how to ask pardon, for the error of some one whom she loves. Then, a new project took form in my mind. Might not this task be utilized to the profit of the enterprise commenced, abandoned, and which the look of Mlle. de Jussat made me think was still possible?

To the question of the marquis upon the choice of the book, I responded that I would consider. And I looked for a work which would permit me to

---

8. *Trictrac* is the French name for backgammon. The *petit jan* and *grand jan* refer to each player's high and low section of the board.

approach the prey around which I turned, as I once saw, near the Puy de Dôme, a kite wheel around and above a poor little bird.

Was not this an opportunity to try by another method this influence of imitation, which I had vainly hoped from my false confidence? It is to you, my dear master, that we owe the strongest pages which have been written upon that which you so justly call the Literary Mind, upon this unconscious modeling of our heart to the resemblance of the passions painted by the poets.

I saw in this then, a means of acting upon Charlotte which I reproached myself for not having thought of before. But how was I to find a romance which was passionate enough to excite her, and outwardly correct enough to be read before the assembled family? I literally ransacked the library. Its incoherent and contrasted composition, reflected the residence of its successive masters and the chances of their taste.

There were all the principal works of the eighteenth century of which I have spoken—then a hiatus. During the emigration the château had remained unoccupied. Then a lot of romantic books in their first editions attested the literary aspirations of the father of the marquis, who had been the friend of Lamartine. Then came the worst of contemporaneous romances, those which are bought on the railway, half-bound, cut sometimes with the finger, or a page lost, and some treatises on political economy, an abandoned hobby of M. de Jussat.

At last I discovered amid all this rubbish *Eugénie Grandet*,[9] which appeared to me to fill the conditions desired. There is nothing more attractive to a fresh imagination than these idyls at once chaste and fervid in which innocence envelops passion in a penumbra of poesy. But the marquis must have known this celebrated romance by heart, and I apprehended that he would refuse to listen to it.

"Bravo!" he replied when I submitted my idea to him, "that is one of the books that one reads once, talks about always and entirely forgets. I saw this Balzac once in Paris, at the Castries. It is more than forty years ago. I was a youngster then. But I remember him well, fat, short and stubby, noisy,

---

9. *Eugénie Grandet* (1833) is a novel by Honoré de Balzac.

important, with beautiful bright eyes and a common air."

The fact is that after the first pages, he fell asleep, while the marquise, Mlle. Largeyx and the *religieuse* knit, and Lucien, who had recently come into possession of a box of colors conscientiously illuminated the illustrations of a large volume.

While reading I observed Charlotte, and it was not difficult to see that this time my calculation had been correct, and that she vibrated under the phrases of the romance as a violin under a skillful bow. Everything was prepared to receive this impression, from her feelings already stirred to her nerves strained by an influence of a physical kind. One cannot live with impunity for weeks in such an atmosphere as that of the château, always warm, nearly stifling.

From that evening, this child hung on my lips as the ingenuous loves of Eugenie and her cousin Charles disclosed their touching episodes. The same instinct of comedy which had guided me in my false confidence made me throw into every phrase the intonation which I thought would please her most.

I certainly enjoyed this book, although I preferred ten other of Balzac's works, such, for example, as *Le Curé de Tours*, which are veritable literary compendiums, each phrase of which contains more philosophy than a scholium of Spinoza.

I forced myself to appear touched by the misfortunes of the miser's daughter, in my most secret fibres; and my voice grew pitiful over the sweet recluse of Saumur.

Here, as before, I gave myself useless trouble. There was no need of an art so complicated. In the crisis of imaginative sensibility through which Charlotte was passing, any romance of love was a peril.

If the father and mother had possessed, even in a feeble degree, that spirit of observation which parents ought to exercise without ceasing, they would have divined this peril of their daughter, more and more captivated during the three evenings that this reading lasted. The marquise simply remarked that characters so black as father Grandet and the cousin did not exist. As for the marquis, he knew too much of the world to proffer any such opinion, he formulated the cause of his ennui during the reading.

"It is decidedly overdrawn. These unfinished descriptions, these analyses, these numerical calculations! They are all very good, I do not say they are not. But when I read a romance I wish to be amused."

And he concluded that he must send to the Library of Clermont immediately for the comedies of Labiche.[10] I was in despair at this new fancy. I would again be powerless to act upon the imagination of the young girl, just at the moment when I could feel success probable. This showed that I did not know the need which this soul, already touched, felt, unknown to herself, the need of drawing near to me, of comprehending me and making herself comprehended by me, of living in contact with my mind.

The next day after that on which the marquis had issued the decree of proscription against analytical romances. Mlle. de Jussat entered the library at the hour I was there with her brother. She came to replace the volume of the Encyclopedia; and with a half-embarrassed smile:

"I would like to ask a favor of you," she said timidly. "I have a great deal of time here, with which I do not know very well what to do. I would like to have your advice in regard to my reading. The book which you chose the other day gave me a great deal of pleasure." She added: "Ordinarily romances weary me, but that one was very interesting."

I felt, at hearing her speak in that way, the joy which Count André must have tasted when he saw the enemy whom he killed during the war put his inquisitive head above the wall. It seemed to me as if I, too, held my human game at the end of my gun.

The response to this request appeared to me so important that I feigned to be very much embarrassed. In thanking her for her confidence I said to her that she had charged me with a very delicate mission for which I felt myself incapable. In brief, I made believe to decline a favor, which I was charmed to intoxication to have obtained. She insisted, and I promised to give her the next day a list of books.

I passed the evening and a part of the night in taking and rejecting in my mind hundreds of volumes. At last I repeated aloud my father's favorite formula: "Let us proceed methodically," and I asked myself how books had

10. Eugène Marin Labiche (1815–1888) was a French dramatist.

acted on my imagination, in my adolescence, and what books?

I stated that I had been attracted most of all toward literature by the unknown of sentimental experience. It was the desire to assimilate unexperienced emotions which had bewitched me. I concluded that this was the general law of literary intoxication. I must then choose for this girl some books which should awake in her the same ideas while taking into account the difference of our characters.

Charlotte was refined, pure and tender. She must be led into the dangerous road of romantic curiosity by descriptions of sentiments analogous to her own heart. I judged that *Dominique* by Fromentin, *La Princesse de Clèves*, *Valérie*, *Julia de Trécoeur*, *Le lis dans la vallée*, *Reisebilder* by Heine, certain comedies of Musset, in particular *On ne badine pas avec l'amour*, the first poetry of Sully Prudhomme and that of Vigny, would best serve my purpose.

I took the trouble to write out this list, accompanying it with a tempting commentary, in which I indicated in my best manner the shade of delicacy proper to each of these writers. That is the letter which the poor child had kept, and of which the magistrates said it seemed like the beginning of courtship. Ah! The strange courtship, and so different from the vulgar ambition of the marriage with which these gross minds have stupidly reproached me! If I had not a reason of pride for refusing to defend myself which I will give you at the end of this memoir, I would be silent from disgust of these low intelligences, of which not one would be able to comprehend an action dictated by pure reason. If they had only made you, my dear master, and the other princes of modern thought, my judges! Then I would speak, as I am speaking now to you.

The works thus designated arrived from Clermont. They were the object of no remark on the part of the marquis. It is necessary to have another reach of mind than that of this poor man to comprehend that there are no bad books. There are bad moments in which to read the best of books. You have a comparison so just in your chapter on "L'âme littéraire," when you liken the sore opened in certain imaginations by certain readings to the well-known phenomenon produced on the body poisoned by diabetes. The most inoffensive prick becomes envenomed with gangrene.

If there were need of a proof of this theory of "the preliminary state," as you say again, I should find it in the fact that Mlle. de Jussat sought in these books for things so diverse, for information about me, my manner of feeling, of thinking, of understanding life and character.

Every chapter, every page of these dangerous volumes became an occasion for questioning me long, passionately, and ingenuously. I am certain that she was sincere, and that she did not imagine she was doing anything wrong when she came to talk with me apropos of such or such a phrase about Dominique or Julia, Félix de Vandenesse or Perdican. I remember the horror which she felt for the young man, the most captivating and the most guilty of Musset's heroes, and the heat with which I stigmatized his duplicity of heart between Camille and Rosette.

Now, there was no personage in any book, who pleased me to the same degree as this lover at once traitorous and sincere, disloyal and loving, *ingénu* and *roué*,[11] who achieved, in his way, his experience of sentimental vivisection upon his pretty and proud cousin.

I have cited this example, among twenty others, to give you an idea of the conversations which we had now in this château in which we were so strangely isolated. No one watched us. The dissimulation in which I had masked myself on my arrival continued to cover me.

The marquis and the marquise had formed from the first an image entirely different from my real nature. They took no pains to verify whether this first impression were exact or false.

The good Mlle. Largeyx, installed in the comfort of her complacent parasitism, was much too innocent to suspect the thoughts of depravity perfectly intellectual which were revolving in my mind.

The Abbé Bartholomew and Sister Anaclet, whom a secret rivalry separated, concealed under the form of an amiability quite ecclesiastic, had only one care, that of pleasing the master and mistress of the château, the priest for the benefit of his church, and the *religieuse* for that of her order.

Lucien was too young, and, as for the domestics, I had not yet learned what perfidy was veiled under the impassibility of their smooth faces and the

---

11. *Ingénu* is a French term implying a lack of sophistication and cunning; and *roué* is a French term for a debauched man, a libertine, especially an elderly one.

irreproachable appearance of their brown livery with its gold buttons.

We were then free, Charlotte and I, to talk the whole day. She appeared first in the morning, in the dining-room where my pupil and I took our tea, and there, under the pretext of breakfasting together, we talked at one corner of the table, she in all the perfumed freshness of her bath, with her hair hanging down in a heavy plait, and the suppleness of her lovely form visible under the material of her half-fitting morning dress.

I saw her again in the library where she always had some excuse for coming; and by this time her hair was dressed, and she had assumed the toilette of the day. We met again in the drawing-room before the second breakfast and still again; and she waited upon us with her customary grace, distributing the coffee a little hurriedly that she might linger near me, whom she served last, which permitted us to talk in an angle of the window.

When the weather would permit we went out, the governess, Charlotte, my pupil, and I, in the afternoon. At five-o'clock tea we were again together, then at dinner, when I sat near her, and in the evening we conversed almost as if we were really alone.

I mentally compared the phenomena which were taking place in this girl, to that which I had observed several times in taming animals. At one time I had written some chapters on animal psychology. A theorem of Spinoza had served me for a starting point. I cannot now recall the text, but this is the sense: to reproduce a movement, you must do it yourself. That is true of man, and it is true of the animal. A savant of rare merit and whom you know well, M. Espinas,[12] has explained that all society is founded on resemblance. I have concluded that for a man to tame an animal, to bring it to live in his society, he must, in his relations with this animal, make only those movements which the animal can reproduce, that is to resemble him.

I have verified this law in establishing the species of analogy of expression between a hunter and his dog, for example. I found—and this was the sign that Mlle. de Jussat was becoming a little tamer each day—that we began to employ analogous expressions, turns of thought almost the same.

---

12. Alfred Victor Espinas (1844–1922) was a French thinker noted for his influence on Nietzsche. He was a student of Comte and Spencer.

I found myself accenting my words as she did hers, and I observed in her gestures which resembled mine. In fine, I became a part of her life, without her perceiving it, so careful was I not to startle this soul just ready to be taken by a word that would cause her to feel her danger.

This life of watchful diplomacy, to which I was condemned during nearly two months that these simply intellectual relations lasted, did not pass without almost daily internal struggles. To interest this mind, to invade this imagination little by little, was not all of my programme. I wished to be loved, and I knew that this moral interest was only the beginning of passion. This beginning ought to lead in order not to remain useless to something more than a sentimental intimacy.

There is in your *Theory of the Passions*, my dear master, a note which I read so much at that time that I know the text by heart: "A well-prepared study of the lives of professional libertines," say you, "would throw a definite light upon the problem of the birth of love. But the documents are lacking. These men have nearly all been men of action, and who, in consequence, did not know how to relate. However, some works of a superior psychological interest, *Histoire de ma vie* by Casanova, *The Private Life of the Marshal Duke of Richelieu*, the chapter of Saint-Simon on Lauzun,[13] authorize us to say that nineteen times out of twenty audacity and physical familiarity are the surest means of creating love. This hypothesis confirms our doctrine on the animal origin of this passion."

Sometimes when we were alone together, and she moved, and her feet approached mine, and when she breathed and I felt that she was a living creature, the feverish wave of intoxication ran through my veins, and I was obliged to turn my eyes away, for their expression would have made her afraid. Often also, when I was away from her, it seemed to me that audacity would be much more easy as it would be more complete. I resolved then to

---

13. Louis de Rouvroy, duc de Saint-Simon (1675–1755), or Saint-Simon, was a French soldier, diplomat and memoirist, who—as the brother-in-law to Antoine Nompar de Caumont, duc de Lauzun (1632–1723)—wrote about Lauzun (the only love interest of the Anne Marie Louise d'Orléans, Duchess of Montpensier). Saint-Simon's memoirs are a classic of French literature, giving the most detailed account of the court at Versailles of Louis XIV.

clasp her in my arms, to press my lips to hers. I saw her feeling badly at my caress, overcome, confounded by this revelation of my ardor. What would happen then? My heart beat at this idea. It was not the fear of being driven from the chateau that held me back. It was more shameful to my pride not to dare. And I did not dare. The inability to act is a trait of my character, but only when I am not sustained by an idea. Let the idea be there and it infuses an invincible energy into my being. To go to my death would be easy. You will see that, if I am condemned. No, what paralyzed me near Mlle. de Jussat as by a magnetic influence was *her purity!* At least I have felt, with singular force, this recoil before innocence.

Often when I felt this invisible barrier between Charlotte and myself, I have recalled the legends of guardian angels, and comprehended the birth of this poetic conceit of Catholicism.

Reduced to reality by analysis, this phenomenon simply proves that in the relations between two beings, there is a reciprocity of action of one upon the other unknown to either. If by calculation I forced myself to resemble this girl in order to tame her, I experienced without calculation the species of moral suggestion which all true character imposes upon us. The extreme simplicity of her mind triumphed at times over my ideas, my remembrances, and my desires.

Finally, although judging this weakness to be unworthy of a brain like mine, I respected her, as if I had not known the value of this word respect, and that it represents the most stupid of all our ignorances. Do we respect the player who ten times in succession strikes the *rouge* or the *noir?* Well, in this hazardous lottery of the universe, virtue and vice are the *rouge* and *noir*. An honest woman and a lucky player have equal merit.

The spring arrived in the midst of these agitating alternations of audacious projects, stupid timidity, contradictory reasonings, wise combinations and ingenuous ardors. And such a spring! One must have experienced the severity of winter among these mountains, then the sudden sweetness of the renewal of nature, to appreciate the charm of life which floats in this atmosphere when April and May bring back the sacred season.

It comes first across the meadows in an awaking of the water which shudders under the thin ice; it bursts through, and then runs singing on, light, transparent and free.

It comes through the woods in a continuous murmur of snow which detaches itself piece by piece and falls upon the evergreen branches of the pines and the yellow and dried leaves of the oaks. The lake freed from its ice takes to shivering under the wind which sweeps away the clouds, and the azure appears, the azure of a mountain sky, clearer, deeper than that of the plain; and in some days the uniform color of the landscape is tinted with colors tender and young.

The delicate buds begin to appear on the naked branches. The greenish aments of hazels alternate with the yellowish catkins of the willows. Even the black lava of the Cheyre appears to be animated. The velvety fructifications of the mosses mingle with the whitening spots of the lichens. The craters of the Puy de la Vache and of the Puy de Lassolas disclose little by little the splendor of their red gravel. The silvery trunks of the birches and the changeable trunks of the beeches shine in the sun with a lively splendor

In the thickets, the beautiful flowers which I had formerly picked with my father, and whose corollas looked at me as if they were eyes, and whose aroma followed me like a breath, began to bloom. The periwinkle, the primrose, and the violet appeared first, then in succession the cuckoo-flower with its shade of lilac, the daphne which bears its pink flowers before it has any leaves, the white anemone, the two-leaved harebell, with its odor of hyacinth, Solomon's seal with its white bells and its mysterious root which walks under the ground, the lily-of-the-valley in the hollows, and the eglantine along the hedges.

The breeze which came from the white domes of the mountain passed over these flowers. It brought with it perfumes something of the sun and the snow, so caressing and so fresh, that only to breathe was to be intoxicated with youth, was to participate in the renewal of the vast world; and I, fixed as I was in my doctrines and my theories, felt the puberty of all nature. The ice of abstract ideas in which my soul was imprisoned melted.

When I read over the pages of my journal, now destroyed, in which I had noted my sensations, I am astonished to see with what force the sources of ingenuousness were reopened in me under this influence, and with what a rushing flood they inundated my heart. I am vexed with myself for thinking of it in this cowardly spirit. However, I experience a pleasure in remembering that at this period I sincerely loved her who is now no more. I repeat it with a real relief, that at least on the day that I dared to tell her of my love—fatal day which marked the beginning of our separation—I was the sincere dupe of my own words.

The declaration on which I had deliberated so much was, however, simply the effect of chance. It was the 12th of May. Ah! It is less than a year ago! In the morning the weather had been even more than usually fine, and in the afternoon Mlle. Largeyx, Lucien, Charlotte and I started to go to the village of Saint-Saturnin through a wood of oaks, of birches and hazels which separated this village from the ruined château of Montredon, and which is called the Pradat woods. We had taken the little English cart which could hold four if necessary.

Never was a day more warm, a sky more blue, never was the odor of spring borne by the wind more exhilarating.

We had not walked a league when Mlle. Largeyx, fatigued by the sun, took her seat in the cart which was driven by the second coachman. The rogue has sworn cruelly against me, and has recalled all that he knew or guessed of what I myself am going to relate to you. Lucien also soon declared himself tired, and joined the governess, so that I was left to walk alone with Mlle. de Jussat.

She had taken it into her head to make a bouquet of lilies-of-the-valley, and I helped her in this work. We were busy under the branches, which were covered with a sort of delicate green cloud of the scarcely opened foliage. She walked ahead, drawn far from the edge of the wood in her search for the flowers. We found ourselves at last in a clearing, and so far away that we could not see the group made by the cart and the three persons. Charlotte first perceived our solitude. She listened, and not hearing the noise of the horse's feet on the road, she cried out with the laughter of a child:

"We are lost. Fortunately the road is not hard to *rembourser*,[14] as poor Sister Anaclet says. Will you wait until I arrange my bouquet ? It would be a pity to have these beautiful flowers spoil."

---

14. *Rembourser* is French for reimburse, to repay.

She sat down on a rock which was bathed in sunlight, and spread the flowers on her lap, taking up the sprays of lilies one by one. I inhaled the musky perfume of these pale racemes, seated on the other extremity of the stone. Never had this creature, toward whom all my thoughts had tended for months, appeared so adorably delicate and refined as at this moment with her face daintily colored by the fresh air, with the deep red of her lips which were bent in a half-smile, with the clear limpidity of her gray eyes, with the symmetry of her entire being.

She harmonized in a manner almost supernatural with the country about us by the charm of youth which emanated from her person. The longer I looked at her the more I was convinced that if I did not seize this occasion to tell her that I had wished to declare for so long a time, I should never again find another opportunity so propitious.

This idea grew in my mind, mingled with the remorse of seeing her, so confident, so unsuspicious of the patient work by which, abusing our daily intimacy, I had brought her to treat me with a gentleness almost fraternal.

My heart beat violently. The magic of her presence excited my entire being. Unfortunately she turned toward me for a moment, to show me the bouquet which was nearly finished. No doubt she saw in my face the trace of the emotion which my pride of thought raised in me, for her face which had been so joyous, so frank, suddenly grew anxious. I ought to say that during our conversations of these two months we had avoided, she from delicacy, I from shrewdness, any allusion to the romance of deception by which I had tried to excite her pity. I understood how thoroughly she had believed in this romance and that she had not ceased to think of it, when she said with an involuntary melancholy in her eyes:

"Why do you spoil this beautiful day by sad remembrances? I thought you had become more reasonable."

"No!" I responded; "you do not know what makes me sad. Ah! It is not remembrances. You refer to my former griefs. You are mistaken. There is no more place in my mind for memories than there is on these branches for last year's leaves."

I heard my voice as if it had been that of someone else, at the same time I read in her eyes that, in spite of the poetical comparison by which I had concealed the direct meaning of this phrase, she understood me.

How was it that what had been so impossible now seemed easy? How was it that I dared to do what I had believed I should never dare to do? I took her hand which trembled in mine as if the child were seized with a frightful terror. She rose to go away, but her knees trembled so that I had no difficulty in constraining her to sit down again. I was so overcome by my own audacity that I could not control myself, and I began to tell her my feelings for her in words which I cannot recall now.

All the emotions through which I had passed, since my arrival at the chateau, yes all, even from the most detestable, those of my envy of Count André, to the best, my remorse at abusing the confidence of a young girl, were dissolved in an adoration almost mystical, and half-mad, for this trembling, agitated, and beautiful creature. I saw her while I was speaking grow as pale as the flowers which were scattered in her lap.

I remember that words came to me which were excited to madness, wild to imprudence, and that I ended by repeating:

"How I love you! Ah! How I love you!"

Clasping her hand in mine and drawing her nearer and nearer to me, I passed my free arm around her waist without even thinking, in my own agitation, of kissing her. This gesture, by alarming her, gave her the energy to rise and disengage herself. She moaned rather than said:

"Leave me, leave me."

And stepping backward, her hands held out in front of her as if to defend herself, she went to the trunk of a birch tree. There she leaned, panting with emotion, while the big tears rolled down her cheeks. There was so much of wounded modesty in these tears, so painful a revulsion, in the tremulousness of her half-open lips, that I remained where I was muttering:

"Pardon."

"Be still," said she, making a motion with her hand.

We remained thus opposite one another and silent for a time which must have been very short, but which seemed an eternity to me. All at once a cry crossed the wood, at first distant, then nearer, that of a voice imitating the cry of the cuckoo. They had grown uneasy at our absence, and it was Lucien who gave the usual signal for rallying.

At this simple reminder of reality Charlotte shivered. The blood came back to her cheeks. She looked at me with eyes in which pride had driven away fear. She looked like one who had just awakened from a horrible sleep. She looked at her hands, which still shook, and, without another word, she took up her gloves and her flowers, and began to run, yes, to run like a pursued animal, in the direction of the voice. Ten minutes after we were again on the road.

"I do not feel very well," she said to her governess, as if to anticipate the question which her disturbed face would provoke; "will you give me a place in the carriage? We are going home."

"It is the heat which has made you feel badly," replied the old demoiselle.

"And M. Greslou?" asked Lucien when his sister had taken her seat and he was in behind.

"I will walk," I answered.

The cart moved lightly on, in spite of its quadruple burden, while Lucien waved me an *adieu*. I could see the hat of Mlle. de Jussat immovable by the side of the shoulder of the coachman, who gave a "pull up" to his horse, then the carriage disappeared and I walked along alone, under the same blue sky, and between the same trees covered with an impalpable verdure. But an extraordinary anguish had replaced the cheerfulness and the happy ardor of the beginning of the walk.

This time the die had been thrown. I had given battle, I had lost; I should be sent away from the château ignobly. It was less this prospect which overcame me than a strange mingling of regret and of shame.

Behold whither my learned psychology had led me! Behold the result of this siege *en règle*[15] undertaken against the heart of this young girl! Not a word on her part in response to the most impassioned declaration, and I, at the moment for action, what had I found to do but recite some romantic phrases? And she, by a simple gesture, had fixed me to my place!

I saw in imagination the face of Count André. I saw in a flash the expression of contempt when they should tell him of this scene. Finally, I was no longer the subtle psychologist or the excited young man, I was a self-love

---

15. *En règle* is a French term meaning in accordance with the rules, in order.

humiliated to the dust by the time I reached the gate of the château.

In recognizing the lake, the line of the mountains, the front of the house, pride gave place to a frightful apprehension of what I was going to suffer, and the project crossed my mind to flee, to go back directly to Clermont, rather than experience anew the disdain of Mlle. de Jussat, and the affront which her father would inflict upon me. It was too late, the marquis himself came to meet me, in the principal avenue, accompanied by Lucien who called me. This cry of the child had the customary intonation of familiarity, and the reception of the father proved that I had been wrong to feel myself lost so soon.

"They abandoned you," said he, "and did not even think of sending the carriage back for you. You must have walked a good stretch!" He consulted his watch. "I am afraid that Charlotte has taken cold." He added, "she went to bed as soon as she came in. These spring suns are so treacherous."

So Charlotte had said nothing yet. She is suffering this evening. That will be for tomorrow, thought I, and I began that evening to pack my papers. I held to them with so ingenuous a confidence in my talent as a philosopher!

The next day arrived. Nothing yet. I was again with Charlotte at the breakfast table; she was pale, as if she had passed through a crisis of violent pain. I saw that the sound of my voice made her tremble slightly. Then this was all. Ah! What a strange week I passed, expecting each morning that she had spoken, crucified by this expectation and incapable of taking the first step myself or of going away from the château! This was not alone for want of a pretext to give. A burning curiosity held me there. I had wished to live as much as to think. Well! I was living, and in what a fever!

At last, the eighth day, the marquis asked me to come into his study.

This time, said I to myself, *the hour has struck. I like this better.*

I expected to see a terrible countenance, and to hear some almost insulting words. I found, on the contrary, the hypochondriac smiling, his eyes bright, his manner young again.

"My daughter," said he, "continues to be very unwell. Nothing very serious, but some odd nervous symptoms. She wishes positively to consult a Paris physician. You know she has been very ill and was cured by a physician in whom she has confidence. I shall not be sorry to consult him also for myself. I am going with her the day after tomorrow. It is possible that we shall take a little journey to amuse her. I desired to give you some particular directions in regard to Lucien during my absence, though I am very well pleased with you, my dear Monsieur Greslou, very well pleased. I wrote so to Limasset yesterday. It is a good thing for me that you are here."

You will judge my dear master, by what I have shown you of my character, that these compliments must have flattered me as evidence of the perfection with which I had filled my role, and by reassuring me after my fears of the last days. I saw this very clear and positive fact: Charlotte had not wished to tell of my declaration, and I asked at once: Why? Instead of interpreting this silence in a sense favorable to me, I saw in it this idea: she did not wish through pity to take away my means of making a living, but it was not the kind of pity which I had wished to provoke.

I had no sooner imagined this explanation than it became evident and insupportable.

No, said I, *that shall not be, I will not accept the alms of this outraging indulgence. When Mlle. de Jussat returns, she will not find me here. She shows me what I ought to do, what I will do. I have desired to interest her, I have not even excited her anger. I will leave at least some other remembrance than that of a vulgar pedant who keeps his place in spite of the worst affronts.*

I was so baffled in my projects; the hope which had sustained me all winter was so dead that I wrote out, on the night following this conversation, a letter in the place of the one in which I had thought to make her love me, again asking for pardon.

I comprehend, said I, *that any relation is impossible between us*, and I added that on her return she would not have to endure the odiousness of my presence. The next morning in the confusion of departure, I found a moment when her mother having called her, I could slip into her room. I hastened to put my letter on her bureau. There, among the books ready to be put into her trunk, was her blotting case. I opened it and found an envelope upon which were the words: May 12, 1886. This was the day of the fatal declaration. I opened this envelope. It contained some sprigs of dried lilies-of-the-valley, and I remember to have given her, in this last walk, some sprigs more beautiful than the others and she had put them in her corsage. She had preserved them then. She had kept them in spite of what I had said to her—because of what I had said to her.

I do not believe that I ever experienced an emotion comparable to that which seized me there, before this simple envelope, to the flood of pride which suddenly inundated my heart. Yes. Charlotte had repulsed me. Yes, she had fled from me. But she loved me! I closed the case, I went up to my room in haste, for fear that she would surprise me, without leaving my letter, which I instantly destroyed. Ah! There was no question of my going away now.

I must wait until she should return, and, this time, I would act, I would conquer. She loved me!

§ V. THE SECOND CRISIS

SHE LOVED ME. The experience instituted by my pride and my curiosity
had succeeded. This evidence—for I did not for a moment doubt the proof,
rendered the departure of the young girl not only supportable, but almost
sweet. Her flight was explained by a fear of her own emotions which proved
to me their depth. And then, by going away for a few weeks, she relieved me
from a cruel embarrassment.

How should I act? By what politic safeguard should I push on to success
from this unhoped for point? I was about to have leisure to think of this
during her absence, which could not last long, since the Jussats had now no
house except in Auvergne.

Deferring then until later the formation of a new plan, I gave myself up
to the intoxication of triumphant self-love which I witnessed in the departure
of Charlotte and of her father. I had taken leave of them in the drawing-room
in order not to embarrass the final adieus, and returned to my room. The
warm, cordial hand-shake of the marquis, proved once more how strongly I
was anchored in the house, and I had divined behind the cool farewell of the
girl the palpitation of a heart which did not wish to yield.

I inhabited in the second story a corner room with a window on the
front of the chateau I placed myself behind the curtain so that I could see
them as they entered the carriage. It was a victoria[1] encumbered with wraps
and drawn by the same light bay horse that had drawn the English cart.
There was also the same coachman on the seat, whip in hand, and with the
same immobility of countenance.

The marquis appeared, then Charlotte. Under the veil and from such a
height, I could not distinguish her features, and when she raised the veil to
dry her eyes, I could not have told whether it were the last kisses of her mother
and her brother which caused this access of nervous emotion or despair at a

---

1. Victoria is an elegant carriage style of French origin; it was light-weight with open sides.

too painful resolution. But, when the carriage turned away toward the gate, I saw her turn her head; and as the family had already gone in what could she be looking at so long, if not at the window from whose shelter I was regarding her? Then a clump of trees hid the carriage, which reappeared at the border of the lake to disappear again and plunge into the road which crosses the Pradat woods—that road where a souvenir awaited her, which I was certain would make her heart beat more quickly—that troubled, conquered heart.

This sentiment of pride satisfied me for an entire month, without a minute's interruption, and—proof that I was still entirely intellectual and psychological in my relations with this young girl, my mind was never more clear, more supple, more skillful in the handling of ideas than at this period.

I wrote then my best pages, a treatise on the working of the will during sleep. I put into it, with the delight of a savant which you will understand, all the details which I had noted, for some months, on the goings and comings, the heights and depths of my resolutions. I had kept, as I have told you, a most precise journal, analyzing, in the evening before going to sleep, and in the morning, as soon as I was awake, the least shades of every state of mind.

Yes, these were days of a singular fullness. I was very free. Mlle. Largeyx and Sister Anaclet kept the marquise company. My pupil and I took advantage of the beautiful and mild days for walking. Under the pretext of teaching I had cultivated in him a love of butterflies. Armed with a long cane and a net of green gauze, he constantly ran after the Auroras with wings bordered with orange, the blue Arguses, the brown Morio's, the mottled Vulcans and the gold-colored Citrons. He left me alone with my thoughts.

Sometimes we took the Pradat road which was now adorned with all the verdure of spring, sometimes we went toward Verneuge, toward the valley of Saint-Genes-Champanelle, which is as gracefully pretty as its name. I would seat myself upon a block of lava, some small fragment of the enormous stream poured out by the Puy de la Vache, and there, without troubling my head about Lucien, I abandoned myself to this strange disposition which has always appeared to me in the midst of this savage nature, as a striking symbol of my doctrines, a type of implacable fatality, a council of absolute indifference to good or ill.

I looked at the leaves of the trees as they unfolded in the sunlight, and I recalled the known laws of vegetable respiration, and how, by a simple modification of light, the life of the plant can be changed. In the same way, one ought to be able at will to direct the life of the soul, if he could exactly know its laws.

I had already succeeded in creating the commencement of a passion in the soul of a young girl, separated from me by an abyss. What new procedures applied with rigor would permit me to increase the intensity of this passion?

I forgot the magnificence of the heavens, the freshness of the wood, the majesty of the volcanoes, the vast landscape spread out before me, in seeing only the formulas of moral algebra. I hesitated between diverse solutions for the next day on which I should have Mlle. de Jussat face to face with me in the solitude of the château.

Ought I on her return to feign indifference, to disconcert her, to subdue her, first by astonishment and then by self-love and grief? Should I pique her jealousy by insinuating that the foreigner of my *soi-disant* romance had returned to Clermont and had written to me? Should I, on the contrary, continue the burning declarations, the audacities which surround, the follies which intoxicate? I replaced these hypotheses successively by still others. I pleased myself by saying that I was not in love, that the philosopher ruled the lover, that myself, this dear self of whom I had constituted myself the priest, remained superior and lucid. I branded as unworthy weaknesses the reveries which at other times replaced these subtle calculations.

It was in the house that these reveries took hold upon me, when I looked at the portraits of Charlotte which were scattered about everywhere on the walls of the salon, on the tables and in Lucien's room. Photographs of all sizes represented her at six years, at ten years, at fifteen, and I could trace the growth of her beauty from the *mignonne*[2] grace of her first years to the delicate charm of today.

The features of these photographs changed, but the expression never. It was the same in the eyes of the child and in those of the young girl, with

---

2. *Mignonne* is a French term meaning daintily small, petite.

something of seriousness, of tenderness and of fixedness which revealed profound sensibility. It was impressed upon me, and the remembrance of it agitates me with a confused emotion. Ah! Why did I not give myself up to it entirely.

But why was Charlotte, in so many of these portraits by the side of her brother André? What secret fibre of hate had this man, by his existence alone, touched in my heart, that simply to see his image near that of his sister dried up my tenderness and left in me only one wish ?

I dared to formulate it, now that I believed I had taken this heart in my snare. Yes, I wished to be Charlotte's lover. And after? After? I forced myself not to think of that, as I forced myself to destroy the instinctive scruples of violated hospitality. I collected the most masculine energies of my mind and I plunged more deeply into my theories upon the cultivation of self.

I would go out of this experience enriched by emotions and remembrances. Such would be the moral issue of the adventure. The material issue would be the return to my mother's house when my preceptorate was ended.

When scruples became aroused, and a voice said: *And Charlotte? Have you the right to treat her as a simple object of experience?* I took my Spinoza, and I read there the theorem in which it is written that our right is only limited by our power.

I took your *Theory of the Passions* and I studied there your phrases on the duel between the sexes in love.

It is the law of the world, I reasoned, *that all existence should be a conquest, executed and maintained by the strongest at the expense of the feeblest. That is as true of the moral universe as of the physical. There are some souls of prey as there are wolves, tigers and hawks.*

This formula seemed to me strong, new and just. I applied it to myself, and I repeated: *I am a soul of prey, a soul of prey,* with a furious attack of what the mystics call the pride of life, among the fresh verdure, under the blue sky, on the bank of the clear river which flows from the mountains to the lake. This exhilaration at my victorious pride was dissipated by a very simple fact. The marquis wrote that he would return, but alone. Mlle. de Jussat, who was still unwell, would remain with a sister of her mother. When the marquise communicated this news to us we were at table. I felt a spasm of anger so violent that it astonished myself, and on the plea of sudden indisposition I left the dinner table.

I should like to have cried out, broken something or manifested in some foolish way the rage which shook my soul. In the fever of vanity which had exalted me since the departure of Charlotte, I had foreseen everything, except that this girl would have character enough not to return to Aydat. The way which she had found to escape from her sentiment was so simple, but so sovereign, so complete.

The marvelous tactics of my psychology became as vain as the mechanism of the best cannon against an enemy out of reach of its shot.

What could I do if she were not there? The vision of my weakness rose up so strong, so painful, that it excited my nervous system so profoundly that I neither ate nor slept until the arrival of the marquis. I should then learn if this resolution excluded all hope of a counter order—if there were any chance that the young girl would return by the end of July, or in August, or in September. My engagement would last until the middle of October.

My heart beat, my throat was choked while we walked, Lucien and I, in the railroad station of Clermont, waiting for the train from Paris. In the excess of my impatience I had obtained permission to come to meet the father. The locomotive entered the station. M. de Jussat put his head through a doorway. I said at the risk of revealing my feelings:

"And Mlle. Charlotte?"

"Thank you, thank you," he answered, pressing my hand with feeling, "the physician says that she has a very serious nervous trouble. It seems that the mountains are not good for her. And I am well only high up! Ah! This is painful, very painful. We shall try for a time, the cold-water cure at Paris, and then at Néris perhaps."

She would not return!

If ever I have regretted, my dear master, the notebook which I burned, it is assuredly now, and this daily record of my thoughts from the evening on which the marquis thus announced the definite absence of his daughter. This record continued until October, when a circumstance brusquely changed the probable course of things.

You would have found there, as in an atlas of moral anatomy, an illustration of your beautiful analysis of love, desire, regret, jealousy, and hate. Yes, during those four months I went through all these phases. It was an insane attempt, but quite natural, persuaded as I was that Charlotte's absence only proved her passion.

I wrote to her. In that letter, deliberately composed, I began by asking her pardon for my audacity in the Pradat woods, and I renewed this audacity in a worse manner, by drawing a burning picture of my despair away from her.

This letter was a wilder declaration than the other, and so bold that once the envelope had disappeared in the box at the village post office whither I had carried it myself, my fears were renewed. Two day, three days, and there was no reply. The letter at least was not returned, as I had feared, without even being opened.

At this time the marquise had finished her preparations to join her daughter. Her sister occupied at Paris in the Rue de Chanaleilles, a house large enough to give to these ladies all the rooms they needed. Hôtel de Sermoises, Rue de Chanaleilles, Paris, what emotions I have had in writing this address, not only once, but five or six times.

I calculated that the aunt would not watch the correspondence of the young girl very strictly, while the mother would watch her. It was necessary to take advantage of the time the latter still remained at Aydat, to strengthen the impression certainly produced by my letter. I wrote every day, until the departure of the marquise, letters like the first, and I found no trouble in playing the lover.

My passionate desire to have Charlotte return was sincere—as sincere as unreasonable. I have known since that, at every arrival of these dangerous missives, she struggled for hours against the temptation to open the envelope. At last she opened it. She read and reread the pages and their poison acted surely. As she was ignorant of the discovery I had made of her secret, she did not think to defend herself against the opinion that I could have conceived of her.

These letters affected her so much that she preserved them. The ashes were found in the chimney of her room where she had burned them the night of her death. I much suspected the troubling effect of these pages which

I scratched off in the night, excited by the thought that I was firing my last cartridges, which resembled shots in a fog, since no sign gave notice that every time I aimed I struck right into her heart.

This absolute uncertainty I at first interpreted to my advantage; then, when the mother had left the château and I saw the impossibility of writing, I found in Charlotte's silence the most evident proof, not that she loved me, but that she was using her whole will to conquer this love and that she would succeed.

Ah, well! I thought, *I shall have to give her up, since I cannot reach her, and all is over.* I pronounced these words aloud alone in my room as I heard the carriage which took the marquise roll away. M. de Jussat and Lucien accompanied her as far as Martris-de-Veyre, where she went to take the train. *Yes,* I repeated, *all is ended. What difference does it make since I do not love her?*

At the moment this thought left me relatively tranquil and with no other trouble than a vague feeling of uneasiness in the chest, as happens when we are annoyed. I went out for the purpose of shaking off even this uneasiness, and, in one of those fits of bravado, by which I was pleased to prove my strength, I went to the place in which I had dared to speak to Charlotte of my love.

In order the better to attest my liberty of soul, I had taken under my arm a new book which I had just received, a translation of Darwin's letters.

The day was misty, but almost scorching. A kind of *simoon*[3] of wind from the south parched the branches of the trees with its breath. As I went on this wind affected my nerves. I desired to attribute to its influence the increase of my uneasiness. After some fruitless search in the Pradat woods, I at last found the clearing where we had been—the stone—the birch.

It trembled constantly in the breath of the wind, with its dentated foliage which was now much thicker. I had intended to read my book here. I sat down and opened the book. I could not get beyond a half page. The memories overcame me, took possession of me, showing me this girl upon this same stone, arranging the sprays of her lilies, then standing, leaning against this tree, then frightened and fleeing over the grass of the path.

---

3. *Simoon* is a term for a hot, dry, dust-laden wind blowing in the desert, especially in Arabia.

An indefinable grief took possession of me, oppressing my heart, stifling my respiration, filling my eyes with scalding tears, and I felt, with terror, that through so any complications of analysis and of subtleties, I was desperately in love with the child who was not there, who would never be there again.

This discovery, so strangely unexpected, and of a sentiment so contrary to the programme I had arranged, was accompanied almost immediately by a revulsion against this sentiment and against the image of her who had caused me this pain. There was not a day during the long weeks that followed that I did not struggle against the shame of having been taken in my own snare and without feeling a bitter spite against the absent one.

I recognized the depth of his spite at the infamous joy which filled my heart when the marquis received a letter from Paris, which he read with a frown and sighed as he said: "Charlotte is still unwell." I felt a consolation, a miserable one, but a consolation all the same, in saying to myself that I had wounded her with a poisonous wound and one which would be slow to heal. It seemed to me that this would be my true revenge, if she should continue to suffer, and I should be the first to cure her.

I appealed to the philosopher that I was so proud of being to drive out the lover. I resumed my old reasoning. *There are laws of life and of mind and I know them. I cannot apply them to Charlotte, since she has fled from me. Shall I be incapable of applying them to myself?* And I meditated on this new question: *Are there remedies against love? Yes, there are, and I have found them.*

My quasi-mathematical habits of analysis were at my service in my project of healing, and I resolved the problem into its elements, after the manner of geometricians.

I reduced this question to this other: *What is love?* to which I answered brutally by your definition: "Love is the obsession of sex." Now, how is this combated? By physical fatigue, which suspends, or at least lessens, the action of the mind.

I compelled myself and I compelled my pupil to take long walks. The days on which he had no lessons, Sundays and Thursdays, I went out alone at the break of day, after having arranged the hour and the place in which Lucien should join me with the carriage. I awoke at two o'clock. I went out from the château, in the cold of the half-twilight which precedes the dawn.

I went straight before me, frantically, choosing the worst paths, ascending the nearest peaks by the most abrupt and almost inaccessible sides. I risked breaking my limbs in descending the yielding sand of the craters, or upon the crests of basalt. No matter.

The orange line of the aurora gained the border of the sky. The wind of the new day beat against my face. The stars like precious stones melted away, drowned in the flood of azure, now pale, now darker. The sun lighted up, on the flowers, the trees and the grass a flashing of sparkling dew.

Persuaded as I am, of the laws of prehistoric atavism, I aroused in myself, by the sensation of the forced march and of the heights, the rudimentary mind of the ancestral brute, of the man of the caves from whom I, as well as the rest of mankind, am descended.

I attained in this way a sort of savage delirium, but it was neither the dreamed-of joy nor peace, and it was interrupted by the smallest reminiscence of my relations with Charlotte. The turn of a road which we had followed together, the blue bosom of the lake seen from some height, the outline of the slated roofs of the château, less than that, even the trembling foliage of a birch and its silvery trunk, the name of a village of which she had spoken, on an advertisement, was sufficient, and this factitious frenzy gave place to the keen regret that she was not near me.

I heard her say in her finely-toned voice: "Look then—" as she would say when we wandered together, through this same region, which was then covered with ice and snow—but the flower of her beauty was then in bloom, now it was adorned with verdure, but the living flower was gone.

And this sensation became more intolerable still when I met Lucien, who never failed to talk of her. He loved her, he admired her so lovingly, and in his ingenuousness he gave me so many proofs that she was worthy of being loved and admired. Then physical weariness resolved itself into a worse enervation, and nights followed in which I suffered from an excited insomnia, in which I would weep aloud, calling her name like one deranged.

It is through the mind that I suffer, I said after having in vain sought the remedy in great fatigue. *I will attack mind through mind.*

I undertook that study the most completely opposed to all feminine preoccupation. I despoiled in less than a fortnight, pen in hand, two hundred pages of that *Physiology of Beaunis* which I had brought in my trunk and the hardest for me, those which treat of the chemistry of living bodies.

My efforts to understand and to sum up these analyses which demand the laboratory, were supremely in vain. I only succeeded in stupefying my intellect and in making myself less capable of resisting a fixed idea.

I saw that I had again taken the wrong road. Was not the true method rather that which Goethe professed—to apply the mind to that from which we wish to be delivered? This great mind, who knew how to live, thus put in practice the theory set up in the fifth book of Spinoza, and which consists in evolving from the accidents of our personal life the law which unites us to the great life of the universe.

M. Taine, in his eloquent pages on Byron, advises the same, "the light of the mind produces in us serenity of the heart." And you, my dear master, what else say you in the preface to your *Theory of the Passions*:

> To consider one's own destiny as a corollary in this living geometry of nature, and as an inevitable consequence of this eternal axiom whose infinite development is prolonged through time and space, is the only principle of enfranchisement.

And what else am I doing, at this hour, in writing out this memoir, but conforming to these maxims? Can they serve me now any better than they did then? I tried at that time to resume in a kind of new autobiography the history of my feelings for Charlotte. I supposed—see how chance sometimes strangely realizes our dreams—a great psychologist to be consulted by a young man; and, toward the last, the psychologist wrote out for the use of the moral invalid a passional diagnosis with indication of causes.

I wrote this piece during the month of August and under the exhausting influence of the most torrid heat. I devoted to it about fifteen séances, lasting from ten o'clock in the evening to one o'clock in the morning, all the windows open, with the space around my lamp brightened by large night-moths, by these large velvet butterflies which bear on their bodies the imprint of a death's head.

The moon rose, inundating with its bluish light the lake over which ran the pearly reflections; the woods whose mystery grew more profound, and the line of the extinct volcanoes. I put down my pen to lose myself, in presence of this mute landscape, in one of those cosmogonic reveries to which I was accustomed. As at the time in which the words of my poor father revealed to me the history of the world, I saw again the primitive nebulousness, then the earth detached from it, and the moon thrown off from the earth.

That moon was dead, and the earth would die also. She was becoming chilled second by second; and the imperceptible consequence of these seconds, added together during millions of years, had already extinguished the fire of the volcanoes from which formerly flowed the burning and devastating lava on which the château now stood.

In cooling this lava had raised a barrier to the course of the water which spread into a lake, and the water of this lake was being evaporated as the atmosphere diminished—these forty poor kilometers of respirable air which surround the planet.

I closed my eyes, and I felt this mortal globe roll through the infinite space, unconscious of the little worlds that come and go upon it, as the immensity of space is unconscious of the suns, the moons and the earths. The planet will roll on when it will be only a ball without air and without water, from which man has disappeared, as well as animals and plants.

Instead of bringing to me the serenity of contemplation, this vision threw me back upon myself and made me feel with terror the consciousness of my own person, the only reality that I could possess, and for how long? Scarcely a point and a moment!

Then, in this irreparable flight of things, this point and this moment of our consciousness remains our only good, we must exalt it by increasing its intensity. I felt, with a frightful force, that this sovereign intensity of emotion Charlotte alone could give me if she were in this room, seated in this chair, uniting her condemned soul to my condemned soul, her fleeting youth to my fleeting youth, and as all the instruments of an orchestra harmonize to produce a single tone, all the separate forces of my being, the intellectual, the sentimental, the sensual united in a yearning for Charlotte.

Alas! The vision of the universe heightened the frenzy of the personal life instead of calming it. I said to myself that without doubt I had been deceived in believing myself a purely abstract and intellectual being. During the months in which I had been entirely chaste had I not lived contrary to my nature?

Under pretext of some family business to regulate I obtained of the marquis a vacation of eight days. I went to Clermont and sought for Marianne. I soon found her. She was no longer the simple working woman. A country proprietor had settled her, dressed her in fine clothes, and coming to the city only one day in eight, left her a sort of liberty. This re-entrance into the world affected me as a renewal of initiation. I was desirous of knowing to what degree the memory of Charlotte gangrened my soul. Ah! How the image of Mlle. de Jussat presented itself at that moment with her Madonna-like profile and the delicacy of her whole being. It was impossible for me to return to these base idols. I passed the days which remained to me in walking with my mother, who seeing me so melancholy became uneasy and increased my sadness by her questions.

I saw the time of my return to the château approach with pleasure. At least I could live there among my memories. But a terrible blow awaited me, which was given me by the marquis on my arrival.

"Good news," said he as soon as he saw me. "Charlotte is better. And there is more just as good. She is going to be married. Yes, she accepts M. de Plane. It is true, you do not know him, a friend of André whom she refused once, and now she is willing." And he continued, going back to himself as usual: "Yes, it is very good news, for, you see, I have not much longer to live. I am broken, very much broken."

He might detail to me his imaginary ills, analyze his stomach as much as he wished, his gout, his intestines, his heart, his head—I listened no more than a condemned man to whom his sentence has been announced listens to the words of his jailer. I saw only the fact so painful to me. You who have written some admirable pages upon jealousy, my dear master, and upon the ravages which the thought alone of the caress of a rival produces in the imagination of a lover, can divine what smarting poison this news poured into my wound.

May, June, July, August, September—nearly five months since Charlotte had gone, and this wound instead of healing had become enlarged, poisoned until this last stroke which finished me. This time I did not have the cruel consolation that my suffering was shared. This marriage proved to me that she was cured of her sentiment for me, while I was agonized by mine for her.

My fury was exasperated at the thought that this love had been snatched from me just at the moment I was about to be able to develop it in its fullness, at the very time of decisive action. I saw Charlotte in Paris, where M. de Plane was passing his leave of absence, receiving her fiancé in the partial *tête-à-tête* with a familiarity permitted under the indulgent eyes of the marquise. They were for this man now, these smiles at once proud and timid, these tender and anxious looks, these passages of paleness and modest red over her delicate face, these gestures of a grace always a little wild.

Finally she loved him, since she was willing to marry him. And he seemed to me like Count André whose detestable influence I found even here, and whom I again hated in the fiancé of his sister confounding these two gentlemen, these two idlers, these two officers, in the same furious antipathy. Vain and puerile anger which I took with me into the woods already reclothed with those vague tints which would soon change to russet.

The swallows were assembling for their departure. As the hunting season had begun there was firing all around them, and frightened, they rose in a flight such as that by which the wild bird had escaped which I had thought to bring down some day.

Toward Saint-Saturnin, the hills were planted with vines whose grapes would soon be ripe for the vintage. I saw the stocks widowed of fruit, those which the hailstorms of the spring had destroyed in their flower. Thus had died on the spot, before being ripe, my vintage of intoxicating emotions, of sweet felicities, of burning ecstasies.

I felt a gloomy and indefinable pleasure in seeking everywhere in the country some symbol of my sentiment, since I was, for a short time, purified from all calculation by the alchemy of grief.

If I was ever a true lover and given up to regrets, memories and despairs, it was in those days which must be the last of my stay at Aydat. In fact, the marquis announced his intention to hasten his departure. He had abdicated his hypochondria, and he cheerfully said to me:

"I adore my future son-in-law. I wish that you could know him. He is loyal, he is brave, he is good, he is proud. True gentlemanly blood in his veins. Do you understand the women? Here is one who is no sillier than the rest, is it not so? Two years ago he offered himself to her. She said no. Then my boy goes away to come back half-dead. And then it is yes. Do you know, I have always thought that there was some love-affair in her nervous malady. I knew it. I said to myself: she is in love with some one. It was he. And what if he had not wanted her, all the same?"

No, it was not M. de Plane whom Charlotte had loved that winter; but she had loved, that was certain. Our existences had crossed at one point, like the two roads which I saw from my window, the one which descends the mountains and goes toward the fatal Pradat woods, the other which leads toward the Puy de la Rodde.

I happened to see, at the close of the day the carriages following these two roads. After almost grazing each other, they were lost in opposite directions. Thus were our destinies separated forever. The Baroness de la Plane would live in the world, at Paris, and that represented to me a whirlpool of unknown and fascinating sensations.

I knew too well my future life. In thought, I awoke again in the little room of the Rue du Billard. In thought I followed the three streets which it is necessary to take to go from there to the Faculty. I entered the palace of the Academy, built in red brick, and I reached the *salle des conferences*[4] with its bare walls garnished with blackboards. I listened to the professor analyzing some author on license or admission. That lasted an hour and a half, then I returned, my *serviette*[5] under my arm, through the cold streets of the old town, for it was necessary for me to pass still another year, as I had not studied hard enough to submit to my examination with success.

I should continue to go and come among these dark houses, with this horizon of snowy mountains, to see the father and mother of Emile sitting at their window and playing at cards, the old Limasset reading his paper in the corner of the Café de Paris, the omnibuses of Royat at the corner of Jaude.

Yes, I come down to that, my dear master, to this misery of minds

---

4. *Salle des conferences* is French for conference room.

5. *Serviette* is a French term for a briefcase.

without psychology which attach themselves to the external form of life without penetrating its essence. I disregarded my old faith in the superiority of science, to which only three square meters of room are necessary in order that a Spinoza or an Adrien Sixte may there possess the immense universe.

Ah! I was very mediocre in that period of powerless desires and conquered love! I detested, and with what injustice, that life of abstract study which I was about to resume! And how I wish today that this might be my fate, and that I might awake a poor student near the Faculty of Clermont, tenant of the father of Emile, pupil of old Limasset, the morose traveler through those black streets—but an innocent man! An innocent man! And not the man who has gone through what I have gone through, and which he finds it a necessity to tell.

§ VI. THE THIRD CRISIS

TOWARD THE END of this severe month of September, Lucien complained of not being quite well, which the doctor attributed at first to a simple cold. Two days after the symptoms became aggravated. Two physicians of Clermont, called in haste, diagnosed scarlet fever, but of a mild character.

If my mind had not been entirely absorbed by the fixed idea which made of me at this period a veritable monomaniac, I should have found material enough to fill my notebook. I had only to follow the evolutions of the mind of the marquis and the struggle in his heart between hypochondria and paternal love.

Sometimes, in spite of the reassuring words of the doctors, he became so uneasy about his son that he passed the night in watching him. Sometimes he was seized with the fear of contagion; he went to bed, complained of imaginary pains, and counted the hours until the visit of the physician. Sometimes, so grave did his symptoms seem to himself, that the marquis must have the first visit. Then he would be ashamed of his panic. He arose, he chastised himself for his terrors with bitter phrases on the feebleness which age brings, and returned to the bedside of his son. His first intention was to conceal from the marquise and Charlotte and André the illness of the child; but after two weeks, these alternations of zeal and of terror having exhausted his energy, he felt the need of having his wife with him to sustain him, and the incoherence of his ideas was so great that he consulted me:

"Do you not think it is my duty?"

There are some lying souls, my dear master, who excel in excusing by fine motives their most villainous actions. If I were of this number I could make a merit of having insisted that the marquis should not recall his wife. Surely I knew the full import of my response and of the resolution that M. de Jussat was about to take. I knew that, if he informed the marquise, she would arrive by the first train, and I also knew Charlotte well enough to be assured that she would come with her mother. I should see her again, I should have a supreme opportunity to reawaken in her the love of which I had surprised the proof. I could say that it was loyalty on my part, the advice to leave Mme. de Jussat in Paris. I should have the appearance of loyalty. Why? If I were not convinced that there is no effect without a cause and no loyalty without a secret egoism, I should recognize a horror in using to the profit of a culpable passion the noblest of sentiments, that of a sister for a brother.

Here is the naked truth: in trying to dissuade M. de Jussat, I was convinced that all effort to regain the heart of Charlotte would be useless. I foresaw in this return only certain humiliation. Worn out by these long months of internal struggle, I no longer felt the strength to maneuver. There was then no virtue in representing to the marquis the inconveniences, the dangers even, of the stay of these two women in the château, near an invalid who might communicate to them his disease.

"And how about me?" responded he ingenuously, "am I not exposed every day? But you are right for Charlotte; I will write that I do not want her."

"Ah! Greslou," said he two days after, on the receipt of a telegram, "see what they do—read." He handed me the dispatch which announced the arrival of Mlle. de Jussat and her mother. "Naturally," moaned the hypochondriac, "she wanted to come, without thinking that I should lie spared such emotions."

The marquis spoke to me in this way at two o'clock in the afternoon. I knew that the train left Paris at nine o'clock in the evening and arrived at Clermont toward five in the morning. Mme. de Jussat and Charlotte would be at the château before ten o'clock. I passed a fearful evening and night, deprived now of that philosophic tension, outside of which I float, a creature without energy, the sport of nervous and irresistible impressions.

Good sense, however, indicated a very simple solution. My engagement would end the 15th of October. It was now the 5th. The child was convalescent. He had his mother and his sister with him. I could return home without any scruple and under any pretext. I could do it and I must—for the sake of my dignity as well as for my repose.

In the morning, I had taken this resolution and I was going to speak about it to the marquis immediately; he did not let me say a word, he was so agitated by the arrival of his daughter: "Very well," said he, "by and by, I have no head for anything now. This willfulness! That is why I have grown old so fast. Always new shocks!"

Who knows? My destiny may have entirely depended on the humor by which this old fool refused to hear me. If I had spoken to him at that moment, and if we had fixed my departure, I should have been obliged to have gone; instead, the sole presence of Charlotte changed the project of going into a project of remaining, as a lamp carried into a room immediately changes this darkness into light. I repeat it, I was convinced that she had absolutely ceased to be interested in me on the one hand, and, on the other, that I was passing through a crisis, not of genuine love, but of wounded vanity, and of morbid brooding.

Ah, well! To see her descend from the carriage before the *perron*, to see that my presence overcame her, as hers affected me, I understood two things: first, that it would be physically impossible for me to leave the château while she should be there; then that she had passed through trouble similar to mine, if not worse. She must have fled from me with the most sincere courage, not to have replied to my letters, not to have read them, to have become betrothed in order to place an insurmountable barrier between us, to have believed even that she no longer loved me, and to have returned to the château with this persuasion.

She loved me!

I had no need of a detailed analysis like those in which I was too complaisant and in which I was so much deceived, to recognize this fact. It was an intuition, sudden, unreasoning, invincible, one to make me believe that the theories in the double life, so much discussed by Science, are absolutely true.

I read it, this unhoped-for love, in the troubled eyes of this child, as your read the words by which I am trying to reproduce here the lightning and the thunderbolt of this evidence.

She was before me in her traveling costume, and white, white as this sheet of paper. I should have explained this pallor by the fatigue of the night passed in the carriage, and by her uneasiness at her brother's illness. Her eyes, in meeting mine, trembled with emotion. That might be offended modesty? She had fallen away, and when she took off her cloak I saw that her dress, a dress which I recognized, was wrinkled around the shoulders.

Ah! I, who had believed so strongly in the method, the inductions, and the complications of reasoning, how I felt the omnipotence of instinct against which nothing could provide.

She had loved me all the time. She loved me more than ever. What matter that she had not given me her hand at our first meeting; that she had scarcely spoken to me in the vestibule; that she went up the grand staircase with her mother without turning her head?

She loved me. This certainty, after so long a period of doubt and anxiety, inundated my heart with a flood of joy, so that I was almost overcome, there, on the carpet of the staircase which I must also climb to go to my room. What was I to do? With my elbows on the table and pressing my hands against my forehead to repress the throbbing of my temples I put this question without finding any other answer than that I could not go away; that absence and silence could not end all between Charlotte and myself; finally that we were approaching an hour in which so many reciprocal efforts, hidden struggles, combated desires on the part of both, was precipitating us toward a supreme scene, and this, I could feel was near, tragic, decisive, inevitable.

At first Charlotte was constrained to submit to my presence. We must meet at the bedside of her brother, and the very morning of her arrival, when it was my turn to keep the invalid company, toward eleven o'clock, I found her there talking with him, while the marquise questioned Sister Anaclet, both speaking in low tones and standing near the window.

Lucien, from whom the coming of his mother and sister had been concealed, showed in his face and in his gestures the excited and almost feverish joy which is seen in convalescents; he saluted me with his gayest smile, and taking my hand said to his sister:

"If you only knew how good M. Greslou has been to me all these days!"

She did not reply, but I saw that her hand, which lay on the pillow near her brother's cheek, shook as with a chill. She made an effort to look at me without betraying herself. Without doubt my face expressed an emotion that touched her. She felt that to leave unnoticed the innocent remark of her brother would make me feel badly, and, in the voice of past days, her sweet and living voice, she said, without addressing me directly:

"Yes, I know it and I thank him for it. We all thank him very much."

She did not add another word. I am sure that if I had taken her hand at that moment she would have fainted before me, she was so moved by this simple conversation.

I stammered a vague response: "It is quite natural," or something similar. I was not very collected myself. Lucien, however, who had noticed neither the altered tone of his sister, nor my embarrassment, continued:

"And isn't André coming to see me?"

"You know he has gone back to his regiment," said she.

"And Maxime?" insisted the child. I knew that this was the name of the fiancé of Mlle. de Jussat. These two syllables had no sooner left the lips of her brother than the paleness of her face gave way to a sudden wave of blood. There was an interval of silence during which I could hear the murmuring of Sister Anaclet, the crackling of the fire in the chimney, the swinging of the pendulum, and the child himself astonished at this silence.

"Yes, Maxime, is not he coming either?"

"M. de Plane has also gone back to his regiment," said Charlotte.

"Are you going away already, M. Greslou?" asked Lucien as I rose brusquely.

"I am coming back," I replied; "I have forgotten a letter on my table." And I went out, leaving Lucien with a smile on his face, and Charlotte with her eyes cast down.

Ah! My dear master, you must believe what I am telling you; in spite of the incoherencies of a heart almost unintelligible to itself, you must not doubt my sincerity in that moment. I have so great need not to doubt it myself; need to say to myself that I was not lying then.

There was not an atom of voluntary comedy in the sudden movement by which I rose at the simple mention of the name of the man to whom Charlotte ought to belong, to whom she did belong. There was no comedy in the tears which burst from my eyes, as soon as I passed the threshold of the door, nor in those which I wept during the night which followed, in despair at this double and frightful certainty that we loved one another, and that never, never, could we be anything one to the other; no comedy in the starts of pain which her presence inflicted on me during the days which followed. Her pale face, her emaciated profile, her suffering eyes were there to disturb me, and this pallor rent my soul, and this spare outline of her body made me love her more, and those eyes besought me.

"Do not speak. I know that you are unhappy too. It would be cruel to reproach me, to complain, to show your hurt."

Tell me, if I had not been sincere in those days, would I have let them pass without acting, when their hours were counted? But I do not recall a single reflection, a single combination. I do recall confusing sensations, something burning, frantic, intolerable, a prostrating neuralgia of my inmost being, a lancination continuous, and growing, growing always, the dream of putting an end to it, a project of suicide.

You see that I truly loved, since all my subtleties were melted in the flame of this passion, as lead in a furnace; since I did not find material for analysis in what was a real alienation, an abdication of my old self in this martyrdom. This thought of death came from the inmost depths of my being, this obscure appetite for the grave of which I was possessed as of physical thirst and hunger, in which, my dear master, you will recognize a necessary consequence of this disease of love, so admirably studied by you.

This instinct of destruction, of which you point out the mysterious awaking at the same time as that of sex, was turned against myself. This was shown first by an infinite lassitude, the lassitude of feeling much but never expressing anything. For the anguish in Charlotte's eyes, when they met mine, defended her better than all words could have done.

Besides, we were never alone, except sometimes for a few minutes in the salon, by chance, and these minutes passed in a silence which we could not break. To speak at such times is as impossible as for a paralytic to move his feet. A superhuman effort would not suffice. One experiences how emotion, to a certain degree of intensity, becomes incommunicable.

One feels himself imprisoned, walled up in his self, and he would like to get away from this unhappy self, to plunge, to lose himself in the coldness of death is where all ended.

That continued with a kind of delirious desire to make on the heart of Charlotte an imprint which could not be effaced, with an insane desire to give her some proof of love, against which neither the tenderness of her future husband nor the magnificence of her social surroundings, could ever prevail.

If I die of despair at being separated from her forever, she must remember the simple preceptor, the poor provincial, capable of sentiments so powerful!

It seems to me that I formulated these reflections. You notice that I say: "It seems to me." For in truth, I did not comprehend myself at that period. I did not recognize myself in the fever of violence and of tragedy by which I was consumed. Scarcely do I discern in this ungovernable come-and-go of my thoughts a kind of auto-suggestion, as you say. I was hypnotized, and it was as a somnambulist that I determined to kill myself at such a day, at such an hour, as I was going to the druggist to procure the fatal bottle of *nux vomica*.

During all these preparations and under the influence of this resolution, I hoped for nothing, I calculated nothing. A force entirely foreign to my own consciousness was acting on me. At no time was I the spectator of my gestures, my thoughts and my actions, with an exterior of the acting "I" in relation to the thinking "I." But I have written a note upon this point, which you will find on the fly leaf, in my exemplar of the book of Brière de Boismont[1] on suicide.

I experienced in these preparations an indefinable sensation of a waking dream, of lucid automatism. I attribute these strange phenomena to a nervous disorder, almost a madness, caused by the ravages of a fixed idea. It was only on the morning of the day chosen for the execution of my project that I thought of making a last attempt to win Charlotte.

I sat down at my table to write her a letter of farewell. I saw her reading this letter, and this question suddenly presented itself to me: *What would she do?* Was it possible that she might not be moved by this announcement of my intended suicide? Would she hasten to prevent it? Yes, she would run to my room and find me dead. At least, should I not wait for the effect of this

---

1. Alexandre Jacques François Brière de Boismont (1797–1881) was a French physician and psychiatrist. He published a comprehensive study on suicide, titled *Du suicide et de la folie suicide*, in 1856.

last proof?

Here I am very sure that I saw myself clearly. I know that hope was born in me exactly in this way and precisely at this point of my project. *Ah, well!* said I, *I will try.*

I resolved that if, at midnight, she had not come, I would drink the poison. I had studied the effects of it, and hoped I should not suffer very long.

It is strange that all that day was passed in a singular serenity. I was as if relieved of a weight, as if really detached from myself, and my anxiety commenced only toward ten o'clock, when, having retired first, I had placed the letter on the table in the room of the young girl.

At half-past ten I heard through my partly-open door the marquis, the marquise and Charlotte ascending the stairs. They stopped to talk a few minutes in the passage, then there were the customary goodnights, and each entered a separate chamber.

Eleven o'clock—a quarter-past eleven.

Still nothing.

I looked at my watch, placed in front of me, near three letters prepared for M. de Jussat, for my mother, and for you, my dear master.

My heart beat as if it would burst; but I wish you to note that my will was firm and cool. I had told Mlle. de Jussat that she would not see me the next day. I was sure of not failing my word if—I did not dare to strengthen what hope this "if" contained.

I watched the second-hand go round and I made a mechanical calculation, an exact multiplication: *at sixty seconds a minute, I shall see the hand go round so many times, for at midnight I shall kill myself.*

A noise of furtive and light steps on the stairs, which I perceived with supreme emotion, interrupted my calculation. These steps approached. They stopped before my door. Suddenly the door was opened. Charlotte was before me. I arose.

We rested thus face to face, both standing. Her face was distorted by the shock of her own action, very pale, and her eyes shone with an extraordinary brilliancy, nearly black, so dilated was the pupil by emotion, almost covering the iris.

I noticed this detail because it transformed her physiognomy. Ordinarily so reserved, her face betrayed the wildness of a being ruled by a passion stronger than her will. She must have lain down, then arose again, for her hair was braided in a large plait instead of being knotted on her head. A white *robe-de-chambre*, fastened by a cord and tassel was folded around her form, and in her haste she had slipped her bare feet into her slippers without thinking.

Evidently an insupportable anguish had precipitated her from her chamber into my room. She did not care what I might think of her nor what I might be tempted to say. She had read my letter, and she came, a prey to an excitement so intense that she did not tremble.

"Ah!" said she in a broken voice after the silence of the first minute. "God be praised, I am not too late. Dead! I believed you were dead! Ah! That is horrible! But that is all over, is it not? Say that you will obey me, say that you will not kill yourself. Ah! Swear, swear it to me."

She took my hand in hers with a supplicating gesture. Her fingers were like ice. There was something so decisive in this entrance, such a proof of love in a moment in which I was so excited that I did not reflect, and, without replying to her, I took her in my arms, weeping, my lips sought her lips, and through the most scalding tears I gave her the most loving, the most sincere kisses; that was a moment of infinite ecstasy, of supreme felicity, and as she drew away from me, with the shame at what she had permitted depicted on her face, always wild.

"Wretched creature that I am!" said she, "Ah! I must go away! Let me go away! Do not come near me."

"You see that I must die," I responded, "for you do not love me, you are going to be the wife of another, we shall be separated, and forever."

I took the dark vial from the table and showed it to her by the light of the lamp.

"Only a fourth of this flask," I continued, "and it is the remedy for much suffering. In five minutes it will be ended," and gently and without making a single gesture that would force her to defend herself. "Go away now, and I thank you for having come. Before a quarter of an hour I shall have ceased to feel what I am feeling now, this intolerable privation of you for so many months. Come, *adieu*, do not take away my courage."

She had trembled when the flame had lighted up the black liquid. She extended her hand and snatched the flask away, saying: "No! No!" She looked at it, read the inscription on the red label and trembled. Her countenance became still more changed. A wrinkle hollowed itself between her eyebrows. Her lips trembled. Her eyes expressed the agony of a last anxiety, then, in a voice almost harsh, jerking her words as if they were drawn from her by a torturing and irresistible power.

"I, too," said she, "I have suffered much, I have struggled hard. No," she continued, advancing toward me and taking me by the arm, "you must not go alone, not alone. "We will die together. After what I have done, it is all that is left." She put the vial to her lips, but I took it away from her, and with a smile almost insane she continued: "To die, yes, to die here, near you, with you," and she approached again, laying her head on my shoulder, so that I felt her soft hair against my cheek. "So! Ah! It is a long time that I have loved you, so long I can tell you the truth now, since I shall pay for it with my life. You will take me with you, we will go away together, both of us."

"Yes! yes," I answered, "we will die together. I swear it to you. But not immediately. Ah! Leave me time to feel that you love me." Our lips were again united, but this time she returned my kisses. Ah! Those were kisses in which the ecstasy of the senses and of the soul were deliciously confounded, in which the past, the present, the future were abolished to give place to love alone, to the painful, the intoxicating madness of love. This frail body, this living statuette of Tanagra[2] was mine in its grace and innocence, and it seemed to me that this hour was not real, it so far surpassed my hopes, almost my desire.

In the softened light of the lamp and of the half-extinguished fire, the delicacy of her features, her consummate pallor, her disordered hair, made her seem an apparition, and it was with a phantom's voice, a voice beyond life, that she spoke to me, relating the long history of her sentiments for me.

She said that she had loved at the first look and without suspecting it;

---

2. Tanagra figurines were a mold-cast type of Greek terracotta produced during the latter half of the fourth century BC, primarily in the town of Tanagra, depicting everyday women. In the nineteenth century, these figures became part of the visual imagination of Europe.

then how she had suffered at my sadness and at my confidence; how she had dreamed of being my friend, a friend who would gently console me; then the fearful light which my declaration in the forest had suddenly thrown upon her heart, and that she had sworn to put an abyss between us.

She recounted her struggles when she received my letters, and her vain resolutions not to read them, and the folly of her engagement in order that all might be irremediable, and her return, and the rest. She found, to reveal to me the secret and cruel romance of her tenderness, phrases modest and impassioned, which fell from the mysterious brim of the soul as tears fall from the brim of the eyes. She said: "I could not if I wished efface these griefs, so much do I need to feel that I have lived for you." She said: "You will let me die first, that I may not see you suffer." And she wrapped me in her hair, and upon her face which I had known so controlled was a kind of ecstasy of martyrdom, a supernatural joy mingled with a profound grief, an exaltation mingled with remorse.

When she was silent, clasped in my arms, absorbed in me, we could hear the wind which moaned outside the closed windows, and this sleeping chateau, in its peaceful silence, was already the tomb, the tomb toward which we were going, drawn out of life by the ardor of love which had thus thrown us heart to heart.

It is here, my dear master, where comes the most singular episode of this adventure, the one which men will call the most shameful; but for you and me these words have no meaning, and I will have the courage to tell you all.

I had been sincere, and sincere without the shadow of calculation, in the resolution of suicide which caused me to buy the *nux vomica*, and then to write to Charlotte. When she had come, when she had fallen into my arms and cried: "Let us die together!" I responded: "Let us die together," with the most perfect good faith. It had appeared so simple, so natural, so easy for us to go away together. You, who have written some strong pages upon the vapor of illusion created in us by physical causes, which is like that intoxication produced by wine, you will not judge me a monster for having felt this vapor dissipate, this intoxication disappear with possession.

Charlotte had placed her head on my breast and she fell asleep, exhausted by the excess of her emotions. I looked at her and I felt, without knowing how, that I fell back from my state before this happiness, to the reflective, philosophic, and lucid one which had been mine, and which a sorcery had metamorphosed into another.

I looked at Charlotte, and thought that in a few hours this adorable body, animated at this moment by all the ardors of life, would be immovable, cold, dead—dead this mouth which trembled still with my kiss, dead these beautiful eyes shaded under their trembling lids, dead this mind filled with me, intoxicated of me!

I repeated mentally several times this word: *dead, dead, dead*, and what it represents of a sudden falling into the night, of an irreparable fall into the darkness, the cold, the emptiness, oppressed my heart.

This entrance into the gulf without bottom of annihilation which had seemed, not only easy, but profoundly desirable when the fury of unfortunate love dominated me—suddenly, and this fury once appeased, appeared to me the most formidable of actions, the most foolish, the most impossible of execution. Charlotte continued to keep her eyes closed. The emaciation of her poor face, rendered more perceptible by the way in which the softened light revealed her features, told too plainly what she had felt for days. And I was going to kill her, or at least, to assist her to destroy herself. We were about to kill ourselves.

A shudder ran through me at the thought, and I was afraid. For her? For myself? For both? I do not know. I was afraid, afraid of feeling to grow numb in my most secret being, the soul of my soul, the indefinable center of all our energy. And suddenly by a sudden facing about of ideas like to that of the dying who throw a last look upon their existence, and who perceive, in the mirage of a secret regret, the joys known or coveted, the vision was evoked of that life, all thought of which I had turn by turn desired and abjured.

I saw you in your little cell, my dear master, in meditation, and the universe of intelligence developed before me the splendor of its horizons. My personal works, this brain of which I had been so proud, this Self cultivated so complaisantly, I was about to sacrifice all these treasures.

"To your pledged word," ought I to have responded? "To a caprice of excitement," I did respond. Strictly, this suicide had a signification, when to be forever separated from Charlotte filled me with despair. But now? We love each other, we belong to each other. Who can prevent us, young and free, from fleeing together, if on the next day we cannot endure separation? This hypothesis of an elopement brought before my mind the image of Count André. Why not make a note of this also? An exhilarating titillation of self-love ran through my heart at this souvenir.

I looked at Charlotte again, and I felt filled with the most ferocious pride. The rivalry instituted by my secret envy between her brother and myself awoke again in a start of triumph. There is a celebrated proverb which says that all animals are sad after pleasure: "*Omne animal.*"[3] It was not sadness that I felt then, but an absolute drying up of my tenderness, a rapid return—rapid as the action of a chemical precipitation—to a state of mind anterior.

I do not believe that this displacement of sensibility could have taken more than half an hour. I continued to regard Charlotte, while abandoning myself to these passage of ideas, with the delight of a reconquered liberty.

The fullness of the voluntary and reflective life flowed in me now, as the water of a river whose dam has been raised. The passion for this absent child had raised up a barrier against which the flood of my old sentiment was dammed up. This barrier thrown down, I became myself again. She was sleeping. I heard her light, equal breath, then suddenly a great sob, and she awoke:

"Ah!" said she, pressing me to her in a convulsive fashion, "you are here, you are here. I had lost consciousness. I dreamed. Ah! What a dream! I saw my brother come toward you. Oh! The horrible dream!"

She kissed me again, and, as her mouth was pressed to mine, the clock struck. She listened and counted the strokes.

"Four o'clock," said she, "it is time—farewell, my love, farewell."

She embraced me again. Her face had become calm in her exaltation, almost smiling. "Give me the poison," said she in a firm voice.

---

3. "*Omne animal*" is Latin for "every animal." The full proverbial phrase is *triste est omne animal post coitum, præter mulierem gallumque* (after sexual intercourse every animal is sad, both the cock (rooster) and the woman) is attributed to Galen of Pergamum (129–c. 216 AD), a Greek physician and philosopher.

I remained immovable without answering.

"You are afraid for me," she resumed; "I shall know how to die. Give it to me." I rose, still without replying. She sat up and clasped her hands without looking at me. Was she praying? Was this the last effort of this soul to extract the love of life which pushes its roots so deeply in a creature of twenty years?

My resolution to prevent this double suicide was now absolute. I had the coolness to seize the brown vial from the table and carry it to a wardrobe and lock it. These preparations of which she took no notice no doubt seemed long to Charlotte, for she turned toward me:

"I am ready," said she.

She saw my empty hands. The ecstatic expression changed to one of extreme anguish, and her voice grew harsh as she said:

"The poison! Give me the poison!" Then as if responding to a thought which suddenly came to her mind, she added feverishly: "No, it is not possible."

"No," cried I, falling on my knees before her, and seizing her hands. "No, you are right, it is not possible. I cannot let you die before me, for I should be your assassin. I pray you, Charlotte, do not ask me to realize this fatal project. When I bought the poison I was mad, I thought that you did not love me. I wished to kill myself. Oh! How sincerely! But now that you do love me, that I know it, that you have given yourself to me, no I cannot, I will not. Let us live, my love, let us live, consent to live. We will go away together, if you will. And if you will not, if you repent of this confession of your regard, well! I will suffer the martyrdom; but, I swear to you, this shall be as if it had never been—I will not trouble your life. But to help you to die, to kill yourself, you so young, so fair, oh no, no, do not ask me to do it."

How many times I spoke thus to her, I do not know. I saw on her face a sweet emotion, a woman's feebleness, the "yes" of the look which gives the lie to the "no" of the mouth. She was silent, then she fixed her eyes on me, and now they were bright with a tragic fire. She had withdrawn her hands from mine, crossed her arms upon her breast, and with her hair falling all around her, as if withdrawn from me by an invincible horror, she said, when I had ceased to supplicate her:

"So you will not keep your word?"

"No," I stammered, "I cannot. I cannot. I did not know what I said."

"Ah!" said she with a cruel disdain on her beautiful lips, "but tell me then that you are afraid! Give me the poison. I will give you back your word. I will die alone. But to have drawn me thus into the snare, you coward! Coward! Coward!"

Why did I not spring up under this outrage, why did I not take the bottle of poison, why did I not put it to my lips there before her and say: "See if I am a coward?" I do not understand why I did not when I think of it, when I remember the implacable contempt printed on her face. It must be that I was afraid, I who would now go to the scaffold without trembling, I who have had the courage to be silent for three months, thus risking my life. But now an idea sustains me, coldly, intellectually conceived while during that frightful scene there was a confusion of all the forces of my mind, between my surcharged sensations of the last months and those of the present hour, and, sitting down on the carpet, as if I had no longer energy enough to hold myself up, I shook my head, and said: "No, no."

This time it was she who did not respond. I saw her mass her beautiful hair and twist it into a knot; put her feet into her slippers, and wrap her white robe around her. She sought with her eyes for the dark flask with the red label, and, seeing it no longer on the table, she walked toward the door, then, without even turning her head, she disappeared after darting at me the terrible word: "Coward! Coward!"

I remained there a long time. Suddenly a frightful uneasiness seized my heart. If Charlotte, exasperated as she was, should attempt her life! A prey to the terrors of this new anguish, I dared to cross the corridors and go down the stairs to her room, and then, putting my ear against the door, I heard a noise, a moaning, a sign of what drama was being acted behind this thin rampart of wood which I could have burst open with my shoulder quickly enough to bring help.

The first noises of the château were rising from the basement. The servants were getting up. I must go back to my room. At six o'clock I was in the garden under the young girl's window.

My imagination had shown me Charlotte, throwing herself from the window, and lying dead on the ground with her limbs broken. I saw her shutters closed, and below, the platband in order with its line of rose bushes on which bloomed the last roses of the autumn.

She had told me, this night, of the charm which she tasted, in her hours of distress, when she loved me in silence, in leaning above this bed of roses and inhaling the aroma of these sweet flowers, spread on the breeze.

I picked one, and its perfume almost made me faint.

To deceive an anxiety which each moment made more intense, I walked straight on, into the country bathed in vapor, in this gray morning of November. I went very far, since I passed the village of Saulzet-le-Froid, and yet, at eight o'clock, I was back taking my breakfast, or seeming to do so, in the dining-room of the château.

This was the time, I knew, for the maid to go into Mlle. de Jussat's room. If anything had happened this girl would call out immediately. With what inexpressible comfort I saw her come down and go toward the kitchen with the *salver*[4] prepared for the tea!

Charlotte had not taken her life.

Hope returned to me then. Upon reflection, and her first feeling of anger passed, perhaps she would interpret as a proof of love my refusal to die and to let her die. I should know that also. It would be sufficient to wait for her in her brother's room. The little invalid was at the end of his convalescence, and, though deprived of walks, he displayed the gaiety of a child about to be born again into life.

He received me with all sorts of pretty ways, and his gracious humor redoubled my hope. He would break the ice between his sister and me. The hands of a young man and of a young girl join so easily when they touch around an innocent and curly head.

But when Charlotte appeared, so white in a dress which brought out her paleness still more, pretending a headache to avoid the pranks of Lucien, the eyes burning with fever, I understood that I had believed too readily in a possible reconciliation.

I saluted her. She found a way to not even respond to my salutation.

---

4. *Salver* is a French term for a flat heavy tray of silver, other metal or glass.

I had known three persons in her already; the creature tender, delicate, compassionate, the young girl easily startled, the lover impassioned almost to ecstasy. I saw now upon this noble visage the coldest, the most impenetrable mark of contempt.

Ah! The old and banal formula: the patrician pride—I was able to account for it and that certain silences kill as surely as the headman's ax. This impression was so bitter that I could not resign myself to it. This very day I watched to have a word with her, and, at the moment when she was going to her room toward the close of the afternoon, to dress herself for dinner, I went to her on the stairs. She put me by with a gesture so haughty, with so cruel a "Monsieur, I do not know you any longer!" upon her trembling lips, a look so indignant in her eyes that I could not find a word to say to her.

She had judged me and I was condemned. Yes, condemned. She despised me for my fear of death; and it was true, I had felt that cowardly chill before the black hole, while she dared face the worst. I certainly had the right to say to myself that this alone would not have arrested me before the suicide of both, if pity for her had not been joined with it and my ambition as a thinker. No matter. She had given herself to me under one condition, and to this tragic condition I had responded "yes" before, and "no" after. Ah, well. She scorned me, but she had been mine. I had held her in my arms, these arms, and I was the first to kiss those lips.

Yes, I suffered cruelly between this night and my definite departure from the house. However, it was not the arid and conquered despair of the summer, the total abdication in distress.

I retained at the bottom of my heart, I cannot say a happiness, but a something of satisfaction which sustained me in this crisis. When Charlotte passed me without noticing me any more than some object forgotten there by a servant, I contemplated her response to my declaration of love. For another experience of that happiness, perhaps, I would have accepted anew the fatal compact, with the cold resolve to keep it. But this happiness had none the less been true.

And was this love really, irremediably ended? In doing as she had done Mlle. de Jussat had proved a very deep passion. Was it possible that nothing remained of it in this romantic heart?

Today and in the light of the tragedy which ended this lamentable adventure, I comprehend that it was precisely this romantic character which prevented any return of love into this heart. She had loved in me a mirage, a being absolutely different from myself, and the sudden vision of my true nature having at a blow dispelled her illusions, she hated me with all the power of her old love.

Alas! With all my pretensions to the learned psychologist, I did not see the evolution of this mind, then I did not even suspect that she would seek at any price the means of knowing me better, and that she would go, in the distraction of her actual disgust, so far as to treat me as judges treat the accused; in fine that she would read my papers and would not recoil before any scruple.

I did not even know enough to guess that she was not the girl to survive such a shock as the revelation of my cold-blooded resolutions written in my notebook brought upon her, and I did not think to destroy the bottle of poison which I had refused to give her.

I believed myself to be a great observer because I reflected a great deal. The quibbles of my analysis concealed from me its falsity. It was not necessary to reflect at this period, but to observe. Instead, deceived by this reasoning which I have just gone over to you, and persuaded that Charlotte loved me still in spite of her contempt, I tried to recall this love by the most simple means, the most ineffective at that moment.

I wrote to her.

I found my letter on my bureau the same day, unopened. I went to her door at night and called to her. This door was locked and no one replied. I tried to stop her again. She waved me off with more authority than the first time, without looking at me.

Finally, the heartbreak of this continuous insult was stronger than the ardors of passion which had begun to kindle in me. On the evening of the day in which she had thus repulsed me, I wept much, then I resolved upon a definite course. A little of my old energy had returned, for it was needed for this part which I had undertaken.

The next week M. de Plane and Count André were coming. This would have decided me if I had still hesitated. Their presence, in this double and sinister disaster of my love and of my pride, no, I would not, I could not endure it.

This, then, is what I had decided: the marquis had asked me to prolong my stay until the 15th of November. It was now the 3rd. I announced, on the morning of this fatal 3rd of November, that I had just received from my mother a letter which made me a little uneasy; then in the forenoon, I said that a dispatch had still further increased my anxiety. I asked then of M. de Jussat permission to go to Clermont early the next day, adding that if I did not return, would he be so good as to box the articles I had left and send them to me. I held this conversation in the presence of Charlotte, assured that she would interpret it in its true significance: "He is going away not to return." I expected that the news of this separation would move her, and, wishing to profit by this emotion, I had the audacity to write to her another note, these two lines only:

"On the point of leaving you forever, I have the right to ask a last interview. I will come to you at eleven o'clock."

It was necessary that she should not return this note without reading it. I placed it open upon her table, at the risk of losing all if the chambermaid should see it. Ah! How my heart beat, when at five minutes to eleven o'clock, I took my way to her room and tried the door.

It was not bolted. She was waiting for me. I saw at the first glance that the struggle would be hard. Her somber countenance showed too plainly that she had not permitted me to come that she might forgive me. She wore a dark silk dress, and never had her eyes been more fixed, more implacably fixed and cold.

"Monsieur," said she as soon as I had shut the door, "I am ignorant of what you intend to say to me—I am ignorant of it and I do not wish to know. It is not to listen to you that I have allowed you to come. I swear to you, and I know how to keep my word—if you take a step toward me and if you try to speak to me without my permission, I will call and you shall be thrown from the window like a thief."

While speaking she had put her finger on the button of the electric bell. Her brow, her mouth, her gestures, her voice showed such resolution that I did not dare to speak. She continued: "You have, monsieur, caused me to commit very unworthy actions. The first has for excuse that I did not believe you capable of the infamy you have employed. Besides, I should have known how to expiate it," she added, as if speaking to herself. "The second. I do not look for any excuse." And her face became purple with shame. "It was too insupportable to think that you had acted thus. I wished to be sure of what you are. I wished to know. You had told me that you kept a journal. I desired to read it and I have done so. I went into your room when you were not there, and forced the lock of your notebook. Yes, yes, I did that! I have been punished, since I have read your infamous plans. The third. In telling you I acquit the debt which I have contracted with you by the second. The third," and she hesitated, "in my indignation, I wrote to my brother. He knows everything!"

"Ah!" cried I, "then you are lost."

"You know what I have sworn," she interrupted; and she put her finger again on the bell. "Be quiet. Nothing worse can befall me than has already happened," she continued, "and no one will do anything more for or against me. My brother will know that also, and what I have resolved. The letter will reach him tomorrow morning. I ought to warn you since you hold your life so dear. And now, go away."

"Charlotte," I implored.

"If in one minute you have not gone out," said she, looking at the clock, "I will call."

§ VII. CONCLUSION

AND I OBEYED!

The next day, at six o'clock I left the château, a prey to the most sinister presentiments, trying in vain to persuade myself that this scene would not be followed by some terrible effect; that Count André would arrive soon enough to save her from a desperate resolution; that she would hesitate at the last moment; that some unexpected thing would happen.

As to fleeing from the possible vengeance of the brother, I did not for a moment think of it. This time, I had resumed my character because I had an idea to sustain me, that of allowing no person to humiliate me any further. Yes, although I had faltered before a loving girl and in the weakness of happy love, I would not do so before the threat of a man.

I arrived at Clermont, devoured by an anxiety which did not last very long, for I learned of the suicide of Mlle. de Jussat and was arrested at the same moment.

From the first words of the Judge of Instruction I reconstructed all the details of the suicide: Charlotte had taken from the flask which I had bought as much as she thought sufficient to cause her death. She had done that on the very day she had read my journal, whose lock I found had been forced. I had not noticed it because my mind was so filled with other things than these sterile notes.

She had been careful, in order to turn away my suspicions, to replace with water the quantity of *nux vomica* thus taken. She had thrown the flask out of the window because she did not wish her father and mother to learn of her suicide excepting through her brother. And I, who know the whole truth of this horrible drama, who could at least give my journal as a presumption of my innocence, destroyed this journal after my first examination; I have refused to speak, to defend myself—because of this brother! I have told you, I have drained to the bottom the cup of humiliation and I will do no more.

This man whom I so much envied from the first day, this man who represents death to me now, and who, knowing the whole truth, must consider me the lowest of the low. I do not wish that he should have the right to quite despise me, and he has not the right. He does not because we both are silent. But this for me, is to risk my life in order to save the honor of the dead, and for him to sacrifice an innocent person to this honor.

Of us two, of me who will not defend myself by taking shelter behind the dead body of Charlotte, and of him who, having the letter which proves her suicide, keeps it, to avenge himself on the lover of his sister by allowing him to be condemned as an assassin, which is the brave man? Which is the gentleman? All the shame of my weakness—if there be any shame, I wipe out by not defending myself, and I feel a proud pleasure, as a revenge for those terrible last days, at not having killed myself, at not asking of death the oblivion of so many tortures.

Count André must also reach the bottom of his infamy. If I am condemned, he knowing me to be innocent, he having the proof of it, he keeping silent, ah well! The Jussat-Randons will have nothing with which to reproach me—we will be quits.

However, I have told all to you, my venerated, my dear master; I have opened my soul to you, and in confiding this secret to your honor, I know too well whom I am addressing even to insist upon the promise I have taken the liberty to exact on the first page of this memoir.

But, you see, I am stifled by this silence; I stifle with the weight which is always, always upon me. To say all in a word, and applied to my sensation, it is legitimate, I stifle with remorse. I want to be understood, consoled, loved; I want someone to pity me and say words to me which shall dissipate the phantoms, the evil spirits, the torturing phantoms.

I made out, when I began these pages, a list of questions which I wished to ask you at the end. I flattered myself that I could recount to you my history as you state your problems in psychology in your books which I have read so much, and now I find nothing to say to you only the word of despair: "*De profundis!*"

Write to me, my dear master, direct me. Strengthen me in the doctrine which was, which is still mine, in the conviction of universal necessity which wills that even our most detestable actions, even this cold enterprise in which

I embarked in the interest of science, even my weakness before the compact of death, are a part of the laws of this immense universe.

Tell me that I am not a monster, that there are no monsters, that you will, if I emerge from this supreme crisis, have me for your disciple, your friend. If you were a physician, and a sick man came to you, you would heal him for humanity's sake. You are a physician, a great physician of souls. Ah! Mine is badly hurt and bleeding. I pray you for a word to comfort me, a word, a single word, and you will be forever blessed by your faithful.

Robert Greslou

V.

TORMENT OF IDEAS

A MONTH HAD passed since the mother of Robert Greslou had brought into the hermitage of the Rue Guy de la Brosse the strange manuscript which Adrien Sixte had hesitated to read. And the philosopher, after these four weeks, was still the slave of the trouble inflicted by the reading, to such an extent that even his humble neighbors noticed it.

There were continual consultations between Mlle. Trapenard and the Carbonnets, in the lodging filled with its odor of leather, where the faithful servant and the judicious concierges discussed the cause of the strange change in the manners of the celebrated analyst.

The admirable, automatic regularity of his goings out and comings in, which had made him a living chronometer for the whole quarter, had been suddenly transformed into a febrile and inexplicable anxiety.

The philosopher, since the visit of Mme. Greslou, went and came, like one who cannot stay in any place, who, as soon as he goes out thinks he will return, and as soon as he has come in, cannot endure his room. In the street, instead of walking along with the methodical step which reveals a nervous machine perfectly balanced, he hurried on, he stopped, he gesticulated, as if disputing with himself. This enervation was betrayed by signs still more strange. Mlle. Trapenard had told to the Carbonnets that her master did not go to bed now, before two or three o'clock in the morning:

"And it is not because he is writing," insisted the good woman, "for he walks and walks. The first time I thought he was ill. I got up to ask him if he wished some infusion. He, who is always so polite, so gentle, that you would not suspect him to be a man who knows so much, he sent me away in a brutal manner."

"And I who saw him the other day," responded Mother Carbonnet, "as I was returning from a course at the cafe! I would not believe my eyes.

He was there, behind the window reading a paper. If I had not known him I should have been afraid. You ought to have seen him—that knit brow and that mouth."

"At the cafe!" cried Mlle. Trapenard. "For the fifteen years I have been with him I have never seen him open a paper but once."

"That man," concluded Father Carbonnet, "has some trouble which overheats his blood. And trouble you see. Mlle. Mariette, is, so to speak, like the tun of Adelaide, it has no bottom. For a fact, it commenced with the summons of the judge and the visit of the lady in black. And do you know what I think? Perhaps it is about a son of his who is doing badly."

"*Mon Dieu!*" exclaimed Mariette, "he has a son?"

"And why not?" continued the concierge, winking one eye behind his spectacles; "don't you think he gallivanted around like other folks when he was young?"

Then he communicated to Mlle. Trapenard the frightful reports which were going about in the *rez-de-chaussées*[1] concerning poor M. Sixte, since his visible change of habits. All the malicious tongues agreed in attributing the trouble of the philosopher to the citation of the judge. The washerwoman pretended to have it from a countryman of M. Sixte, that his fortune proceeded from a trust which his father had abused, and that he would have to return it. The butcher told those who would listen that the savant was married, and that his wife had made a terrible scene and was going to bring a suit against him. The coal merchant had insinuated that the worthy man was the brother of an assassin whose execution under the false name of Campi still tormented the popular mind.

"I will never go to their houses again," moaned Mlle. Trapenard; "is it possible to imagine such horrors!"

And the poor girl left the lodge completely heart-broken. This great creature, high in color, strong as an ox in spite of her fifty-five years, with her big shoulders, her blue wool stockings which she had herself knit, and her cap fitting closely over her compact chignon,[2] felt a strong affection for

1. *Rez-de-chaussées* is a French term for the ground story of a building along a street.

2. Chignon is a term for a knot or coil of hair arranged on the back of a woman's head.

her master because all the different elements of her frank and simple nature were involved in it.

She respected the gentleman, the educated man who was often mentioned in the papers. She cherished, in the old bachelor who never examined his accounts, and left her mistress of the house, an assured source of comfort for her old age. Finally, this solid and robust creature protected the man, feeble in body and so *simplet,*[3] as she said, that a child ten years old might have cheated him.

Such words mortified her pride at the same time that the sudden change of humor of the philosopher rendered their residence together uncomfortable. From genuine affection she became anxious because her master did not eat or sleep. She saw that he was sad, anxious, and ill, but she could do nothing to make him cheerful, nor even guess the cause of his melancholy and agitation.

What did she think when, one afternoon in the month of March, M. Sixte came in about five o'clock, after having had his breakfast outside, and said to her: "Is the valise[4] in good order, Mariette?"

"I do not know, monsieur. Monsieur has not used it since I came into the house."

"Go and get it," said the philosopher. Mariette obeyed. She brought from a loft which served as lumber-room and wood-house together a small, dusty-leather trunk, with rusty locks and keys entirely lacking.

"Very well," said M. Sixte, "you may go and buy a little one like that, immediately, and you may put into it whatever is necessary for a journey."

"Is monsieur going away?" asked Mariette.

"Yes," said the philosopher, "for a few days."

"But monsieur has nothing that he needs," insisted the old servant, "monsieur cannot go away like that, without any traveling rugs, without—"

"Procure what is needed," interrupted the philosopher, "and hasten—I take the train at nine o'clock."

"And is it necessary that I accompany monsieur?"

---

3. *Simplet* is French for simple, basic.

4. Valise is term for a small traveling bag or suitcase.

"No, that is useless," said M. Sixte, "come, you have no time to lose."

"Oh! If he only does not think of killing himself," said Carbonnet when Mariette had told of this new move, almost as extraordinary in this little corner of the world as if the philosopher had announced his marriage.

"Ah!" said the servant, following up his idea, "if he only would take me with him! If I have to pay out of my own pocket, I will go."

This sublime cry, in the mouth of a creature who had come from Péaugres in Ardèche, to be a servant and who carried economy so far as to make her home dresses from the old redingotes of the savant, will demonstrate better than any analysis what uneasiness the metamorphosis of this man who was passing through a moral crisis, which was terrible for him, inspired in these humble people.

Not realizing that he was observed, he showed the intensity of it in his slightest gestures as well as in the features of his face. Since the death of his mother he had not known such unhappy hours, and the suffering inflicted by the irreparable separation was entirely sentimental; but the reading of Robert Greslou's memoir had attacked him in the center of his being, his intellectual life, his sole reason for living.

At the moment he gave Mariette the order to prepare his valise, he was as much overcome by fright as on the night he turned over the pages of the notebook of confidences. This fright began from the first pages of this narrative in which a criminal aberration of mind was studied, as if spread out for display, with such a mixture of pride and of shame, of cynicism and of candor, of infamy and of superiority.

At meeting the phrase in which Robert Greslou had declared himself united to him by a cord as close as it was unbreakable, the great psychologist had trembled, and he had trembled at every repetition of his name in this singular analysis, at every citation of one of his works, which proved the right of this abominable libertine to call himself his pupil.

A fascination made up of horror and curiosity had constrained him to go straight through to the end of this fragment of biography in which his ideas, his cherished ideas, his science, his beloved science, appeared united with acts so shameful.

Ah! If they had been united! But no, these ideas, this science, the accused claimed them as the excuse, as the cause of the most monstrous, the most complaisant depravity! As he advanced into the manuscript he felt that a little of his inmost person became soiled, corrupted, gangrened; he found so much of himself in this young man, but a "himself" made up of sentiments which he detested the most in the world. For in this illustrious philosopher the holy virginities of conscience remained intact, and, behind the bold nihilism of mind, the noble heart of an ingenuous man was hidden.

It was in this inviolate conscience, in this irreproachable honesty, that the master of this felon preceptor felt himself suddenly lacerated. This sinister history of a love affair, so basely carried on, of a treason so black, of a suicide so melancholy, brought him face to face with the most frightful vision; that of his mind acting and corrupting, his, who had lived in voluntary renunciation, in daily purity.

The whole adventure of Robert Greslou showed to him the complexities of a hideous pride and of an abject sensuality, to him who had labored only to serve psychology, to him a modest worker in a labor which he believed beneficent, and in the most severe asceticism, in order that the enemies of his doctrines could not argue from his example against his principles.

This impression was the more violent as it was unexpected. A physician of large heart would experience an anguish of an analogous order if, having established the theory of a remedy, he learned that one of his assistants had tried the application of it, and that all in one ward of the hospital were in agony from its effects. To do wrong, knowing it and willing it, is very bitter to a man who is better than his deeds. But to have devoted thirty years to a work, to have believed this work useful, to have pursued it sincerely, simply, to have repelled as insulting the accusations of immorality thrown at him by his angry adversaries, and, suddenly, by the light of a frightful revelation, to hold an indisputable proof, a proof real as life itself, that this work has poisoned a mind, that it carries in it a principle of death, that it is spreading this principle to all the corners of the earth—ah! What a cruel shock, what a savage wound to receive, if the shock should last only an hour, and the wound be closed at once!

All revolutionary thinkers have known such hours of anguish. But most pass quickly through them, and for this reason it is rare for a man to be thrust into the battle of ideas without his becoming soon the comedian of his first sincerities. He sustains his role. He has partisans, and more than all he soon comes, by friction with life, to that conception of the *à peu près*[5] almost, which makes him admit, as inevitable, a certain falling away from his ideal. He says to himself that one does evil here, right elsewhere, and sometimes, that after all, the world and the people will always go the same.

With Adrien Sixte sincerity was too complete for any such reasoning to be possible. He had neither role to play nor faithful adherents to manage. He was alone. His philosophy, and he made only one, and the compromises by which all great fame is accompanied, had in no way impaired his fierce and proud mind.

We must add that he had found the means, thanks to his perfect good faith, of passing through society without ever seeing it. The passions which he had depicted, the crimes which he had studied, he saw as persons who designate medical observation, "A, thirty-five years, such profession, unmarried." And the exposition of the case is developed without a detail which gives to the reader the sensation of the individual.

Always the rigorous theorizer on the passions, the minute anatomist of the will, he had never fairly seen face to face a creature of flesh and blood; so that the memoir of Robert Greslou did not speak only to his consciousness as an honest man. So, during the eight days which followed the first reading, there was a continual obsession, and this increased the moral pain by uniting it with a sort of physical uneasiness.

The psychologist saw his ill-fated disciple as he had looked upon him here in this same room, with his feet on the same carpet, leaning his arms on this same table, breathing, moving.

Behind the words on the paper he heard that voice a little dull which pronounced the terrible phrase: "I have lived with your mind and of your mind, so passionately, so completely;" and the words of the confession, instead of being simple characters written with cold ink upon inert paper, became animated into words behind which he felt a living being: "Ah!" thought he when this image became too strong, "why did the mother bring

---

5. *à peu prés* is a French phrase meaning nearly, approximately.

this notebook to me?"

It would have been so natural for the unhappy woman, a prey to mad anxiety, to prove the innocence of her son by violating this trust. But no, Robert had without doubt deceived her with the hypocrisy of which he so boasted, the miserable fellow, as if it were a psychological conquest.

The haunting hallucination of the face of the young man would have sufficed to overcome Adrien Sixte. When the mother had cried: "You have corrupted my son," his learned serenity had been scarcely disturbed. In like manner, he had opposed only contempt to the accusation of the elder Jussat, repeated by the judge, and to the remarks of the latter on moral responsibility.

How tranquil he had gone out of the Palais de Justice! And now there was no more contempt in him; that serenity was conquered, and he, the negator of all liberty, he the fatalist who decomposed virtue and vice with the brutality of a chemist studying a gas, he the bold prophet of universal mechanism, and who until then had always experienced the perfect harmony of mind and heart, suffered with a suffering in contradiction to all his doctrines—he felt remorse, he felt himself responsible!

It was only after these eight days of the first shock, during which the memoir had been read and re-read, so that he could repeat all the phrases of it, that this conflict of heart and mind became clear to Adrien Sixte, and the philosopher tried to recover himself.

He walked to the Jardin des Plantes, one afternoon toward the end of February, an afternoon as mild as spring. He sat down on a bench in his favorite walk, that which runs along the Rue de Buffon, and at the foot of a Virginia acacia, propped up with crutches, adorned with plaster like a wall, and with knotty branches like the fingers of a gouty giant.

The author of *Psychology of God* loved this old trunk whose sap was all dried up because of the date inscribed on the placard and which constituted the civil status of the poor tree. "Planted in 1632." The year of the birth of Spinoza.

The sun of the early afternoon was very soft and this impression relaxed the nerves of the promenader. He looked around him absently, and was pleased to follow the movements of two children who were playing near their mother. They were collecting sand with little wooden shovels with which to build an imaginary house. Suddenly one of them rose up brusquely and struck his head against the bench which was behind him. He must have hurt himself, for his face contracted into a grimace of pain, and, before bursting into tears, there were the few seconds of suffocated silence which precede the sobs of children. Then, in a fit of furious rage, he turned to the bench and struck it furiously with his fist.

"Are you stupid, my poor Constant," said his mother to him, shaking him and drying his eyes; "come, let me wipe your nose," and she wiped it; "it will do you much good to be angry at a piece of wood."

This scene diverted the philosopher. When he rose to continue his walk under this pleasant sun, he thought of it for a long time.

I am like that little boy, said he to himself. *In his childishness, he gives life to an inanimate object, he makes it responsible. And what else have I been doing for more than a week?*

For the first time since the reading of the memoir, he dared to formulate his thought with the clearness which was the proper characteristic of his mind and of his works: *I have believed myself responsible for a part in this frightful adventure. Responsible? There is no sense in that word.*

While passing toward the gate of the garden, then in the direction of the Île Saint-Louis and toward Notre-Dame, he took up the detail of the reasoning against this notion of responsibility in *Anatomy of the Will*, above all his critique of the idea of cause.

He had always particularly held to this piece. *That is evident*, he concluded.

Then, after he was once more assured of the certainty of his own intellect, he constrained himself to think of the Robert Greslou, now a prisoner in cell number seven in the jail of Riom, and of the Robert Greslou formerly a young student of Clermont leaning over the pages of *Theory of the Passions* and of *Psychology of God*.

He felt anew an insupportable sensation that his books should have been thus handled, meditated upon, loved by this child.

But we are double! thought he. *And why this powerlessness to conquer illusions which we know to be false?*

All at once a phrase of the memoir came to his mind: *I have remorse, when the doctrines which form the very essence of my intelligence make me consider remorse as the most foolish of human illusions.*

The identity between his moral condition and that of his pupil appeared so hateful to him that he tried to get rid of it by new reasoning.

Ah, well! said he to himself, *let us imitate the geometrician, let us admit to be true what we know to be false. Let us proceed by absurdity. Yes, man is an agent and a free agent. Then he is responsible. Maybe. But when, where, how have I acted badly? Why do I have remorse because of this scoundrel? What is my fault?*

He returned, resolved to review his whole life. He saw himself a little child, working at his tasks with a minuteness of conscientiousness worthy of his father the clock maker. Then when he had begun to think, what did he love, what did he wish? The truth. When he had taken the pen, why did he write, to serve what cause, if not that of truth? To the truth he had sacrificed everything; fortune, place, family, health, love, friendship. And what did even Christianity teach, the doctrine the most penetrated by ideas different from his own? "Peace on earth, to men of good will," that is to those who have sought for the truth. Not a day, not an hour in all that past, which he scrutinized with the force of the most subtle genius put to the service of the most honest conscience, had he failed in the ideal programme of his youth formulated in this noble and modest device: "To say what he thought, to say only what he thought."

This is duty, for those who believe in duty, said he, *and I have fulfilled it.*

The night after this courageous meditation, this great, honest man slept at last and with a sleep that the remembrance of Robert Greslou did not trouble.

On awaking, Adrien Sixte was still calm. He was too well accustomed to study himself not to seek for a cause for this facing about of his impressions, and too sincere not to recognize the reason. This momentary lull of remorse must arise from the simple fact of having admitted as true some ideas upon the moral life which his reason condemned.

There are then beneficent ideas, and malevolent ideas, he concluded. *But what? Does the malevolence of an idea prove its falsity? Let us suppose that the death of Charlotte be concealed from the Marquis de Jussat, he is quieted by the idea that his daughter is living. The idea would be salutary to him. Would it be true for that reason? And inversely.*

Adrien Sixte had always considered as a sophism, as cowardly, the argument directed by certain spiritualistic philosophers against the fatal consequences of new doctrines, and generalizing the problem, he said again: *As is the mind so is the doctrine. The proof of it is that Robert Greslou has transformed religious practices into an instrument of his own perversity.*

He again took up the memoir to find the pages consecrated by the accused to his sentiments for the church, then he became again fascinated and reread this long piece of analysis, but giving particular attention this time to each passage in which his own name, his theories, his works were mentioned.

He applied all the strength of his mind to prove to himself that every phrase cited by Greslou had been justified by acts absolutely contrary to those which the morbid young man had justified by them.

This reperusal, attentive and minute, had the effect of throwing him into a new attack of his trouble.

With his magnificent sincerity, the philosopher recognized that the character of Robert Greslou, dangerous by nature, had met in his doctrines, as it were, a land where were developed his worst instincts, and that Adrien Sixte found himself radically powerless to respond to the supreme appeal made to him by his disciple from the depths of his dungeon.

Of all the memoir, the last lines touched the deepest chord. Although the word debt had not been pronounced, he felt that this unfortunate had a claim on him. Greslou said truly: a master is united to the mind that he has directed, even if he has not willed this direction, even if this mind has not rightly interpreted the teaching, by a sort of mystic cord, and one which does not permit of casting it to certain moral agony with the indifferent gesture of Pontius Pilate. Here was a second crisis, more cruel perhaps than the first. When he had been fully impressed by the ravages produced by his works, the savant became panic-stricken. Now that he was calm, he measured, with frightful precision the powerlessness of his psychology, however learned it might be, to handle the strange mechanism of the human soul.

How many times he began letters to Robert Greslou which he was unable to finish! What could he say to this miserable child? Must he accept the inevitable in the internal as well as in the external world—accept his mind as one accepts his body? Yes, was the result of all his philosophy. But in this inevitable there was the most hideous corruption in the past and in the present.

To advise this man to accept himself, with all the profligacy of such a nature, was to make himself an accomplice in this profligacy. But to blame him? In the name of what principle had he done it, after having professed that virtue and vice are additions, good and evil, social labels without value; finally that everything is of necessity in each detail of our being as well as in the whole of the universe.

What counsel could he give him for the future? By what counsel prevent this brain of twenty-two years from being ravaged by pride and sensuality, by unhealthy curiosity and depraving paradoxes? Would one prove to a viper, if it could comprehend reasoning, that it ought not to secrete venom? "Why am I a viper?" it would respond.

Seeking to state his thought with precision, Adrien Sixte compared the mental mechanism taken to pieces by Robert Greslou, with the watches which he had seen in his father's establishment. A spring goes, a movement follows, then another, and another. The hands move. If a single part were touched the whole would stop.

To change anything in the mind would be to stop life. Ah! If the mechanism could only modify its own wheels and their movement! But if the watchmaker take the watch to pieces and make it over again!

There are persons who turn from the evil to the good, who fall and rise again, who are cast down and are again built up in their morality. Yes, but there is the fallacy of repentance which presupposes the delusion of liberty and of a judge, of a Heavenly Father. Could he, Adrien Sixte, write to this young man: "Repent; cease to believe that which I have shown you to be true?"

And yet it was frightful to see a soul die without trying to do something to save it. At this point of his meditation the thinker was brought to a stand by the insoluble problem of the unexplained life of the soul, as desperate for the psychologist as is the unexplained life of the body for the physiologist.

The author of the book upon God and who had written this sentence:

"There is no mystery; there are only ignorances," refused the contemplation of the beyond, which, showing an abyss behind all reality, leads science to bow before the enigma and say: "I do not know, I shall never know," and which permits religion to interpose.

He felt his incapacity for doing anything for this young soul in distress, and who had need of supernatural aid. But to only speak of such a formula, with his ideas, was as foolish as to talk of squaring the circle, or of giving three right angles to a triangle.

A very simple event rendered this struggle more tragic by imposing the necessity for immediate action. An anonymous hand sent him a paper which contained an article of extreme violence against himself and his influence in regard to Robert Greslou. The writer, evidently inspired by some relation or some friend of the Jussats, branded modern philosophy and its doctrines, incarnated in Adrien Sixte and in several other savants.

Then he called up an example. In a final paragraph, improvised in the modern style, with the realism of imagery which is the rhetoric of today, as the poesy of the metaphor was that of the past, he showed the assassin of Mlle. de Jussat mounting the scaffold, and a whole generation of young decadents cured of their pessimism by this example.

In any other circumstances the great psychologist would have smiled at this declaration. He would have thought that the *envoi* came from his enemy Dumoulin, and resumed his work with the tranquility of Archimedes tracing his geometrical figures on the sand during the sack of the city. But in reading this chronicle, scribbled without doubt on the corner of a table in the Tortoni cafe by a moralist of the boulevard, he perceived one fact of which he had not thought, so much had the folly of abstraction withdrawn him from the social world: that this moral drama was becoming a real drama.

In a few weeks, perhaps in a few days, he of whose innocence he held the proof, would be judged. Now, according to the justice of men, the supposed assassin of Mlle. de Jussat was innocent; and if this memoir did not constitute a decisive proof, it offered an indisputable character of veracity which was sufficient to save a life.

Would he allow this head to fall, he, the confidant of the misery, the shame, the perfidy of the young man, but who also knew that this intellectual scoundrel was not an actual murderer?

Without doubt he was bound by the tacit engagement contracted in opening the manuscript; but was this engagement valid in the presence of death? There was, in this solitary being assailed for a month by moral torment, such a need of escaping from the ineffectual and sterile corrosion of his thoughts by a positive volition, that he felt it a relief when he had at last decided on a part.

From other journals which he anxiously consulted, he learned that the Greslou case would come before the assizes[6] of Riom, on Friday, March 11th.

On the 10th he gave Mariette the order to prepare his valise, and the same evening he took the train after posting a letter addressed to M. the Count André de Jussat, Captain of Dragoons in garrison at Lunéville. This letter, not signed, simply contained the lines:

"Monsieur, Count de Jussat has in his hands a letter from his sister which contains the proof of the innocence of Robert Greslou. Will he permit an innocent man to be condemned?"

The nihilistic psychologist had not been able to write the words *right* and *duty*. But his resolution was taken. He would wait until the trial was ended, and if M. de Jussat were still silent, if Greslou were condemned, he would place the memoir in the hands of the president.

"He took his ticket for Riom," said Mlle. Trapenard to Father Carbonnet on returning from the station whither she had accompanied her master, almost in spite of himself, "but the idea of his going away off there, alone, and in this cold, when he is so comfortable here!"

"Be easy, Mlle. Mariette," said the astute porter. "We shall know all someday. But nothing will make me think that there is not an illegitimate son in it somewhere."

---

6. Assizes refers to the sittings or sessions (Old French *assises*) of the judges, known as "justices of assize,"who traveled commissions, setting up court and summoning juries at various assize towns.

VI.

COUNT ANDRÉ

AT THE MOMENT when the note which had been put into the box by Adrien Sixte arrived at Lunéville, Count André was himself at Riom. Chance willed that these two men should not meet, for the celebrated writer, on leaving the train, took his place at a venture in the omnibus for the Hôtel du Commerce, while the count had his apartment at the Hôtel de l'Univers.

There in a parlor furnished with old furniture, hung with a faded paper, with worn curtains and a patched carpet, and on the morning of this Friday, March 11, 1887, on which the Greslou trial opened, the brother of poor Charlotte was walking up and down. Noon was about to strike from the clock of ornamented copper, which decorated the chimney-piece.

Outside, the sky was covered with clouds, one of those Auvergne skies which brings the icy wind of the mountains.

The count's orderly, a dragoon with a jovial physiognomy, had brought a little military order into this salon, and, after having wound the clock stirred up the fire he began to set the table for two. From time to time he watched his captain, who, stroking his mustache with one hand, biting his lips, wrinkling his brow, wore the expression of the most painful anxiety. But Joseph Pourat, this was the orderly's name, simply thought that the count was scarcely master of himself, while they were trying the assassin of his sister. For him, as for all who were in any way connected with the Jussat-Randons and who had known Charlotte, there was no doubt of Robert Greslou's guilt. What the faithful soldier less understood, knowing the energy of his officer, was that he had allowed the old marquis to go to the trial alone.

"That will do very well," said the count, and Pourat, who placed the plates and forks after having wiped them, a necessary preliminary, thought in presence of the visible agony of his master:

"He has a good heart all the same, if he is a little brusque. How much he loved her!"

André de Jussat did not seem to even suspect there was any one in the room beside himself. His brown eyes close to his nose, which had astonished, almost disturbed Robert Greslou, by their resemblance to those of a bird of prey, no longer shot forth that proud look which goes straight to an object, and takes hold of it. No, there was a species of shrinking back, almost a shame, like a fear of showing his inmost suffering. They were the eyes of a man whom a fixed idea possesses and whom the sting of an intolerable pain constantly touches in the most sensitive part of his soul.

This pain dated from the day on which he had received his sister's letter revealing her terrible project of suicide. A dispatch had arrived almost at the same moment, announcing the death of Charlotte, and he had taken the train for Auvergne precipitately, without knowing how to inform his father of the fearful truth, but decided to have a just revenge on Greslou. And the marquis had received him with these words: "You received my dispatch? We have the assassin."

The count had said nothing, comprehending that there must be a misunderstanding; and the marquis had stated the suspicions against the preceptor, also the fact that he had just been arrested.

Immediately this idea imposed itself upon the brother, who was mad with grief, that destiny offered him this vengeance, the only object of his thought since he had read the confession of the dead and the detail of her misery, of her errors, her resistances her atrocious deception, of her fatal resolution.

He had only not to hide the letter, and the cowardly moral assassin of the young girl would be accused, imprisoned, no doubt condemned. The honor of Charlotte would be saved, for Robert Greslou could not prove his relations with the girl. The marquis and the marquise, the father and the mother, so confiding so penetrated by the truest love for the memory of their poor child, would at least be ignorant of the fault of this dear one which would be to them a new despair greater than the girl's tragic death.

And Count André was silent. Not, however, without a violent effort over himself. This courageous man who possessed by nature and by will the true virtues of a soldier, detested perfidy, compromises of conscience, all expedients and all dastardliness.

He had felt that it was his duty to speak, not to allow an innocent person to be accused. He had in vain said to himself that this Greslou was the moral assassin of Charlotte, and that this assassination merited a punishment as well as the other; this sophism of his hate had not quite controlled the other voice, that which forbids us to become accomplices in an iniquity, and the condemnation of Greslou as a poisoner was certainly iniquitous.

An unexpected and to him an almost monstrous circumstance had completely overwhelmed André de Jussat; the silence of the accused.

If Greslou had spoken, recounted his amours, defending his life at the price of the honor of his victim, the count could not have despised him enough. By a contrast of character which must appear still more inexplicable to a simple mind, this infamous man suddenly displayed the generosity of a gentleman in not speaking a word which could soil the memory of one whom he had drawn into so detestable an ambuscade.[1]

This scoundrel was brave in the presence of justice, almost heroic in his way. In any case he ceased to be worthy of disgust only. André said to himself that this might be the tactics of the Court of Assizes, a proceeding to obtain an acquittal in the absence of proofs. But, on the other hand, he knew by the letter of his sister of the existence of the journal in which the details of the scientific experiment had been consigned hour by hour. This journal singularly diminished the chances of conviction, and Greslou did not produce it.

The officer could not have explained why this dignity of attitude on the part of his enemy so angered him, that he had a frantic desire to rush to the magistrate, in order that the truth might be brought to light, and the dead should owe nothing, not an atom of her posthumous honor to this scoundrel who had won her love.

When he thought of his sister, the sweet creature whom he had loved, with so virile and noble an affection, that of an elder brother for a frail refined child, in the possession of this clown, this chance preceptor, him who had inflicted on his race an outrage so abject he could have roared with fury,

---

1. Ambuscade is an archaic term for an ambush.

as when, during the war, it had been necessary to assist at the capitulation of Metz and to give up his arms.

He felt then a solace in thinking that the bench of infamy on which were seated burglars, swindlers, and murderers was waiting for this man, and then the scaffold or the galleys. And he stifled the voice which said: "You ought to speak."

My God! What agony for him in these three months, during which there had not been five minutes in which he had not struggled against these contradictory sentiments.

On the field of drill, for he had returned to service; on horseback, galloping over the roads of Lorraine; in his room thinking, over this question: "What was he to do?"

Weeks had passed without any answer, but the moment had come when it was necessary to act and to decide, for in two days—the trial must occupy four sessions—Greslou would be judged and condemned. There would be still some time after the conviction; but what of it! The same debate would only have to be gone over again. He had not decided to be silent until the last. He refrained from speaking, but he had not vowed to himself that he would refrain from speaking. This was the reason it had been physically impossible for him to accompany his father to the Palais de Justice during this first session, of which he should soon hear the account, as twelve was striking, twelve very harsh strokes followed by a carillon in the steeple of a neighboring church.

"My captain, here is M. the Marquis," said the orderly, who had heard the rolling of a carriage, then its stop before the hotel, after which he took a look out of the window.

"Ah, well, my father?" asked André anxiously as soon as the marquis had entered.

"Ah, well! The jury is for us," responded M. de Jussat. He was no longer the broken-down monomaniac whom Greslou had so bitterly mocked in his memoir. His eyes were brilliant and there was youth in his voice and gestures. The passion for vengeance, instead of breaking him down, sustained him. He had forgotten his hypochondria, and his speech was quick, impetuous, and clear. "They were drawn this morning. Among the twelve jurors, there are three farmers, two retired officers, a physician, two shopkeepers, two proprietors, a manufacturer, and a professor, all good men, men of family, and who would wish to make an example. The procureur général is sure of a conviction. Ah! The scoundrel! But I was happy, the only time in three months, when I saw him between two gendarmes![2] But what audacity! He looked around the hall. I was on the first bench. He saw me. Would you believe it, he did not turn away his eyes? He looked at me fixedly as if he wished to brave me. Ah! We must have his head, and we will have it."

The old man had spoken with a savage accent and he had not noticed the painful expression that his words had brought to the face of the count. This last, at the picture of his enemy, thus conquered by public force, seized by the gendarmes, as if caught in the gear of that anonymous and invincible machine of justice, trembled with a chill of shame, the shame of a man who has employed bravos in a work of death.

These gendarmes, and these magistrates, were really the bravos employed in doing what he would so much have liked to do himself, with his own hands and upon his own responsibility. Decidedly, it was cowardly not to have spoken.

Then the look thrown by Greslou at the Marquis de Jussat, what did it mean? Did he know that Charlotte had written her letter of confession the evening before her suicide? And if he knew it, what did he think? The idea alone that this young man could suspect the truth and despise them for their silence lighted a fever in the blood of the count.

No, said he to himself when the marquis had gone back for the afternoon session after a dinner eaten in haste, *I cannot keep silent. I will speak, or I will write.*

He seated himself and began to trace mechanically these words at the head of a sheet: "Monsieur le Président."

The night fell while this unhappy man was still in the same place, his brow in his hand, and not having written the first line of this letter. He waited

---

2. Gendarmes is a term derived from the medieval French expression *gens d'armes*, which translates to "men-at-arms" (literally, armed people). It refers to military guards with law enforcement duties among the civilian population.

for the news of the second session, and it was with a shock that he heard his father recount the details of it.

"Ah! My dear André! You were right not to come! What infamy! Ah! what infamy! Greslou was questioned. He continues his system and refuses to say anything. That is nothing. The experts reported the results of their analyses. Our good doctor first. His voice trembled, the dear man, when he described his impression at seeing our poor Charlotte, you know, in her room. And then Professor Armand; you could not have endured this horrible thing, this autopsy of our angel in that room in which there were certainly five hundred persons. And then the Paris chemist. If there could be any doubt after that! The bottle which that monster used, was on the table. I saw it. And then—how did he dare? His lawyer, an official advocate, however, and who has not even the excuse of being the friend of his client. His advocate. But how shall I tell you? He asked if Charlotte had had a lover. There was a murmur of disgust in the hall, of indignation from everybody. She, my child, so pure, so noble, a saint! I could have choked the man. Even the assassin was moved, he whom nothing touches. I saw him. At that moment he put his head in his hands and wept. Answer, ought it not to be forbidden by law, to speak in that way of a victim in open court? What did this rogue believe then, that she had a lover? A lover! She a lover!"

The old man's indignation was so strong that he suddenly burst into tears. The son, in presence of this touching grief felt his heart melt and the tears fill his eyes, and the two men embraced one another without a word.

"You see," resumed the father when he was able to speak, "this is the dreadful side of these trials, the public discussion of the most private matters. I have told you before that I was sure she was unhappy all winter because Maxime was absent. She loved him, but was not willing that it should be seen. It was this that aroused Greslou's jealousy when he came to the house and found her so gracious, so unpretentious, he believed that he could win her. How could she have suspected such a thing, when I who have had so much experience of men, never saw or guessed anything?"

Once started on this subject the marquis talked all through the dinner, then during the whole evening. He enjoyed the consolation, the only one possible in certain crises, of recollecting aloud. And the religious worship which the unhappy father preserved for the dead was for the son, who listened without responding, something tragically at this moment when he was preparing to do what? Was he really about to bring this terrible blow on the old man? In his own room, with the great silence of a provincial city around him, he took up his sister's letter and read it again, although he knew by heart every phrase in it. There arose from these pages traced by the hand forever still, a sigh so profound, a breath of agony so sad and so heartrending! The illusion of the girl had been so mad, her struggles so sincere, her awakening so bitter, that the count felt again the tears flow down his cheeks. This was the second time that he had wept that day, he who, since the death of Charlotte, had kept his eyes dry and burning with hate.

He said: "Greslou has deserved—" He remained motionless some minutes, and, walking toward the chimney in which the fire was just extinguished, he placed on the half-consumed log the leaves of the letter. He struck a match and slipped it under the paper. He saw the line of flame develop all around, then again the frail writing, then transform this only proof of the miserable amour and suicide into a blackish mass.

The brother finished by mixing this debris with the ashes. He lay down saying aloud: "It is done," and he slept, as on the night after his first battle, the exhausted sleep which succeeds with men of action, great expenditure of will, and he did not open his eyes until nine o'clock the next day.

"Monsieur, the marquis forbade me to wake you," said Pourat when, called by his master, he opened the shutters. The sunlight entered, the bright sunlight instead of the sad and lowering sky of the evening before. "He has been gone an hour. My captain knows that today they are going to take the accused by the subterranean passage, everybody is so excited against him."

"What subterranean passage?" asked André.

"That one which goes from the jail to the Palais de Justice. They use it for great criminals, those who might be torn to pieces by the public. Faith, captain, if I saw that fellow go by, I believe I should feel like knocking him over on the spot. Those enraged dogs do not judge, they kill. But," he continued, "I have forgotten the morning's letters in the salon."

He returned in a minute, having in his hand three envelopes. André, who threw a glance at the first two, saw at once from whom they came.

The third was in an unknown hand. It had been addressed to Lunéville, from Paris, then sent on to Riom. The count opened it, and read the three lines which Sixte had written before taking the train for Riom. The hands of this brave officer who did not know the meaning of the word fear, began to tremble. He became as pale as the paper which he held in his trembling hands, so pale that Pourat said to him with fear:

"My captain is ill."

"Leave me," said the count brusquely. "I will dress myself alone."

He had need to recover from the sudden blow which had just struck him. There was some one in the world who knew the terrible secret, some one who knew the mystery of Charlotte's death and who was not Robert Greslou, for he had seen some of the young man's writing and this was quite unlike it.

This was a shock of terror such as the most courageous might feel before a fact so absolutely unexpected that it takes on a supernatural character. If the brother of Charlotte had seen his sister, alive there before him, he could not have been more prostrated with astonishment.

Someone knew of the suicide of the young girl, and of the letter written by her before her death, and possibly all the rest. And this someone, this mysterious witness of the truth, what did he think of him? The question with which the note ended told plainly enough.

Suddenly the count remembered what he had dared to do. He remembered the letter thrown into the fire, and the purple of shame rushed to his cheeks. The resolution, taken the evening before, could not be kept. That any man should have the right to say: "The Count de Jussat has committed a cowardly act," was more than this gentleman so proud of his honor, was able to endure. The trouble of the night before, that he had believed ended, revived, and was rendered more intolerable by the return of his father who said:

"They have heard all the witnesses. I have deposed. But what was very hard was to find myself in the small hall with Greslou's mother. It is a chance if she does not come down here. She is at the Hôtel du Commerce, where she has begged me to come to talk with her. Ah! What a scene! She has a face not to be forgotten, a severe face, with black eyes which have, as it were, a fire in their tears. She walked up to me and spoke to me. She adjured me to say that her son was innocent, that I knew it, that I had no right to depose against him. Yes, it was a terrible scene, and the gendarme interrupted it. The unhappy woman! I cannot feel hard toward her. He is her son. What a strange thing that a rascal like him can still have in the world a heart that loves him, even as I loved Charlotte, as I love you! Alas!" continued the old man. "It is one o'clock. The attorney general is going to speak. Then the defense. Between five and six o'clock we shall have the verdict. Ah, but that will satisfy the heart to see him when the sentence is pronounced! It is only just. He has committed murder. He ought to die."

When the count was again alone, he began to walk up and down, as the evening before, while Pourat with the valet of M. de Jussat, cleared away the table. These two men have since declared that their master had never seemed so violently uneasy, as during the thirty minutes that they were busy in the room. Their astonishment was very great when he asked to have his uniform got ready.

In a quarter of an hour he was dressed and left the hotel. One detail made the brave Pourat shiver. He stated that the officer took his revolver with him which had been placed for two nights on the nightstand. The soldier communicated his fears to his companion.

"If this Greslou is acquitted," said he, "the captain is the man to blow his brains out on the spot."

"We ought to follow him, perhaps?" responded the *valet-de-chambre*.

While the two servants were deliberating, the count followed the main street which led to the Palais de Justice. He knew it, for he had often been to Riom in his childhood. This old parliamentary city, with its large hotels with the high windows, built in black Volvic stone, seemed more empty, more silent, more dead than usual as the brother of Charlotte walked toward the court.

Near the approaches to Palais there was a dense crowd which filled the narrow Rue Saint-Louis by which one reaches the hall of assize. The Greslou case had attracted all who had an hour to spare. André could scarcely force his way through the mass of people, composed of countrymen and small shopkeepers who were conversing with passionate animation.

He arrived at the steps which lead to the vestibule. Two soldiers guarded the door, charged to keep back the crowd. The count seemed to hesitate, then, instead of entering, he pushed on to the end of the street. He reached a terrace, which, situated between the sinister walls of the central building and the dark mass of the Palais, gave a view of the immense plain of the Limagne.

A fountain charmed the silence of this spot, and the sound of its murmuring could be heard even above the noise of the crowd in the neighboring street. André sat down on a bench near the fountain. He was never able to tell why he remained there more than half an hour, nor the exact reason why he arose, walked toward the Palais, wrote his name and some words on a card, and gave this card to a soldier to be carried by the bailiff to the president.

He had the very distinct feeling that he must act, almost in spite of himself, and as in a dream. His resolution nevertheless was taken and he felt that he should not weaken again, although he apprehended with horrible anguish the meeting with his father, who was over there, beyond those people whose heads were bent forward, their shoulders curved.

He felt in his agony the only solace he could experience when the bailiff came for him. For, instead of introducing him at once into the hall, this man led him through a passage to a small room which was, without doubt, the office of the president. Some packets were lying on the table. An overcoat and a hat hung on a peg. Arrived there, his guide said to him:

"Monsieur le Président will come to you as soon as the attorney general has finished." What unexpected consolation in his pain! The punishment of deposing in public and before his father would be spared him! This hope was of short duration. The officer had not been ten minutes in the office of the president when the latter entered: a large old man, with a face yellow from bile and with gray hair, whom the contrast of his red robe made look greenish. After the first words and before the affirmation of the count that he brought proof of the innocence of the accused:

"On these conditions, monsieur," said the president, "I cannot receive your confidences. The audience is to be resumed and you will be heard as a witness, provided neither the prosecution nor the defense object."

Thus none of the stations toward his Calvary could the brother of Charlotte avoid. He was about to come in contact with this impassible machinery of justice, which does not stop, which cannot stop on account of human sensibility. He must seat himself in the witness chamber, and recall the scene which had passed there between his father and the mother of Greslou, then enter the hall of assize. He could see the bare wall with the image of the crucified which overlooked this hall, the heads turned toward him in supreme attention, the president among his judges, and the attorney general, all in their red robes; the jurors on the left of the court. Robert Greslou was on the right on the prisoner's bench, his arms folded, livid but impassible, and everybody crowded everywhere, behind the magistrates, in the tribunes.

On the witness bench André recognized his father and his white hairs. Ah! How this sight cut him to the heart—the heart which did not falter however, when the president, after asking the counsel and attorney general if they did not object to hearing the witness, asked him to state his name and title and take oath according to the formula. The magistrates who assisted at this scene are unanimous in declaring that they never experienced an emotion in court at all comparable to that which seized the audience and themselves when this man, whose heroic past all were acquainted with through the articles published in the journals, began in a firm voice, but one which betrayed excruciating grief:

"Gentlemen of the jury; I have only a few words to say. My sister was not assassinated, she killed herself. The night before her death she wrote me a letter in which she announced her resolution to die, and why. Gentlemen, I believe that I had the right to conceal this suicide, I burned this letter. If the man whom you have before you," and he indicated Greslou with his left hand—"did not give the poison, he has done worse. But this is not for your justice to consider, and he ought not to be convicted as an assassin. He is innocent. In default of material proof which I can no longer give, I bring you my word." These sentences fell one by one, amid the anguish of the whole audience. There was a cry followed by groans.

"He is mad," said a voice, "he is mad, do not listen to him."

"No, my father," replied Count André, who recognized the voice of the marquis, and who turned toward the old man, who lay back, crushed, on his bench. "I am not mad. I have done what honor compelled. I hope, Monsieur le Président, that I may be spared from saying any more."

There was entreaty in his voice, the voice of this proud man, as he uttered this last sentence, and it so affected the hearers that a murmur ran through the crowd when the president replied:

"To my great regret, monsieur, I cannot grant what you ask. The extreme importance of the deposition which you have just made does not permit justice to rest upon the information which is our duty—a very painful duty—to ask you to state precisely."

"That is well, monsieur, I also will do my duty to the end."

There was in the accent with which the witness uttered this sentence such resolution that the murmur of the crowd gave way suddenly to silence, and the president was heard saying: "You spoke of a letter, monsieur, which your sister had written to you. Permit me to say that it is at least extraordinary that your first idea was not to enlighten justice by communicating it at once."

"It contained," said the count, "a secret which I would have been willing to conceal at the price of my blood."

He has since told the friend who remained so true to the end of this drama, Maxime de Plane, that this was the most terrible moment of his sacrifice—but his emotion was suppressed by its very excess. He was obliged to give all the details of the letter— and recount his own sensations, and confess all his agonies. As to what followed, he has declared that he could recall only a few material details—and those the most unexpected— the coldness to his hand of an iron column against which he was leaning when he ought to have been sitting on the witness bench from which some one came to take him to his father who had fainted at the last words of his deposition. He noticed also the drawling Lorraine accent of the procureur général who had risen to abandon the prosecution.

How much time elapsed between the speeches of the procureur and of Greslou's counsel, the retiring of the jury and its re-entrance with a negative verdict, he never knew. He has never known how he employed his evening, after the doorkeeper had invited him to leave. He remembers to have walked a great distance. Some citizens of Combronde met him on the road to this village. He went to an inn where he wrote some letters, addressed, one to his father, one to his mother and a third to his colonel, and a last to Maxime de Plane. At nine o'clock he knocked at the door of the Hôtel du Commerce, where his father had told him the mother of Greslou had gone, and he asked the concierge if M. Greslou was there. This fellow had heard of the dramatic scene. He guessed from the uniform of the captain who he was, and had the good sense to reply that M. Robert Greslou had not appeared. Unfortunately he thought it right to inform the young man, who was at that moment with his mother and M. Adrien Sixte. This last could not resist the supplications of the widow who, having met him in the corridor of the hotel, had conjured him to aid her in comforting her son.

"Monsieur," said the concierge to Robert after having asked permission to speak to him apart, "be careful, M. de Jussat is looking for you. "

"Where is he?" asked Greslou feverishly.

"He cannot have left the street," responded the concierge, "but I told him that you were not here."

"You did wrong," replied Greslou. And taking his hat, he rushed toward the stairs. "Where are you going?" implored his mother. The young man did not answer. Perhaps he did not even hear this cry, he was in such haste to go down the stairs. The idea that Count André believed him cowardly enough to hide himself maddened him. He had not long to look for his enemy. The count was on the opposite side of the street, watching the door. Robert saw him and walked straight up to him.

"You have something to say to me, monsieur?" he asked proudly.

"Yes," said the count.

"I am at your service," continued Greslou, "for whatever reparation that it may please you to exact. I will not leave Riom, I give you my word."

"No, monsieur," responded André de Jussat, "one does not fight with such men as you, one executes them."

He drew his revolver from his pocket, and as the other, instead of fleeing, remained standing before him and seemed to say: "I dare you," he lodged a bullet in his head. The noise of the report, and a cry of agony were heard at the same time at the hotel, and when they ran to see the cause, they found Count André standing against the wall, who, throwing down his pistol and, folding his arms said simply, pointing to the body of his sister's lover at his feet: "I have executed justice."

And he allowed himself to be arrested without any resistance.

During the night which followed this tragic scene, the admirers of *Psychology of God,* of *Theory of the Passions,* and of *Anatomy of the Will,* would have been astonished if they could have seen what was passing in room No. 3 of the Hôtel du Commerce, and in the mind of their implacable and powerful master. At the foot of the bed on which lay the dead man, with his brow bandaged, knelt the mother of Robert Greslou.

The great negator, seated on a chair, looked at this woman praying, and at the dead man who had been his disciple, sleeping the sleep which Charlotte de Jussat was also sleeping; and, for the first time, feeling his mind powerless to sustain him, this analyst, almost inhuman by force of logic, bowed before the impenetrable mystery of destiny. The words of the only prayer he remembered: "Our Father who art in heaven," came to his mind. Surely he did not pronounce them. Perhaps he never will pronounce them. But if He exist, then the only father toward whom they could turn in their hours of distress and in whom was their only resource, was their heavenly Father. And voices of prayer the most touching went up. And if this heavenly Father did only exist, should we have this hunger and not insist for Him in such hours as this? "Thou wouldst not seek Me, if thou hadst not found Me!" At that very moment, thanks to the lucidity of mind which accompanies the scholar into all crises, Adrien Sixte recalled this admirable sentence of Pascal in his *Mystérie de Jésus,* and when the mother arose from her knees the philosopher was also weeping.

THE END